About the Author

Paul Kiritsis, PsyD, is a licensed clinical psychologist in the SF Bay Area. He has authored six other books, including the creative compendium *Confessions of a Split Mind*, and the award-winning titles *The Creative Advantages of Schizophrenia* and *A Critical Investigation into Precognitive Dreams*. His diverse academic interests straddle cognitive neuroscience, neuropsychology, and the philosophy of mind on one end of the spectrum and esotericism, comparative religion, history, and mythology on the other. He enjoys cycling, playing the keyboard, reading, drawing, and scuba diving in his spare time.

Tales of a Spiritual Sun

Paul Kiritsis

Tales of a Spiritual Sun

Olympia Publishers
London

www.olympiapublishers.com
OLYMPIA PAPERBACK EDITION

A CIP catalogue record for this title is
available from the British Library.

ISBN: 978-1-80439-005-4

First Published in 2023

Olympia Publishers
Tallis House
2 Tallis Street
London
EC4Y 0AB

Printed in Great Britain

Dedication

This book is dedicated to my godson, Alexander.

Acknowledgements

My first expression of gratitude belongs to my cousin, Harry Toulacis, who encouraged me to take off from where *Shades of Aphrodite* concluded by navigating through the Greek myths and selecting my very favorites to work with. I thank him for his inspirational words, but above all, his tutored ears for listening to my work and offering useful suggestions. Gee Butcher, my close friend and work colleague, for her unyielding passion, enthusiasm, and inspiration. My mother and father, Chryssoula and Christos, for their love and support, I thank them always. I am eternally indebted to my late editor, Ron Kenner, former metro staff writer of the Los Angeles Times, for his editing prowess, continued support, and guidance. Finally, my last and most heartfelt acknowledgement goes to the God through which we all live, strive for, suffer, love, experience the world find meaning in, and have our being.

Contents

PREFACE

Choosing to contemporize or reconstruct any ancient myth, particularly a fragment of universally recognized mythological discourses such as Homer's *The Iliad* and *Odyssey* or Hesiod's *Theogony*, can be an incredibly daunting experience. Yet for any writer who intuitively penetrates the dark veil of entertainment, or explanatory devices, and sees myth as a primal mover in the narrative or story-telling process, one who can acknowledge the intrinsic powers of myth in reshaping and recasting the cosmic clay which forms the mold of knowledge, the cultural attitudes, behaviors and values of any society, and for any writer who appreciates the political ramifications that may ensue, retelling these extraordinarily powerful and timeless stories somehow mimics a thermometer. The thermometer—measuring and reflecting the increment and nature of our collective consciousness—acts as a necessary precursor to our evolutionary leap in critical thinking, inquiry, and the way we process and evaluate information as a whole.

But before we go onto my preferred choice of subject, it is necessary to define the physiology, the internal components or "stuff" of what might be defined as "myth." Strictly speaking, myths are sacred, timeless stories that attempt to make sense of an otherwise confusing and chaotic universe. They also define and delineate the central "Self" from the unconscious matrix, illuminate the relationship between the microcosm of the "Self" and the macrocosm of the greater cosmos, and recount events pertaining to the origins and functions of the universe and all things, living or inanimate, contained within it.

Most of the questions inexplicably linked with myth are abstract, philosophical in nature, and highly resistant to localization in the three-dimensional, corporeal region of time and space. Myth consciousness might be viewed as a baby struggling to make sense of its immediate environment despite its own helpless state of passivity in a world of meaningless associations. Information processing belonging to this level of evolving intelligence would inevitably raise the following questions: Who am I? Who are we? How did I come to be? What is the world? How did it come to be? Who created it, and what are the moral, and social codes of conduct that govern our behavior and society as a whole? What are the consequences of law-making and law-breaking?

The term *mythos* itself, derived from the Greek "mythos," denotes a word or story. Apparently, the pre-Socratic philosophers only referenced it in passing and the concept didn't really gain eminence in the intellectual world until the life and times of Plato, who perceived it to be a literary vehicle encapsulating allegorical truth, i.e., the *mythos* of Atlantis. The Platonic and Neo-Platonic schools of thought, despite some significant differences and unlike the dark age separating them, are inextricably linked with the exploration of reality. This exploration divided the cosmos into an eternal world of "being" which encompassed the intellect, divine forms and ideas, and the ever-fluctuating, temporal, and chaotic world of "becoming." It goes without saying that Platonic thought flirted openly with a psychological, ahistorical approach to mythography, though little to no attention had been given to the hermeneutics of myth until well into the nineteenth century.

In 1890, Sir James Frazer published his now-classic book, *The Golden Bough,* as a quasi-anthropological work which defines mythological discourse as a preserved body of oral folklore, embodying the unconscious projections of pastoral dilemmas and traditions. Emerging in the twentieth century, Carl Gustav Jung and Sigmund Freud, taking a more holistic approach, saw myth as an exploration of psychological terrain in which archetypal content of the human psyche emerged from the unconscious, subsequently forging dynamic relationships with one another and with the macrocosm at large. Joseph Campbell, the author of *The Hero with a Thousand Faces,* took the psychoanalytic point of view a step further; he professed that the characters of myth and dream were urgent heroes who embarked on a long journey, underwent a struggle of some sort, and successfully emerged from it enlightened and anew with a refined, resilient and altogether more evolved identity. On the polar end of this hermeneutical or interpretative scale sat French anthropologist Claude Levi-Strauss, who rejected the psychological internalization of myth for a more impersonal model, one that emphasizes narrative strategy and plot device as the bone which forms the skeletal framework of all stories, be they compelling fiction or dramatic non-fiction.

My purpose here is not to analyze the scope of hermeneutical interpretation that has typified the study of mythography over the last few centuries but to give a millisecond flash, a fleeting glimpse, if you like, of the onion-skinned layers composing the mythological sphere; in this way, readers may garner a greater appreciation of its interdisciplinary, multifaceted nature. Thus, entering the labyrinth of mythology, one must tread the winding passages which harness a worm's eye view of political, social, literary, performative, textual, psychological, astronomical, seasonal, and structural aspects, and all the while he or she must never lose sight of the birds-eye view, an impartial trajectory which succeeds in taking all into account without becoming localized.

Present-day Western society is eclectic in its choice of subject, with most academics and students harboring an unconscious bias toward Greek, Roman, and Norse myths. If one elects to study mythology at a postgraduate level, they'll be surprised to find the subject reader askew with a profusion of classical texts. This is one reason I've chosen to contemporize a selection of Greek myths. Another is because simplified and unaltered children's versions of classical myths comprised my first ever experience of active story-telling. It's downright impossible to forget the page-turning suspense and anticipation evoked by masterful tales absorbed during one's formative years, and I am no different. Who could overlook memories of the twelve death-defying feats of Heracles, Jason's adventures in finding the Golden Fleece, Theseus's courage in squaring off against the dreaded Minotaur, Perseus's subjugation of Medusa, the snake-haired Gorgon, and the lamentable fate of Oedipus who killed his birth father and unknowingly married his own mother? Myths are narratives that reflect universal laws of being that no human can transcend, and so carry, widescale appeal. We are fascinated by them because we are them, individually and collectively.

The collection of short stories in this tome is *Tales of a Spiritual Sun*. As an avid lover of multiple meanings, my choice of a pun is self-explanatory. Just as the sun is the heart-center of the solar system that makes life on earth possible, so, too, is the Divine Mind, or what many would term as *God,* the source of the transient human soul which makes personal growth and transformation possible. These are the stories whose nuclei have their roots in esoteric spirituality as well as mystical philosophy, and the writer who transcribed them is merely a transitory vessel for an everlasting spiritual world. One might say, then, that they are cogitations of the spirit world written by one of its mortal children, a spiritual son. Functioning mythically, these cogitations aren't true in the literal sense of the word. They are allegories comprising philosophical and spiritual truths about the anatomy of the individual and collective human psyche. In other words, they are unconscious archetypal projections that find expression through the contingencies of chance, time, and time again.

There are thirteen retellings in this collection, all written within the space of a year. In terms of content and proximity to the old myths, they range from marginally transformed versions that stay faithful to the original plots to versions whose skeletal frameworks and compositions are virtually unrecognizable. Whichever the case, the contemporary versions can be linked to their ancient counterparts through ideologies, philosophies, characters, or narrative fragments held in common.

The reader is first dropped into the mystical marshes of the Minoan world and the inner chthonic workings of Hellenistic fatalism before a change of scenery brings him or her to a variegated landscape of star-crossed lovers; a landscape that includes inwardly-turned reinterpretations of Orpheus and Eurydice, Pygmalion and Galatea, Eros and Psyche, and Narcissus and Echo. Following this is a transposition into turbulent waters where the reader encounters such dreadful villains as the Minotaur, the shape-shifting Proteus, the Theban Sphinx, and the Gorgon Stheno. The mythological journey then changes trajectory once again, wheeling a Trojan horse of a different kind before the reader. Finally, an ethereal narrative built around a Pandora's Box of the latter-day intellect unleashes a cosmic paradox into consciousness.

I hope you enjoy reveling in these tales as much as I enjoyed breathing life into them.

In the beginning, was the Word and the Word was with the Imagination, and the Word was the Imagination.

So, let the Imagination begin....

To Propitiate the Earth

Potinija wove her way in and out of the water, propelling herself forward with the powerful muscles in her tail. There was no way any human being could ever swim like this; their bodies just didn't allow for it.

The sense of inhabiting a foreign body was still somewhat eerie, though it was a feeling she'd grown used to with time. Long ago, she'd mastered the art of separation, meandering in disembodied states, encroaching upon, and then possessing, the bodies of the unassuming zodiacal beasts. Some of these ventures were quite enjoyable, like little quests to explore some of the lesser-known paths that the divine she manifested in, though the aftermath was always tainted by a sense of guilt.

The truth of the matter was that she didn't quite know how she felt yet about usurping the minds of other creatures. There was something rude and entirely unbecoming about it. To intrude upon, and take possession of a being without its consent, went against her will, the natural ordering of things in the cosmos. Thus, a while back, Potinija came to the conclusion that she would only engage in the activity as a last resort or when a desirable outcome could not be arrived at by other means. Along with the notion that it was somewhat sacrilegious, the projection also encompassed the danger of becoming entrapped in the body of a decaying carcass. At one time, she'd been unlucky enough to project herself into a rabbit at the exact moment it was being ambushed by a white eagle. Thankfully, she'd been able to eject herself from the throne of the animal's consciousness before its life force deserted it. Potinija shuddered at the thought of imprisonment in a festering heap of matter.

Further, it required a profuse and intense effort of concentration to disarm and then hold the reigns over the throne of the intellect when the creature's consciousness equalled, if not surpassed, that of human beings. Actually, keeping the porpoise's jaws sealed tight as it plunged toward the seashore was starting to become an insurmountable task. Not only was the vessel struggling to free itself from her stranglehold, it was beginning to tire. She could feel every bit of the spasm which wracked its tail fluke. Potinija drew upon every reserve of strength the creature had and urged herself on, desperate to deliver the Stone which would save her people from the wrath of the Earth-shaker.

Snapping out of her reverie, Potinija was surprised to see that she had reached her destination. Careful not to beach the porpoise upon the shore, she rolled onto her side and spat the Stone onto the swirling sands. Then she relinquished her hold upon the creature's mind by diffusing out through the individual field of its life-force and into the ambient background of fields that, united, all created Nature. Soon, she was soaring above the skies like a whooping crane. From here she had a bird's eye view of the ceremony: nineteen chanting priestesses, still holding hands and dancing around her inanimate body–slender, tall and powdered over with chalk–which lay atop the sacrosanct stone table. The sacrificed bull was beside her; a river of blood ran from its neck, feeding an adjoining sacred pool which would soon manifest soul force in the guise of bees and butterflies. The vision, fleeting, lasted all of about a fraction of a second before her wafting consciousness was sucked rudely back into its mortal vessel. She could now hear the rhythmic beating of drums and the intermittent ululation that came from the dishevelled priestesses as they beat their breasts and danced about her.

Potinija wiped beads of sweat which had formed under her brows.

"I have it! I have it!" she cried out.

"Where is it?" asked the Wise One, peering down upon her naked body in anticipation. "Where is the Stone of the moon?"

"By the sea," said Potinija. "It's been dropped by the sea."

Two priestesses helped her to her feet. The psychic energy spent in going walkabouts was often significant, and a common side effect of the practice was to suffer a mild case of disorientation and dizziness afterwards. Nevertheless, Potinija overcame the nasty aftereffects as well as the pitch darkness and stumbled all the way to the shore without losing her bearings.

Soon her eyes had adjusted to the subtle moonlit tones of the night. She scanned the area in which froth and seaweed had been spewed out from the sea by the waves and that was when she saw it. About the size of a small plum, it glimmered with a supernal opalescence that rivaled, if not surpassed, that of the moon when it was at the height of its generative powers.

Potinija snatched it up and curled her fingers around it. It was cool and smooth to touch as if the waves had washed over it a billion or so times. Sensing that the priestesses were standing right behind her, she pivoted and thrust her hand out towards the heavens, holding the Stone between her thumb and forefinger. Gasps of awe and shrieks of reverence came from the women, and each proceeded to prostrate herself on the ground to commemorate, yet again, the magical powers that could be yielded by tapping into the nervous system of the Earth Goddess, the electromagnetic currents that coursed through the earth and passed beneath the stone table. These were forces which only Potinija, as the figurehead of the Great Mother Goddess, could appropriate.

For a while, there was a deep, graveyard silence. What little light there was illuminated the colored sands of Keftiu, stained a reddish-pink from incessant sacrifices which hoped to placate the Earth's proliferating anger and restore it to its former quietude through the violent, spontaneous release of vital energy. Potinija lifted her gaze to the great cliffs which lined the seashore and which had been nibbled on by the sea for time immemorial. Giant cypresses, olive groves and oak trees were rooted on the furthest edges of the dramatic ravine, steadfast in their effort to resist a fatal tumble into the brackish chaos below. Down there, one could marvel at the violence of creation and uncreation, the place where the returning waters polished dross and detritus into a brilliant glass of obsidian and hewed out slabs of rock into intricate labyrinths. These were places where the voice of the Mother Goddess could be heard, dark and damp places in which she revealed to the seeker innumerable reasons as to how and why the human soul incarnates over and over again.

Many a time, Potinija had climbed to the top to enjoy daytime views of mighty Kairatos, the magic mountain Juktas, and the green-blue sea; by night-time, she would gaze at the star gods which wove the threads of human fate together as they circumnavigated the heavens and then charted the wanderers as they displaced the etheric gases in their search for everlasting love. More often than not, the moon would sprinkle its romance, its invisible silver dust onto the land and ignite the ravenous flames of desire within both the female, Melissae, and the male, Essenes. Even she, Queen Melissa, was not immune from its intoxicating assault.

Suddenly a weight was on her shoulder. Potinija peered down. Eileithyia, the Wise One, had descended from the stone table to confer with the oracle. She held in her hands a sacrosanct of double axes made of pure bronze. The priestesses had dressed her in a black robe which draped over her shoulders and hung quite low, touching the ground. As with all ceremonial attire, her rounded breasts and dark nipples remained exposed to the elements. Her headdress was a spherical mirror of copper and obsidian, held in position by a pair of polished bull horns which sprung up symmetrically from either side. The entire headpiece was decorated with large peacock feathers.

Aside from its aesthetic appeal, the headdress encompassed a practical purpose. The Wise One would use the mirror to concentrate moonlight onto the surface of the sacred pool by the stone table and obtain messages from the other world.

"Tell me," Potinija prompted her.

"I see darkness," the Wise One said, lifting the bronze double axes toward the heavens.

"Can you see our birth time?"

"Yes, it's encoded in the stars. It was a long, long time ago."

"Have we appeased Her?" Potinija asked.

"There will be no conception," the Wise One declared, holding her navel. "I cannot feel it growing inside of me."

"It cannot be."

"I see tears," the Wise One continued. Tears were

streaming down her eyes. "I am the moon that is wounded."

"But you will wax," said Potinija.

Eileithyia's voice deepened; her tone grew graver. She held her arms out toward the skies. "I can't. There's absolutely no light, no fire. The only thing I see is darkness after darkness. Nothingness."

"How can it be? We have offered the Earth-shaker so many bulls. Search deeper. Go deeper still," Potinija prompted her.

"Darkness," she whispered.

"Go deeper," Potinija ordered. "To the time origin."

After a few seconds, she said, "They will come after the great fire."

"Who will?"

"The red people," the Wise One said.

"Who are they?"

"They are like our Essenes but there are many of them," the Wise One said. "They have eyes of the sea and wear the skins of the wolves. They're on the rise. Their nature is not white, it is red. They are betrayers of the white light, shadows in the sea. They're from the north."

"What do they look like?" Potinija asked.

"I can't see their features," the Wise One said, "but know that there are many. One wears the skin of a lion. The rest call him their lamb."

"What is he?"

"Dangerous," said the Wise One. "They will come on the day of the Sacred Marriage, a day with darkness in the light of day, to take arms against our temples."

"When?" Potinija asked.

"The fourth of the month."

"Three days from now?" asked Potinija. Suddenly, she was

overcome by a strong sense of urgency.

"Yes. On this day there will be fire and darkness. I cannot see new birth," Eileithyia reiterated.

"But I have retrieved the Stone from the treacherous depths of the sea," Potinija insisted. "There must be a new birth."

"No," the Wise One said. "You are barren."

"What are we to do? Tell me, Eileithyia," Potinija pleaded.

"There is much to be done," the Wise One advised. "You must go to Her and ask how she may be appeased before it is too late."

"How?"

"You will grind the Stone into a fine white powder, mix it with the mead we use for the New Year ritual and ingest it. It will open up the way to Her."

"Is this the only way?"

"It is the only way," the Wise One confirmed. "The moment must be accompanied by a colossal release of energy."

"More bulls?" Potinija asked.

"No, for this, Essenes will be needed," the Wise One revealed, clenching the axes tightly in her hands. "The Earth-shaker is still angry. She has not been appeased."

"We have yet to see the great Hive," Potinija pointed out. "Let alone enter it."

"I know," the Wise One said. "And that is why our faith will have to be bigger."

"What's that noise?" Potinija said, looking down.

The ground began to tremble. Parts of it formed fissures, opening up into gaping mouths ready to swallow anything in the immediate vicinity.

"It's the Earth-shaker," the Wise One screamed, dropping the axes. "Everybody, face down on the ground."

Potinija felt the vibrations welling up from deep within the cavernous depths of the earth. They seeped into her inner being, filling her with a primitive resolve, a carnal desire to enact violence upon the so-called red peoples.

A loud bang erupted from somewhere in the distance. Potinija looked up. The stone table, used to enact magical feats by the ancestors since the laying of the foundation stone of the empire, had snapped in half.

Potinija watched the priestesses closely as they busied themselves about the sacrosanct, innermost sanctuary of the Juktas temple. The laborious procedures associated with the ritual had to be enacted with great love, passion and attention to detail, otherwise, the invocation would not work. No doubt the Wise One Eileithyia was to be commended for her brilliance in discerning a method whereby a homologous enterprise would generate a twofold, and hopefully favorable consequence; by enacting the human sacrifice and projecting her being into the great Hive of the Great Mother Goddess by the manner of the Stone, Potinija hoped to propitiate the fuming earth whilst at the same time evoking the all-omniscient, fiery eye of the Lady. The latter, a powerful weapon, would be used mercilessly to subjugate the red peoples who, according to the Wise One, were expected to arrive on the shores of Keftiu just after the great conflagration.

From where Potinija stood, she could see that they had cleaned and polished the sacrificial implements. These included a large, gilded double-axe, a golden labrys, which usually hung inside the north wall of the innermost sanctuary of the mountain shrine, and two bronze knives engraved with the heads of winged griffins; one was made of stone and the other of copper, both able to slice through flesh and bone with great precision and accuracy. Two blood buckets had been hauled up along the side of the mountain and placed beside the sacrificial victim, a young Essene, who had recently been purified in a lustral basin and then bound tightly to a stone table, itself fashioned to look like a bull.

The magic potion, made from the grated powder of the Stone and honey collected from the surrounding forests and caves of Juktas had been placed inside a small chalice made of copper and engraved with bucrania. It was subsequently mounted onto a holder formed by the adjoining arms of a wasp-waisted, life-sized statue of the Great Mother Goddess, standing near the center of the sanctuary. Potinija stared at the veiled goddess for some time, trying to imagine what Her face might look like. It was forbidden to lay eyes on any incarnation of Her supernal brilliance, animate and ethereal or inanimate and concrete.

Potinija became so transfixed by the black veil that shrouded the statue's head that she didn't notice the priestesses leave the mountain sanctuary and begin their descent along the mountain in a bid to continue the bull sacrifices at Cnossos. Lamentably, the ground began trembling not long after they left. The vibrations themselves, emanating from deep within the earth, were more vehement than ever.

"We're here," the Wise One said, bursting into the sanctuary with her assistant, a priestess named Ida. "We must begin at once!"

"This time the Earth-shaker is serious," said Ida, "and the sacrifices at Cnossos aren't working."

"Quick! Quick!" the Wise One yelled. "Drink the potion Potinija."

Potinija snatched the chalice up, itself inlaid with gold, silver, and other precious stones. She stared at the opalescent mixture suspiciously.

"Drink it now!" the Wise One screamed. "We haven't a moment to lose. The Sacred Marriage is about to unravel."

Somewhat befuddled, Potinija lifted the chalice to her lips and emptied the contents into her mouth. The lunar potion was electric, sickeningly sweet. She swallowed it in one gulp.

"Now do exactly as I tell you. Lie directly beneath the symbols of the sun and moon etched on the sanctuary roof," the Wise One said. "Lie on your back and turn your concentration inward, as you have done many times before. Then wait until I give you the signal to begin separation. Blood must feed the earth before you induce separation."

"This isn't going to work," said Ida.

"You dare to question me?" the Wise One asked, pointing the golden labrys at her. "Remain silent and do as you're told."

"But we've given her the blood of many a bull," Ida pushed on. "Much more than any human could offer. Why should anything less work?"

"Quality is much more important than quantity, Ida," the Wise One asserted. "She has revealed it to me in a dream. She wants mortal blood, the blood of our young Essenes."

"Are you sure about this, Eileithyia?" Potinija asked, positioning herself on the ground before the statue of the goddess. "The oracle has served us well and I am not one to doubt its integrity, but we have indeed seeded the ground with life-force the past two seasons without reprise. Her will is yet to be appeased."

"And our will is yet to come to fruition," Ida added.

"What has gotten into the both of you?" the Wise One said.

"You're supposed to be falling into a slumber, ready to be sucked into the vortices that will lead us to Her the moment blade finds flesh."

Dropping to her knees beside the stone table, Eileithyia tore away the golden sheath that covered the Essene's member. She cupped it with her palm, using her fingers to stimulate the tip. Then she lowered her head and took him into her mouth, sucking on his erect phallus like a vacuum. The Essene squirmed in titillation as she swirled her tongue around him.

Working herself up into a frenzied state, the Wise One seemed oblivious to the severity of the quakes which increased in magnitude. If anything, the quakes had done nothing but let loose a primitive rage, a lascivious drive from deep within her. They had supplanted her higher senses, her sanity, and the intellectual reigns of her consciousness.

The temporary insanity which had suddenly seized her relinquished its hold. Eileithyia pulled her head away from the Essenes shaft and scrambled to her feet. The white lilies on her breasts trembled as she snatched up the golden labrys from the ground. With a primitive cry that made Potinija's skin crawl, the Wise One retracted the axe above the Essene with one long, fluid motion.

The Essene screamed. He powered his bound feet into her stomach before she could deliver the blow, knocking her backwards.

"Stop, Eileithyia!" Ida yelled.

Eileithyia was stoic, unwavering in her resolve to fertilize the earth with mortal blood. Dishevelled, she scurried to her feet and came rushing toward the Essene again. But Ida tackled her from behind before she could swing the axe down, wrestling the sacrificial instrument from her hands.

"Stop this!"

"No!" the Wise One clenched her teeth. "It's mine!"

"Let go of it," Ida yelled, powering a kick into her knee.

The roar was getting louder and the tussle between the two priestesses more violent, but Potinija remained oblivious to both. She had already slipped into a self-induced trance and was now ruminating in perfect solitude, waiting for her projection into the realm of the Great Mother Goddess. Above her, the chunk of gypsum, upon which the symbol of reconciliation between the moon and sun was etched, had already separated from the rest of the ceiling. Being synthesized of weaker material, it was designed to break off so that light from the Sacred Marriage could reach the sacrosanct chamber. Now it was precariously suspended above them and would come crashing down at any minute.

"The roof is going to collapse," said Ida. "We're going to die."

"Not before the Essene does!" the Wise One remarked.

"You'll have to get through me first, Eileithyia," said Ida.

"Gladly."

Rubble continued to rain down around them but that didn't seem to bother Eileithyia who kept swinging the axe toward Ida. But the latter was equal to the task of retaliation. She dodged the assault by stepping sideways and then powering a kick into her assailant's arm. There was a loud shriek as the golden labrys went spinning off across the sanctuary.

"You fool!" the Wise One shrieked. "Look what you've done. Now we'll—"

The chunk of gypsum that had come loose was suddenly airborne. Squealing, the priestesses dropped onto the ground, retracting their limbs, and covering their heads in a protective pose, somewhat reminiscent of a developing embryo. Their soul-wrenching screams were silenced by the force of the block as it crashed down on top of them.

Directly overhead, the moon had eclipsed the sun.

After concentrating her energies in the region of her solar plexus, Potinija felt herself diffuse out of her own body. At first, the schism incited a sense of disorientation, of dizziness. She was gyrating, spinning around and around in circles at the speed of light. This was closely followed by an ululation that came from somewhere beneath her. It jolted her out of her inert position, shuttling her skyward. Her disembodied consciousness floated upwards, expanding outwards like helium gas. Before long, her personal energy field was hovering above the mountain temple like a bulbous cloud, witnessing the slab of gypsum at the precise moment it tore away from the roof and landed on the three bodies inside, one of which was still in a state of suspended animation.

What happened next was rather puzzling, as if she'd somehow slipped through a mirror, walked through a time warp or been sucked through a black hole even. She was zapped through mountains and deserts of iridescent dust to the heart of an amorphous black heap, a Stygian darkness that started off as a three-dimensional spherical whole but then began to divide and further subdivide into tiers of hexagonal cells, like those of an earthly beehive.

In fact, when Potinija pondered the reality of her situation, it was as if she'd become entrapped inside the polygonal chambers of a colossal beehive which were boundless and whose being extended as far back as the primaeval time origin, if not further. An ethereal quietude overlaid with rapturous vibration reverberated through the darkness, stirring within the intuitive feeling that this was her eternal home. Potinija was by nature a curious being, and so the desire and temptation to pry deeper into the hive and discover "truths" about the cosmos was ever-present. But as she was to find out, something stood in the way of that understanding.

Another presence wanting to make itself known suddenly materialized in the Stygian darkness. At first, Potinija thought that the movement was coming from amongst the hexagonal cells of the beehive, but that conviction soon went the way of the Golden Age. No, the presence didn't originate from the hexagonal cells at all but rather from the nucleus of the Stygian unity. The unity multiplied itself over and over until it had acquired a shape that was part-humanoid, part-bee. It began to form definitive features; an elongated head with thin lips and large, beady eyes, a wasp-waisted body and a thick abdomen. Potonija could almost hear the fluttering of its translucent wings as they sprouted a new along its back.

A very powerful sensual energy radiated from the divine being. There wasn't anything that this being remained ignorant of nor anything which could remain occult before its all-pervading justice. It could inhabit a single locale, a pinprick of time and space, or alternatively, encompass the entire diffuse background of energy fields that made up the cosmos. It was omniscient, empathic, and telepathic.

"Are you our White Queen?" Potinija asked.

"It is I."

"You're really speaking to me, aren't you?" Potinija was elated.

"We speak the same language Potinija."

"We have discovered the moon milk," Potinija said, "and the moon milk has finally opened the portal which leads to you."

"I know."

"Of course, you know, forgive me."

"The language of the white people will be lost, Potinija."

"Why, oh Queen?" Potinija asked. "I have only ever used it for the sake of good."

"Because it challenges the absolute authority and will of the creator," the divine being revealed. "It challenges the threads of fate that are woven from the fabric of the cosmos."

"How?"

"You tamper with the contingencies and inclinations of Nature. It is unlawful."

"I need your powers to fight the red people," said Potinija. "They will come to desecrate our temples and destroy us."

"The time of the red people is very near," the being said. "It cannot be helped."

"You must defend us from the ravages of the red people," Potinija insisted. "Our ways are the ways of truth."

"They are only half the truth," the being revealed. "Blood sacrifice will not influence the heavenly order. If anything, they defile the sanctity of created life."

"Oh, Great Mother," Potinija sighed. "We have been cursed."

"Nothing is ever accursed in Nature," the divine being said. "It merely runs its course and fulfils its destiny."

"I, too, oh Queen, must return to fulfil my destiny," Potinija said. "My people need me."

"You cannot return to earth, Potinija," the being revealed.

"Why not?"

"Your body has been rendered too weak to contain your life force."

"You mean I'm dead?" Potinija asked.

"If you chose to regard it as such," the divine being said. "You can choose to return, but the plight will most likely be an unsuccessful one."

"What do you propose I do?"

"You must let yourself go," the being instructed. "You must

forfeit your personal history, your memories and unique vibrations, your very life force to me. You must beach yourself upon the shores of pure consciousness until the seasons change again. There will come a time when the stars will call for the conferral of the lunarized powers upon the reddened peoples, powers which will be forgotten completely. That is when you will be allowed to descend, to return, to incarnate—"

Potinija remained silent.

"If you return, you will suffer the second death, non-existence," the divine being revealed. "You will not be able to diffuse back through the portal."

"Fine," Potinija said. "I accept your offer."

"You agree with all your being?"

"With all my being," Potinija repeated.

"So, let it be done."

Potinija resisted every attempt to hold herself together. Bit by bit, the shards of her personal energy field broke off from her nucleus and were absorbed by the wasp-waisted divinity's self-generated vortices. It wasn't long before she was one with the noetic matter of which the entire cosmos had been hewn. There, she entered that much-desired condition known as nirvana, a dream-like state that was entirely indigenous to divinity itself.

In time, she would incarnate to deliver the golden Logos of the Goddess, to spur human beings to the remembrance of who they once were and what they could become.

Fate Came in Three

Once upon a "fate" there lived a very wealthy, insolent, and selfish man named Andros, who, like most suffering from the dangerous affliction of material wealth, was always disgruntled and never at peace. He was rich in all things: large fields to grow fruit and vegetables; animals such as cows, sheep, donkeys, and goats to fill them; properties with single and multi-storey houses; and a great many horse carriages. But despite these prodigious assets, he was void of happiness.

Now there came a time when Andros was required to travel to the neighboring town to resolve issues surrounding the inheritance of his dead brother's properties. Andros of a self-serving, stingy disposition, thus avoided seeking out the hospitality of other wealthy or influential individuals for fear of attracting to himself the contingency of reciprocating favors of any sort. Although he abhorred it, he much preferred the refuge of the filthy and plague-ridden neighborhood slum where one was bound to commune with the lower mortals who embraced and loved all without expecting anything in return. Their sentiments suited Andros just fine.

Instead of seeking hospitality in the rich quarters, Andros began his door-knocking enterprise in the dilapidated downtown. He was dutifully received on his third attempt by a vibrant couple who made room for their overnight guest by laying a mattress in the corner of their two-room home. Before long, he became aware of a third presence in the home, a newborn baby. If Andros had known this from the beginning, he would have turned down the offer. He wasn't particularly enthused by the idea of sleeping in the same space as an infant prone to high-pitched outbursts throughout the night.

Andros didn't even like kids, save for his own. After the young couple went to bed in the adjoining room, he found himself scowling repeatedly at the infant in the crib every time it laughed, burped, or whimpered. The night brimmed with all sorts of bothersome noises: Andros could hear the hoot of an owl as it soared above the house in search of prey and the neighing of horses as they pulled carriages urgently along the dirt road which passed directly in front of the cottage. It appeared Hypnos, the god of sleep, had forgotten to sprinkle his nocturnal dust over Andros's eyes tonight.

Huddling in his corner of the room, Andros pondered on how best he could fool his brother's wife into signing over her inherited possessions to him. He became so entangled in these fantasies that he failed to see three snow-colored entities materialize from the slivers of moonlight that seeped into the room from the window and illuminated the baby's crib. The three entities morphed from vaguely discernible human figures into seductive femme fatales, to skin-wrinkled crones, to little girls with gold-colored hair. Then they were femme fatales again.

The sight mortified Andros. He cupped a hand over his mouth to muffle his own scream.

"Look at this little cherub," one of them whispered, stroking the infant's head. "Isn't he gorgeous?"

"He is Clotho," another agreed.

"Cute and adorable," said the third.

"Too cute and adorable to be poor, that's for sure," said the one who went by the name Clotho. "Lachesis and Atropos, are you two thinking what I'm thinking?"

"Sure." The other two nodded.

"Let's take the biological parents out of the picture and weave this little bundle of joy into the graceless life of that miserable old fool lying in the corner over there," said Clotho.

"Yes," the others agreed. "This little cutie will inherit the mister's wealth."

The three entities exchanged looks and giggled. Clotho withdrew a magic wand, waved it around and muttered some words over the baby's crib. Then the three dematerialized into slivers of moonlight and disappeared.

Andros, who'd been conscious, had heard every word that had been whispered in the preternatural dark. He was immediately gripped by a fear that took on a more tangible form and formed a stranglehold around his neck. He began to hyperventilate and it wasn't long before his whole body became saturated by a veil of perspiration.

What possessed them to think that the son of an old nobody, a peasant, had any rights to the riches and glories that another had acquired through hard work and perseverance? No, he thought. There would be none of that. He would either beat the "fates" at their own game or take "fate" into his own hands.

When dawn came, he scurried to his feet and stumbled into the adjoining room, having rehearsed the dramatic script in the recesses of his own mind.

"Good morning!" the young peasant said. "Did you sleep well?"

"Couldn't have slept better," Andros lied. "I have a proposition for you."

"What proposition?"

"As I lay on the comfortable mattress you two cherished people offered me last night," he said, "I had time to mull things over, to think about why I'd been unhappy all these years! The realization struck me like a ton of bricks. I knew what had been missing from my life."

"What had been missing from your life?" the peasant asked.

"A child," Andros said. "You see, my wife and I have no children of our own. Watching your son as he slept peacefully last night, I came to realize that what was missing from my life was the presence of a child. I knew it, felt it. For what greater joy could exist in this world to rival the reward and honor that comes with being a good parent? I always sought happiness and splendor in gold instead of seeking in the laughter of an infant. If you give me your son, I will raise him as my own. I would dearly love to be a father. Your son will be raised amongst wealth and nobility; he will be showered in gifts. He will be given opportunities that other children born to humble parents like you can only dream about."

The peasant laughed. "I couldn't just hand you my son."

"Sure, you could," Andros said. "You and your wife are still young and will have many children. My wife and I, on the other hand, are way past our primes. And besides, the "fates" revealed it in my dream last night. They led me to you so that I could give your son a chance at life; a chance at happiness."

"But riches don't necessarily make one happy," the peasant argued.

"It depends," Andros said. "It certainly creates the conditions necessary for happiness to grow. If you don't have money, your chances of being happy are slim to none."

The peasant looked at his wife. "What do you think?"

She shrugged. "The stranger speaks the truth, husband. He can give our child things that we can't."

"But ...."

"If it is the decree of the mighty Fates as you say, then I willingly accept their will on condition that you allow us to see him as often, and as quickly as we like."

"Have no fear," Andros said. "You can see him whenever you choose."

"Then he is yours."

But Andros never had any intention of adopting and raising the child. His ploy was merely a theatrical ruse to separate the baby from its parents. As soon as he reached the outskirts of the city, he ordered his obedient servant to hurl the baby onto a sharp rock.

"I won't," the servant argued. "God will cause misfortune to rain down upon me for having committed the most heinous of crimes."

Andros yanked the servant to his feet by his shirt. 'Do it you low life filth, of I'll humiliate you in front of your own children."

"Let go of me," the servant said, staggering backwards.

Taking the child with him, the servant stumbled toward the cornfields, torn between the act he was compelled to commit and the repercussions of not following through with it. Thankfully, he was the kind of man who could weed his way out of unruly situations by thinking laterally. And think laterally he did, for the minute he reached the cornfields, he picked up a rock and threw it against another with all his might, issuing a cacophonous noise to confuse his master. Leaving the infant hidden in the grasses, he raced back to the dust road where Andros stood waiting beside the horse carriage.

"What happened?" Andros asked him.

'I did it, but I think someone saw," the peasant panted.

"Quick, let's get out of here then!" Andros yelled.

Never once thinking that the servant may have deceived him, Andros made haste for his hometown.

A great many years elapsed before Andros returned to the site of the alleged crime, this time for business. A blue-eyed, blond-haired youth, no more than about sixteen or seventeen years of age, greeted him at the tall iron gates which guarded the entrance to the farmhouse.

"Is this the Nicholais residence?" Andros asked the youth.

"This is it," the youth replied. "My parents aren't here today but they said you were coming to pick up some cedar wood for your fireplace. Is that right?"

"Yeah."

"Come with me. I'll show you where it is."

"Nicholais never told me he had a son," said Andros.

The youth smiled. "My parents are very private people."

As they walked, Andros noticed a golden chain around the youth's neck. His eyes dropped lower. A gold-plated coin swung over his pectorals as he walked. Andros noticed that the word "Naidis" was inscribed around its rim.

"What's that thing around your neck?" Andros asked. "It says Naidis on it. Doesn't that mean Foundling?"

"Oh, that's my name," the youth replied. "My dad hung it around my neck, days after he found me."

"Found you?"

"Yes, right over there," Naidis said, pointing towards the cornfields. "I was a wee little thing when they found me, barely four days old. My mother said she'd seen a dream in which God bestowed a gift upon the household. In fact, God told my mother that she and my father should expect to find a bundle of joy in the most unlikely of places."

"Oh."

"I'm not sure how much of it I believe," Naidis went on, fumbling the coin around his neck, "but I do know that I'm adopted. I look nothing like my mother or father."

Andros felt blood rush up to his head. How could this have happened? How could that damned servant of his have betrayed him like this? There could be no question that this was the same child he'd conspired to murder aeons ago. He knew that time was running out. He had to act fast to halt the unraveling prophecy dead in its tracks.

"What's wrong?" Naidis asked him. 'You look like you've seen a ghost."

"Um… well… there's also another reason why I'm here. One your parents don't know about," said Andros.

"Go on."

"I've got an important message that needs to reach home as soon as possible," Andros winced, "and there's simply no way that I can deliver it in time. My carriage was stolen by some armed thieves back there. Walking will take me days…"

Naidis rubbed his back. "Don't let that bother you. I'll deliver it."

"Are you sure?"

"Yes," Naidis said. "We've got a horse all saddled up and ready to go."

Andros withdrew a small parchment from his pocket and scribbled something onto it using a black-feathered quill. He folded the letter neatly in half and handed it over to Naidis.

"It's for my wife's eyes only," Andros told him. "It's for her and only her."

"Understood," said Naidis. "I can't read so you have nothing to worry about."

The journey back to Andros's residence was full of surprises. He'd been propositioned by a fortune-telling gypsy; he'd attempted communion with foreigners who spoke in strange tongues, and he'd brushed shoulders with the archbishop of the Greek Orthodox Church.

But one specific event stood out, one that he couldn't quite jettison from his thoughts throughout the duration of the trip. It had occurred near water. His intentions to stop for a brief hiatus had been sabotaged by his lethargy, and his exhaustion was such that he fell asleep beside the river, lulled to sleep by the running waters. He awoke to the realization that the position of the letter inside his jacket had moved. It was now inside the front pocket of his pants. Had somebody moved it whilst he lay on the ground, completely unaware? Stranger still was that it didn't even look like the same letter. It had changed somehow.

In any case, he attributed the phenomenon to his tired mind and pushed on, arriving at his intended destination before nightfall. The residence was an oppressively opulent mansion, framed by beautiful balustrades and decorated with stone lions, eagles and mythological creatures of every kind. It was a residence fit for the noblest of kings and queens.

As he dismounted his animal, he caught sight of a supernal maiden looking out from one of the windows. Naidis guessed that it was Andros's daughter. He was entirely transfixed by her gaze. Desire began to well up from the fountainhead of his psyche. It fueled a ravenous fire that burned in the pit of his heart and loins. It was love at first sight.

An elderly woman with sharp features was waiting for him

at the door.

"Good evening, madam, would you happen to be Andros's wife?"

"It is I, yes," she said.

"I have an urgent message for you," he said, handing the letter over.

"Thank you."

Naidis watched as her eyes scanned the document. The creases around her eyes and lips deepened as her lips curled into a smile.

"Finally!" she said, throwing the letter into the air. "Oh, I so knew that sooner or later, God would shed his light upon my husband and he'd change his mind about our daughter. Finally, she will be wed."

"To whom?" Naidis asked, feeling a tight knot form in his stomach.

"To you, my boy!" she yelled, pulling Naidis towards her. "You are the bearer of good news! He wants me to summon a priest and marry the two of you before his return."

Naidis couldn't believe his fruit-laden luck. He'd struck gold.

Andros returned home a week afterward, expecting to find Naidis dead, buried and confined to existence in the terrible past. Instead, he was greeted by an entourage that included his wife, son, daughter, and an uninvited guest. He nearly had a coronary when he glimpsed the rings that hugged the index fingers of the latter two. He opened and closed his eyes rapidly and scrunched his face, but the hallucination wouldn't disappear. It merely grew more concrete by the passing second. Naidis was still alive, and, worse, he was now part of the family, a son-in-law and possible heir to his kingdom.

Andros cussed under his breath. His wife was certainly the primal cause of this inveiglement. It was she who was the cause of this evil, for she had openly flouted his authority. He waited until they were alone afterwards to vent his mounting fury.

"What possessed you to do such a thing?" he yelled at her. "Why didn't you do what I asked of you?"

"Stop screaming. I did exactly what you asked of me," she replied, throwing the letter at him. "That's your writing, isn't it?"

Andros scanned the letter. He stared at it aghast, staring at the words inscribed on the page in utter disbelief.

"It is," he heard himself whisper.

"So, what has angered you?" she asked.

"It doesn't matter," he said. "In the morning, I need an urgent message to be delivered to the lumberjacks working our land up north."

"Yes."

"I'll leave a letter on the kitchen table first thing in the morning before I head into town," he continued. "You make sure that Naidis is up to deliver it, you hear?"

"Sure."

"Naidis is to deliver it," Andros repeated, walking out of the mansion, slamming the door shut behind him.

The following morning, Andros returned from completing some errands to find his wife picking dandelions, sunflowers, and roses from the garden.

"Look!" she prompted her husband. "Do you like what I've picked for Naidis and our daughter? I'm going to put them in a vase and take it up to the room now. I want to surprise them."

"Wait a second!" Andros yelled. "Didn't you send Naidis to the lumberjacks with the letter I left on the kitchen table?"

"Oh yeah," she said. "I forgot to tell you. He was still asleep when I went upstairs this morning. I didn't want to wake him, for he looked so peaceful beside our daughter…"

Andros's heart was beating so hard that he thought it might explode.

"…so, I sent it up with our son."

"You did what?" he screamed. "You stupid, stupid woman."

"Why are you upset?" she asked.

"How long ago did you send him?" Andros asked.

"About half an hour ago," his wife answered.

Andros hastened to the lumberjacks, running as fast as his legs could carry him in a bid to overtake the tragedy which loomed so tangible in the air now, but it was too late. The letter was addressed to the rustic, heartless mountaineers who worked for him and it was a threatening order which sanctioned the death and dismemberment of the person who handed it to them. When Andros arrived, they had already disposed of his son's body parts in a nearby well.

Letting out an ululation of despair, Andros threw himself into the well and perished. After the grim news of the horrific deaths reached the household, his wife jettisoned all sanity and became possessed by a madness which drove her to commit suicide in the heat of the moment.

They say that everything comes in threes. If we so adhere to this philosophy, then it might not be so surprising to know that on that fateful day, the personification of death known to the Greeks as Charos came to collect the souls of the father, and unfortunately, those of the innocent mother and son. This left Naidis and his newly wedded wife as the sole inheritors of a dowry fit for the noblest of kings and queens.

On the whole, Naidis had little to complain about, for the "fates" were indeed ruminating in bliss at the same time he was born. Hence, their smiles were in his every breath and his every train of thought. They pervaded everything that Naidis did and carried him aloft on a magic carpet to worlds where everything he touched just turned to gold.

And this concludes the incredible story of the man called Naidis who was favored by the three Fates.

A Golden Moment

Told that one possesses the Midas touch, one infers that he or she is a harbinger of good luck and serendipity or proliferator of 'gold'. Many have heard this figure of speech, yet it is impossible to understand without knowledge of the beautiful myth which underpins the saying. The tale itself, retold here in my own way, first appears in Ovid's Metamorphoses.

One might think of King Midas of Phrygia as the universal archetype of an imprudent and senseless man who temporarily succeeded in plunging neck-deep into the sugar-laid oppressive opulence of unprecedented riches. However, as good old Mother Nature would have it, since Midas' intellectual capacity and ability to reason were vastly limited, he was robbed of the opportunity to enjoy the far-reaching riches. The story of King Midas serves to illuminate the ironic tragedy at the heart of the human condition and to bring to our collective awareness the unusually high incidence of human stupidity. Moreover, it offers a reverberating moral, that the acquisition of affluence means absolutely nothing if its inheritor is mentally and spiritually ungrounded or devoid of the astute and adroit judgment so characteristic of intellectual thought.

Midas was blessed because he had been raised in Phrygia, the land of milk and honey. The latter was like the womb of the Earth Mother; even the stubbornest plants and trees which might demand very explicit weather conditions for growth would take root there. Phrygia's floral emblem was the rose, and rightfully so, given that the famed flower grew there in profusion. Midas's palace was decked in lush gardens containing roses of every shape, size, and description. There were rusty and scarlet five-petalled reds, golden yellows, inbred blues, coral pinks, and creamy virgin whites. Even more remarkable was the intoxicating fragrance that emanated from them. Walking through the labyrinth pathways that circumscribed the gardens was akin to experiencing nitrogen narcosis when one dived down into the cavernous depths of the sea.

One afternoon, whilst Midas's servants were out and about enacting their usual maintenance duties, they discovered an elderly man sleeping amongst a grove of roses. They aptly concluded he was a casualty of the Dionysian rites of the evening before. The intoxication intrinsic to the Dionysian way had robbed him of his noonday senses and separated him from the long train of orgiastic dancers which passed near the Midan gardens tracing out invisible S-bends and meanders in the early morning hours. Wishing to amuse and impress their king, the servants garnered a spectacle fit for royal eyes by entwining the drunken man in rose garlands and decking him in a crown of bird feathers. They proceeded to hoist him to his feet and carry him to Midas's royal chambers in a semi-conscious state. The only thing that issued from the elderly man's mouth during the small pilgrimage to the palace was a verbal sandwich of "oohs" and "ahhs" and the occasional groan. Miraculously the servants succeeded in extracting a name–Silenus–or old Silenus, as most of the townsfolk identified him.

Midas, himself a self-proclaimed adherent and fan of the Dionysian rites, found Silenus to be immensely flamboyant and entertaining and he decided on the spur of the moment to accommodate him in the residential quarters of his palace as an honored guest. About ten days elapsed before the novelty of his newfound entertainment had worn off, at which time Midas happily agreed to escort old Silenus back to the gargantuan grapevines in northern Phrygia, Dionysus's corporeal home. Midas had never been in the presence of a god before, so one can imagine his surprise and awe at seeing the divinity suddenly acquire an anthropomorphic form from a clump of grapes that dangled from a colossal vine to his side.

"Thanks for bringing back one of my most faithful proselytes," said Dionysus.

"No problem," Midas said, smiling.

"No. Thank you," he said, stepping forward and putting a hand on his shoulder. "And to show you how grateful I am, I shall bestow any gift your heart desires."

"Are you for real?" Midas's eyes widened. "You're not just pulling my leg, are you?"

"Try me," the god prompted.

"Anything I want?"

"Sure," Dionysus assured. "Like anything?"

"Yes."

Midas's mouth curled up into a grin. "I want everything I touch to turn to gold."

"You sure about that, Midas?"

"Of course, I'm sure," Midas said. "Why else would I ask for it if I wasn't sure?"

"Think about it."

"I have," Midas said. "Just do it already."

"Fine," Dionysus said, stepping forward and exhaling onto Midas's face. "All done."

"What's done?"

"What you asked," Dionysus said. "Check it out."

Midas was puzzled. "How?"

"Touch something, Your Majesty."

Midas reached out and touched a chair, which instantly began to phosphoresce with a golden hue. "It's gold!"

"So, it is!"

"Look at this," he said, trudging up to a cup and putting his index finger on it. The cup's internal composition changed instantly. "It's made of gold now."

"Riveting," said Dionysus.

"You!" Midas sprinted towards a sluggish-moving lizard. "You'd make a great addition to my collection of animal statues," he blurted, tapping the lizard on its head. "You're gold now."

"You have been blessed!" Dionysus ridiculed.

"Oh, for sure," Midas said. "What else around here should I turn into gold?" Midas asked. "Gold, gold, gold!"

"Hmm... I think your gold-making efforts have exhausted you, Midas," Dionysus teased, offering him a platter of lush grapes. "Here's a little something to replenish your reserves."

"Thanks," Midas said, taking the grapes from Dionysus. After a few seconds, his smile vanished.

"What's wrong?"

"Well, they're gold."

"You like stating the obvious, don't you?" Dionysus asked.

"I can't eat these," said Midas.

"Not unless you render the yellow metal into a colloidal solution," said Dionysus, taking a sip of wine from his chalice.

"What in Zeus's name are you talking about? Midas asked. "I need to be able to turn it off so I can eat and drink, otherwise

I'll die of thirst or starvation."

"That wasn't part of the deal," Dionysus pointed out.

"I hadn't thought about it," Midas admitted.

"I don't believe you encompass that possibility," said Dionysus.

"Excuse me?"

"Thinking," Dionysus said, taking another sip of wine. "It's not indigenous to your being."

"What will I do now?" Midas asked.

"Start thinking for a start," Dionysus said. "Wishing is such a barren enterprise when it is a by-product of thoughtlessness."

"Help me."

"Or nonsensicalness," Dionysus continued.

"Please help me," said Midas, dropping to his knees.

Dionysus ignored him. "Or stupidity, Midas, a quality which you express in profusion."

"I don't want it anymore," said Midas.

"What? The gift or the gold you just made?"

"Both."

"You'll need a time machine to go into the future and discover the secrets of colloidal gold, which is edible... drinkable I should say. There you go, problem solved."

"Why are you doing this to me?" Midas asked. "I made a mistake; surely you can see and forgive that. Don't let me starve, I beg you."

"I'd help you, Midas, but I can't," Dionysus informed. "Once a god bestows a divine gift or power upon a mortal, it can never be retracted."

"So, I'm going to die," said Midas "Great."

"Look," Dionysus said. "There is one way to jettison the gift."

"How?"

"Go to the origin of Pactolus," Dionysus said. "Go to the great spring which feeds that great river. Once you are there, submerge yourself entirely in its waters."

"Will the River Pactolus take it away?"

"It will cleanse you of divine touch," Dionysus said. "Sadly, that's the only thing it will cleanse you of."

"What's that supposed to mean?"

"Think about it," Dionysus said. "You need to start thinking, remember."

"I will go to Pactolus," Midas said. "Soon—tonight even."

"Go then," Dionysus prompted him, "and never forget that the art of wishing is an art that brings gold to the ripened intellect, one with a functioning moral compass attached to it that always points due north."

Midas scratched his head. "Due north?"

"Yes, the direction you'll be moving in later today and for the remainder of your life," Dionysus said. "Literally and spiritually."

Through Dionysus's kind intervention, Midas was able to jettison the gold-making gift that had finally revealed itself as a curse. What he never managed to lose, though, was his mental incapacity. From that perspective, he never got anywhere near the north. Just as a leopard may never change its spots, so, too, was King Midas forever bound to foolishness. Sometime after his wishing folly, Midas was approached by the Olympian godhead and asked to judge a musical contest between Apollo, the god of music, light and poetry, and Pan, the god of fertility and sexual gratification. The latter was no stranger to music and could belt out some very pleasing tribal and rustic tunes on his reed pipes, but he was often made to look amateurish and untutored before the music of the heavenly spheres spawned by the supernal Apollo. Anyone who ever heard Apollo strumming his silver lyre became entranced; his melodies were so sweet and syrupy, so harmonic and otherworldly, so readily able to evoke the spectrum of emotions, that the only compositions that could compare were those spun by the choir of the Muses.

With no faculty of higher intellect to guide him, Midas espoused an honest affinity with Pan's performance and indicated this preference by handing him his palm. One might say that Midas's decision exemplified just how low he would have scored on a modern IQ test. Not only did he prefer a lesser, rudimentary form of musical entertainment to a lyre that sounded like the orchestra of the rotating heavenly spheres, but he also made the tragic mistake of unwisely electing a lesser powerful entity as his victor. Judging a lesser being as being nobler or "fairer" in appearance or ability than an Olympian was foremost of the ways one attracted themselves to the anger or vehemence of the latter. Nonetheless, Apollo did not take offence at Midas's decision, for it was devoid of the ambrosial and intellectual commodity known as thought. He did, however, make his feelings known by changing Midas's ears into those of an ass. Through no fault of its own, and pertaining to its own intrinsic nature, the ass is an animal equipped with very limited intellectual capacity, as well as having a pair of ears untutored to higher understanding and learning that prove the rule. Given that Midas encompassed both, Apollo reasoned that he may as well adopt some of the ass's physiognomy.

Midas's newfound ears embarrassed him so much that he had a hat specifically made to shroud them. Nobody ever saw them, save the poor servant responsible for his physical maintenance. On many occasions, the servant would snigger quietly to himself as he snipped the hair around the king's ears. Midas had managed to convince him to take an obligatory oath of silence regarding the disfigurement, but the grossly misshapen ears were of such an intriguing and mesmerizing nature that the servant's will to speak openly about them could not be contained. One day, the servant dashed out to a nearby plantation where he dug a shallow pit and whispered into it the words, "King Midas has asses' ears." The act of blurting out the secret in the presence of only Mother Nature herself relieved the servant of the sudden urge to divulge the secret without actually breaking the oath, but it also had the adverse effect of imprinting the surrounding soil with knowledge of the fact. When spring finally came, the reeds that sprouted from the small pit would disclose Midas's unfortunate condition each time they were rustled by the breeze, rendering the secret common knowledge to all who loitered about.

In hindsight, it would be fitting to suggest that the tale of Midas is an allegory for the most tragic aspect of the human condition; the seed of wisdom, knowledge and an antidote to inanity might very well be latent in those deemed ignorant by the philosopher or spiritual teacher, but it is entirely absent in the idiot or imbecile. One cannot make gold from lead or dust if the kernel of becoming isn't contained from the very beginning; an adult cannot be expected to make moral choices in life if they have not been properly fitted with the correct ethical compass from birth. Utilizing one's thought processes goes a very long way, too. They were bestowed to human beings by the superior intellect for a reason.

The Therapist

Orpheus, the progeny of a Thracian prince and one of the Muses, appears twice in the annals of classical literature: as a guardian for Jason and the Argonauts on the Argo, and in a short-lived romance involving his chosen life partner, Eurydice. The first is transcribed by a third-century Hellenic poet, Apollonius of Rhodes; the second is by two Roman literary greats, Virgil and Ovid.

Jim Sweeting was quite fond of quoting the axiom, "Chemotherapy destroys ailing cells and psychotherapy ailing thought patterns." The vast corpus of his professional opinion hinged on those golden words. According to Jim, using antipsychotics, barbiturates, narcotics, and other wonder drugs, which most clinicians were vastly dependent upon in treating their patients, was bereft of formative power. This merely blanketed the symptoms of psychiatric and psychological dysfunctions, dressing them in superficial garments of normalcy so as to provide the illusion of restored health. For a professional whose chosen medium was merely an avenue for financial gain, the answers offered up by drugs sufficed; alternatively, for a compassionate humanitarian like Jim, the latter was merely an intermediary until humanity experienced another fundamental leap in its understanding of neuroscience. But being of an impatient disposition, he wasn't just going to fold his hands across his chest and wait for that glorious moment to transpire; that would be an immense waste of time and energy. Instead, he would initiate a radical departure from the reductionist approach of Western medicine, opting for herbal preparations which brought recuperative effects on the nervous system. Many of these he'd learned whilst living and travelling through the Hindu Kush.

Jim was, amongst other things, intensely ambitious and profound—a beacon of light in Stygian darkness. He lived, breathed, and practised clinical psychiatry and psychology with an evangelical zeal. There wasn't much he wouldn't attempt for the sake of curing his patients. He was a devoted advocate of conventional psychotherapy, but unlike other practitioners in the field, he didn't mind listening to the nonsensical, eccentric ramblings that typified many consultations and took up thick slices of his day. He was a good listener and his high success rate in exacting cures attracted the admiration and respect of his peers. It also brought the enmity and jealousy of those towing their dreams along the same denomination of inquiry.

Lately, he'd become deeply involved with Orpheus, a Greek-Australian musician suffering from acute night terrors and mild hallucinations. The severity and longevity of Orpheus's anxiety and unrest didn't disconcert Jim; not yet anyway. He'd dealt with many such cases in the past and all of them could be explained in the context of Freudian theory; just like the physical body came equipped with immune defenses to mend and protect it from foreign invasion, so, too, was the human mind wired with a psychic mechanism that became activated when a median threshold for traumatic and hurtful experiences was surpassed. In such instances, individual memories pertaining to the trauma were isolated from the conscious role of psychic film and were buried deep in the vast and oceanic territories of the unconscious. When the individual experienced an event whose internal composition or anatomy was identical or near identical to the repressed memory, details of the former trauma erupted into consciousness again like a landmine being trotted on.

As a therapist, Jim's role was to access the contents of repressed memories through the application of techniques such as guided fantasy, expressive therapy through art, word association, and hypnosis. Being the language of the unconscious, dreams often held the key to identifying and harmonizing the traumatic contents which in effect healed the individual by fusing together the two fragmented halves of the personality. Thanks to his intimate knowledge of Freudian ideology and Jungian archetypes, Jim was especially good at interpreting dream symbols and had, this way, identified innumerable phobias, past traumas, complexes, and disorders. If the working theory had served him so well in the past, there was no reason why it should meander about and cease as an intellectual dead end now.

He picked up the dream journal and flipped through it again, looking for distinct patterns in this pictorial sequence of strains and dissatisfactions that might betray the nature of the trauma. Determined to get to the root of Orpheus's problem, Jim could not, would not, fail. A future promotion to the position of Director of the Faculty of Clinical Psychology could very well be contingent on the outcome here.

After meditating on one of the recurring images, he clasped his eyes shut and rubbed his face with both hands.

"Dr. Sweeting?" sounded a familiar voice from the door.

"Amara, you're early."

"No traffic."

"Oh, yeah, it's nearly six."

"You shouldn't work so hard, Jimmy. Liz might end up filing for divorce," she joked.

"Yeah, I wouldn't blame her. Did you get the chance to look at this?" Jim held up the diary.

"Just the samples you sent me."

"Wacky stuff, hey?"

"I don't know if I'd want to sleep if I had to endure dreams like that every night," Amara said. "Some of them make horror flicks like Paranormal Activity seem lame and tame by comparison. The poor guy must be mortified."

"Well, it's got me kind of edgy and I'm not even the one experiencing them. Liz thinks I'm becoming it."

"Becoming what?"

"The diary."

"True, that," said Amara, shaking her head. "I seriously don't know how you do it. I mean, the dream where he's talking about all those invisible hands groping him everywhere really sent shivers up my spine. The one where his fingers are blown off doesn't fall too far behind either."

"That's just a fear of losing what he loves most."

"His fingers?"

Jim laughed. "No, the ability to play the harp and mandolin. He's a musician, remember?"

"Oh, I'd forgotten about that. Anyhow the dream which really got me jittery was the one where he's trapped in a cellar with all those cockroaches crawling all over him. That made the hair on my skin rise. I can't stand creepy crawlies."

"Is there anything that really stood out?"

"In the diary, you mean?"

"Yeah."

"There was one thing."

"Go ahead."

"The recurring vision in the cave," said Amara. "You know, the one where he's trapped underground."

"Exactly my thoughts," said Jim. "That one is fascinating because it always occurs just before waking. In the diary, he explains that it's a fragmented vision; there's no beginning to it. It just starts off midpoint as if he's a passive observer who has been dropped smack bang into the middle of an action scene. It's always pitch dark in there, and ghastly. He's always running away from something, too. He doesn't quite know what he's running from, except that it's something evil, very evil. Then he sees the pinprick of light, which is the exit, the mouth of the cave leading to freedom...."

"But he awakes just before passing through it," Amara added.

"Right."

"There's someone with him too, isn't there? Someone who's running directly behind him."

"Yeah, that's Eurydice."

"Who is that?"

"It's his wife."

"I didn't know he was married," said Amara.

"Was," said Jim. "She died a few years ago."

"Oh."

"It happened while they were on their honeymoon," said Jim. "They went exploring and discovered a deserted mine that hadn't been in use since God knows when. After such a long time of disuse, the shafts had become highly unstable. Orpheus and Eurydice ignored the signs of wear and tear and decided to go walkabouts anyway. They didn't get very far though; one of the ceilings collapsed and the breakdown rained onto Eurydice, killing her instantly."

"That's sad," Amara sighed.

"I know."

"Do you think the vision is an admittance of guilt then? You know, the guilt that comes with having survived such a tragic event; the guilt of having done nothing to save her, even though he couldn't."

"Maybe," said Jim. "I still haven't figured out whether he's leading her out of the cave or whether he's running from her."

Amara frowned. "Why would he run from her? That doesn't make any sense at all."

"It does when you look at it as a whole," said Jim. "Think about the psychosomatic symptoms. Orpheus said that when he's running through the cave, he feels like there's someone biting and scratching his arms and legs. The marks on his body correspond precisely to those positions."

"Yeah? And you're sure that they're genuine?" asked Amara. "I mean, someone in his condition could easily self-mutilate and then make up wild stories and embellishments about how they'd come about."

"No, I'm pretty sure that they're genuine. I've had him under close observation."

"If the trauma is manifesting physically then it must be something very deep," said Amara.

"How much deeper can it be than watching a loved one die in front of you?"

"I don't think we've quite gathered all the pieces of this puzzle yet," said Amara. "There's something else. There's got to be."

"You're reading my mind and I don't like it. That's my

job!"

"We've missed something for sure," said Amara.

"Yes," said Jim. "That's why I called you, remember?"

"You're just looking for new and wonderful ways to spice up my life, aren't you, Dr. Sweeting?"

"How did you know?" Jim asked, grinning. "We need to exhaust the possibilities. We need to get to the bottom of this."

"We will," said Amara. "But don't expect the bottom to be a bouquet of flowers, a box of chocolates or a cheerful face."

Orpheus barged into the consultation room looking dishevelled and glum. His shirt was furrowed, open and untucked. He'd obviously been running in the rain; strands of wet hair were glued to his forehead. Gobs of fresh mud splashed onto his pants. Sweat ran along his temples. Jim was always thankful that Orpheus never used deodorant sparingly.

"I'm really sorry, but practice finished late."

"Not a problem," said Jim. "We haven't been waiting long anyway. Orpheus, I'd like you to meet a colleague of mine, Dr. Amara Edmonton."

"Hi, Dr. Edmonton."

"Pleased to meet you, Orpheus."

"Dr. Edmonton is a clinical hypnotherapist and will be guiding the hypnosis today. Are you ok with that?"

Orpheus shrugged. "Sure."

"We're going to approach this in a very simple manner," said Jim. "There seems to be a blockage of sorts in your subconscious."

"We're hoping that the hypnosis will clear it," Amara added.

"Once we know what it is, we'll talk about it and hopefully

it will stop."

"Do you think it will stop?" asked Orpheus, a glimmer of hope in his eyes.

"Don't see why not," said Jim. "Much of it depends on your own attitude."

"I hope I can beat it."

"No...."

"I'm going to beat it."

"That's better," said Jim. "And you will."

"It's been a long while since I've had a good night's sleep, Dr. Sweeting."

"How long, Orpheus?"

"Oh, years," he said. "It all started when my wife died."

"Why did you let it linger for so long without seeking professional help?"

"I was scared."

"Of what?"

"The dream," he said.

"The dream isn't real. It can't hurt you."

Orpheus remained silent for a few seconds. "I know, but it might be something embarrassing."

"You've got nothing to worry about," said Jim. "My colleague and I are professionals. Everything is strictly confidential; whatever you say in this room stays in this room."

Orpheus was staring directly at Jim, his eyes blank and unnerving.

"Tell me more about Eurydice."

"What would you like to know?"

"Anything,' said Jim. "What was she like?"

"I loved her very much. She was a decent girl, very pretty,

a bit stubborn; she was a Taurus, you see. She was a bit queer, too."

"Queer?"

"Yeah, into pentacles and all this Gothic stuff," said Orpheus. "She used to keep these weird-looking wax figures in the wardrobe."

"Witchcraft?"

"No, she wasn't a pagan."

"What was she then?"

"Greek Orthodox."

"You're Greek Orthodox, aren't you?"

"I'm not quite sure anymore."

"Faith in a higher purpose can be a powerful thing," said Jim.
"Do you believe in life after death?"

"You mean whether or not somebody can continue to exist in an alternate dimension?"

"Yeah," said Orpheus. "Do you think someone can cheat death, continue to exist in an alternate dimension, and then find a way to come back into our world?"

"Are you referring to reincarnation?"

"Yeah."

Jim sighed. "No, I don't believe in reincarnation, Orpheus. What about you, do you believe in it?"

"I never used to believe in it but now I'm not so sure."

"Sorry to interrupt," said Amara, "but how is reincarnation related to your wife?"

"She said she knew how to cheat it."

"Cheat what?" asked Jim.

"Death."

"When did she tell you this?"

"When we first got together," he said. "I don't think there was a day that I wasn't reminded of the fact."

"That's not a fact, Orpheus."

"No."

"So, you never took her claim seriously?"

"Never, but I'm less certain now than I used to be."

"Why would you entertain it now?"

"Well things have started happening," said Orpheus. "Things I can't explain."

"Do you think there's a chance that these things come from your own self?"

"Are you trying to say that I'm crazy?"

"I never use that word, Orpheus."

"But that's what you think."

"I don't think that at all, Orpheus. I'm just curious if you think they could be irruptions of your own subconscious."

"Possibly."

Jim watched from his reclining chair as Amara put Orpheus into a hypnotic trance with the use of a swinging pendulum. Once he was under, she regressed him to a date and time consistent with the recurring vision in his dream journal.

"Where are you, Orpheus?"

"I don't know."

"Can you see anything?"

"No, it's dark."

"Start walking forward."

"What if I trip over a rock?"

"A rock? You must be outside somewhere."

"It feels like it."

"Start walking."

"Oh, hold on a second."

"What is it?"

"There's something in the distance. It looks like a bonfire."

"A bonfire?"

"Yeah, it's ablaze next to a stone table. The stone table is enclosed in a circle of tombstones. No wait, they're not stones. They're people prostrated on the ground."

"Why?"

"They're praying."

"To whom?"

"A tall, hooded figure, with horns, in a red robe. She's holding a stiletto knife."

"Is this a cult of some sort?"

"She's holding the knife over an infant which they've strapped onto the table. Oh no! She can't do that! For God's sake, don't let her do it!"

"You need to calm down, Orpheus. Calm down, ok? You're reliving a dream. Nothing can hurt you here. Breathe in, breathe out. Breathe in, breathe out."

"I'm breathing."

"Very good. Now, without getting too caught up in the experience, I want you to tell me exactly what happens next."

"They're all chanting in a language I don't understand. It sounds a lot like Latin. Th—There's blood splattered everywhere."

"Go on."

"P-people are walking around the table, h-howling at the top of their voices and s-stabbing it with their knives. It's s-still alive."

"Go on."

"Oh, J-Jesus... No, I c-can't look!"

"You need to stay calm, Orpheus. Tell me what's going

on."

"The horned woman with the red face is using the stiletto knife to cut out the beating heart... Oh, J-Jesus Ch-Christ."

"Relax, Orpheus."

"I'm relaxing."

"You're hyperventilating."

"Oh my God."

"What's happening now?"

"A woman has flopped onto the stone table. The horned woman has sliced a leg off the dead infant and is inserting it into the woman's vagina with a pair of pliers. Oh, I think I'm going to be s-sick..."

"Do you see anyone you recognize?"

"No."

"Are you sure? What do the people attending look like?"

"I can only see their shadows. There isn't enough light."

"What about the horned woman? Do you know who she is?"

"Her head is always lowered. I can't see her face."

"Orpheus, is this what you see every night before waking?"

"Yes, this is the vision I see."

"But is it only a vision?"

"What do you mean?"

"Is this something you've witnessed before in real life?"

"Y-yes."

"When?"

"Many years ago. Right after I got married."

"Where did you witness this?"

Orpheus remained silent.

"Where, Orpheus? A cave?"

"No."

"A courtyard?"

"No."

"An abandoned warehouse?"

"No."

"A mine, maybe?"

"Yes, that's it. There are wagons loaded with coal beside me. It's a mine."

"An abandoned mine?"

"Yes."

"Where is this mine?"

"I'm frightened."

"Nothing's going to happen to you. You're perfectly safe."

"Wait a second she's lifting her head up."

"Who?"

"The woman with the horns."

"The high priestess?"

"Yes."

"Who is she?"

"Oh, my G-God."

"Who is she, Orpheus?"

"It's... it's…"

"Tell me."

"Eurydice."

Jim felt the hair on his skin begin to rise. He exchanged glances with Amara, who was equally flustered. Nevertheless, her calculated psychic probing was proving very successful and she wasn't about to let up. Jim couldn't discern anything in her overall demeanor to suggest that the session should be terminated.

"Oh!" he exclaimed.

"What's wrong, Orpheus?" asked Amara.

"She's looking straight at me!"

"Eurydice?"

"She knows I'm here, huddled near a wagon."

"You need to stay calm, Orpheus. Remember, nothing can hurt you so do you're best to ditch the emotion. Breathe in, breathe out. You're completely relaxed now, right?"

After a few seconds of graveyard silence, he said, "She's coming."

"She can't hurt you."

"She's coming."

"Orpheus, lie down on the sofa."

"I need to get out of here, out of the darkness and into the light. She'll kill me if I stay here. I need to get to the light…"

"Orpheus, you need to listen to me. I'm commanding you to lie down on the sofa."

"She's coming for me. She knows that I know."

"Orpheus, stop!"

"If I can only… get out of here… they won't be able… to… to follow," he wheezed.

"I order you to stop running around the room! Orpheus, listen to me!"

"I can hear her… sh-she's behind me… g-gaining on me. She's gaining on me. Oh, J-Jesus Christ!"

"Orpheus, I am commanding you to calm down. You will listen only to the sound of my voice, you understand? Let my voice guide you…."

"She's coming…"

Jim watched Orpheus scuttle to a corner of the room and curl himself up in a fetal position as if the act might insulate him from the ravages of his invisible assailant. He was trying to yell, yet only a few garbled croaks sprung from his mouth. Fear had apprehended his vocal chords. For a long while, he just sat there, imprisoned in a cataleptic state between sleeping and waking. Had they gone too far?

Jim tried to keep his hand from shaking as he handed Orpheus a cup of water.

"How are you feeling?"

"Better."

"We thought we'd lost you for a second. You really scared us!"

"I scared me," said Orpheus. "The last thing I remember before going under is being on the couch and when I finally awoke, I was hunched over in the corner there. It freaked me out."

"I'll say," said Amara. "I've never experienced anything quite like that before and I've regressed hundreds of people."

"I don't remember any of it."

"Really?" she asked.

"Nothing at all."

"It was intense," said Jim. "But you'll remember quite soon."

"How?"

Jim waved a note-taker about.

"Oh, you taped it."

"I tape all of our sessions, Orpheus," said Jim. "You consented to it when we first started, remember?"

Orpheus remained silent for a few seconds. During that time, a strange clicking noise issued from the nape of his neck. Jim could see that he was pouting and fluttering his eyes, the latter now glistening like orbs of pure obsidian. He crossed one leg over the other and placed both hands atop one knee. The gesticulations were way out of character. Stranger still, they were typically feminine.

"Did you tape all of it?" asked a voice that wasn't Orpheus's.

"Yes."

"You'll be handing that over to me."

What happened next was preternatural and fast, like an electric shock. Orpheus's left arm darted out and clasped tightly around Amara's neck, squeezing until her face went blue. He then hurled her across the room with brute force, like a fuming child punishing a battery-powered toy for its refusal to work. Her limp body crashed onto the floor with a loud thud.

"What's going on here?" asked Jim, backing up against the wall.

"Orpheus didn't make it out this time, Dr. Sweeting," said the strange voice. "No thanks to you and your colleague. He stayed behind with all the others."

"Wh-who are you?"

"Eurydice."

"Somebody help me!" Jim screamed. "Security, help me! I'm being attacked!"

"Dr. Sweeting, you need to listen to me. Listen to me, ok? You're reliving a dream. Nothing can hurt you here."

Animating the Statue

The myth of Pygmalion and Galatea appears in Ovid's narrative poem Metamorphoses as the story of a sculptor who becomes enamored with his own creation, an ivory statue of a woman. The skeleton of the myth has stayed faithful to the original. However, I've taken the liberty that comes with creative license to alter the narrative style, introduce new scenes, and inject it with themes and ideas indigenous to twenty-first-century philosophical and metaphysical inquiry.

Pygmalion regarded his masterpiece in the slivers of moonlight which passed through the windowsill. He pressed the palm of his left hand, so as to cover the entire forehead from temple to temple, placed his right on the shoulders, and breathed heavily onto the clay statue. Imagining a fourfold division of the prime element into Earth, Water, Air, and Fire, he repeated several times, "Your name, my love, is Galatea."

Earth, the thickest and densest of the elements, was like a black mist which contained, within itself, the qualities of cold, sleep, falsehood and death, and Pygmalion imagined it diffusing into the legs of the statue. Then he visualized Water, a volatile fabric which smelt of green, blue, sound, the moon, and hydrogen, soaking into the statue's abdominal region. Air, an element which usually signaled its eternal presence through rustling noises, revealed itself as a constellation of active qualities such as life, heat, white, electricity and heat, and

Pygmalion invited it into his creation through the breast region. The last and mightiest, Fire, vibrated with light, red, truth and phosphorus, and was steadfastly prompted by the sculptor to take its place in the holy shrine of the wax statue, the head.

After a brief hiatus of continual free-flowing, energetic thought Pygmalion, he brushed his hand casually over the statue's pudendum. Blood welled into his manhood like an inflating, jumping castle. He stripped naked, clenched his eyes firmly shut and beat his thick, purpled and vein-coated flesh off with a dozen strokes, rubbing the throbbing head against his lover's wax vagina and tonguing its salmon-colored lips.

As he jerked himself, he began projecting a barrage of mental images toward the impending soul of the statue. She will encompass immense emotional understanding, he thought. Her intellectual comprehension will be second to none. Her cosmic awareness, creativity, imagination, and intuition will be like an act of sudden light banishing the pitch darkness. The depth and breadth of her wisdom and knowledge will be more glorious than a Swiss alpenglow. She will be physically and mentally powerful, he thought, more powerful than a pod of orcas caught in the vortex of a feeding frenzy. Her personality will be circular and mysterious, but void of any sharp, over-reactive corners and irrational sharp edges that typify the vast majority of females in the population. There will be no exaggerated tides, no wild mood swings, or overt expressions of dependence. Instinct would not override the state of being that is true and unrequited love. Pygmalion wished for a woman of intense, unique, explosive, and multidimensional vision. He was so turned on by his own visualization and powerful will that he soon tumbled over the threshold of pleasure, spurting his wad all over the bronze skin of the clay statue.

After cleaning up the mess, he dropped to his knees and impressed his forehead against the statue's navel. It took a few seconds to regain his composure before generating the image of a burning star in the recesses of his own imagination. This he symbolically exhaled onto the clay statue whilst concurrently whispering the chosen name of his female entity. "Galatea," he called out as if the intonation of the name would instantaneously animate the statue. Placing both hands onto the statue's breasts, Pygmalion visualized a flash of thunder and a bolt of lightning which ripped through the inanimate figure and jump-started the heart. The heart began to thump, pumping fresh oxygen-rich blood through the body and altering the fundamental nature of inert matter. He breathed in and out, in and out, invigorating the clay with the fiery spark of activity, silently urging it to use its mimetic facial features to physically channel the ethereal senses of its astral and mental bodies.

Pygmalion knew that the clay statue would be permanently energized with a conduit of life force from the parent body of his own being if the psychic river of concentration was tempered long enough for the blood to symbolically flow through the entire statue and return to the heart area at least once. For this to eventuate, he had to respire as if he had just completed an extended session of vigorous exercise. On the ninth breath, a part of the endeavor deemed of utmost importance to magical invigoration, Pygmalion exhaled so violently that a gob of spit flew out of his mouth and struck the statue just below the jaw.

"Galatea, awaken! Live! Live! Live!" he screamed aloud, somewhat astonished by the unshakable conviction in the tone of his own voice.

Nothing....

"Live!" he called out again, stamping his foot against the ground.

Nothing....

"Live, damn it!" he screamed, punching the statue in the thigh.

Again nothing....

Despite the incessant plea and coercion on the part of its creator, the statue remained faithful to its material composition, in other words, inactive and lifeless. It just stood there, solemn in its intellectual and mental incapacity, its soulless, unblinking eyes staring him down unsympathetically in the moonlit tones of the night. He waited and waited until his eyes watered and his head became so heavy that it was no longer possible to resist the earthward pull of gravity. In time, enthusiasm gave way to disappointment, disappointment to despair, and despair to loneliness and desolation. His meticulous, drawn-out attempts at invigoration had failed dismally. Perhaps he was remiss with the practical execution or with the magical implements deemed necessary for the endeavor to have any chance of success. Whichever the case, the tiredness had sedated him to such an extent that he was beyond knowing or caring.

Scrambling to his feet, Pygmalion wheeled the multipurpose trolley, upon which the clay statue rested, to the queen-sized bed in the adjoining room. He lifted the statue from its portable base, tipped it horizontally onto its back, pushed it onto the left-hand side of the bed, and then pulled the heavy doona over it. Once he had finished arranging the pillows about his static lover's head, he scooted on over to the opposite side and climbed in beside her.

It was a frigid winter's night and the cold seeped down through the covers and into the marrow of his very bones. His extremities were in a lamentable state, feeling as if they'd been dipped repeatedly in buckets of icy water. His chattering teeth wouldn't as much as stand up to the cold either. Pygmalion remedied both problems by rubbing his hands and feet together, an act which generated body heat rather quickly.

He pivoted and stared at the profile of his beautiful lover.

"At least one of us is free from the ravages of the elements," Pygmalion uttered, his arm darting across the bed to caress her. "I guess that's another good thing about not being alive."

"You couldn't be more right about that," said a female voice from the region of his wax lover's mouth. "It's freezing tonight."

Pygmalion nearly lost control of his bowels.

An opaque aura of pulsating purple light differentiated from the clay statue and sat up, turning its head to face a startled Pygmalion.

"The living space in here is horrid... almost as uncomfortable as being trapped in a magical lamp."

Pygmalion gulped. "Galatea?"

"At your service."

"It worked!"

"Yeah, it did," she said. "Would you mind not spitting on me next time? That was most unbecoming of you."

"Sorry."

Galatea swiveled and stared down at the naked wax statue lying on the bed beside Pygmalion. She screamed.

"What's wrong?"

"Is that me?" she asked.

"It's your image, yeah."

"Could you have made me any uglier?"

"You've got to be kidding me," Pygmalion said, throwing the doona off and hopping out of bed. "Either that or you're blind. It took me many years of hard work to get you to look like that."

"I look awful."

"What are you talking about?" he fumed. "I collected pictures of the best-looking models from *Dolly*, *Cosmopolitan*, *Women's Weekly*, *Playboy*. I chose the most flawless of their features and molded them into you. There's not a woman on this planet that's as gorgeous as you, Galatea."

"Don't be so sure…."

"I went out and bought you the most expensive designer clothes, underwear, shoes, hats, handbags, purses, makeup, perfume, deodorant, bags, gloves, sunglasses, jewels, and everything else a beautiful woman like you might want. There's nothing that I've denied you."

"Don't always assume that's what a girl wants."

"That's what all women want!" Pygmalion cried.

"Maybe in your experience of the world they do," she said, "but that doesn't automatically make it a fact. You've obviously forgotten what you wished for. You're a funny man."

"Why?"

"You must sculpt and paint full-time, yeah? Only an artist of the sort would have such confidence in and take such impudent pride in both their judgement and lofty powers."

"I'm good at what I do," said Pygmalion, pointing at a vast collection of lifelike statues in the adjoining room. "Everyone who comes to my workshop tells me so. I perfect the art of nature."

"You perfect the art of mimicry, Pygmalion."

"I select the most aesthetically pleasing features and motifs from the natural world and sculpt them into the simulacra of human beings," he said, ignoring her comment. "I perfect nature, Galatea."

"You've perfected the skin-deep."

"Meaning?"

"Well, what is art?" Galatea asked.

"An artificial representation of the natural world," said Pygmalion.

"There," she said. "You said it with your own tongue."

"What are you talking about?"

"You said the artificial representation of the natural world," said Galatea. "By artificial, you mean a copy, right?"

"What's your point?"

"Art copies nature," she said. "It's Mother Nature's artificial mirror. Imitation belongs to art and originality to nature. The first is inferior to the second."

"Some imitations happen to be better than their originals," said Pygmalion.

"In cases where it concerns only the artificial, perhaps so," said Galatea. "But not when you stack it up against a natural product."

"Why not?" Pygmalion questioned. "Hasn't artificial intelligence been shown to be superior to human intelligence?"

"Another illusion."

"Meaning?"

"The two are spawned from dissimilar properties," said Galatea. "They are fundamentally different, the same only in outward appearance."

"An illusion is as good as its model," said Pygmalion.

"Come on, don't be unreasonable," said Galatea. "Look at your statues, Pygmalion. They might resemble Sophia, Athena, or Aris to the extent that glancing at them might incite a case of mistaken identity, but in the end, the copy is counterfeit and the original or model genuine."

"Okay, I get it." Pygmalion sighed. "You're so opinionated!"

"Like you," said Galatea. "They say likeness causes friction."

"It's true," said Pygmalion. "In any case, you're here to love me. You're not supposed to challenge me like that, so openly and boldly. A created entity should never challenge its creator."

"So now we're a creator, are we?"

"I created you, didn't I?" Pygmalion asked.

"Are you sure about that?" asked Galatea. "I think I've existed for time immemorial."

"Now we're playing mind games," said Pygmalion. "Typical woman."

"That wouldn't fit into the scheme of what you wished for," said Galatea. "I'm simply challenging your own beliefs about yourself. I think you're overconfident."

"Creating is a big part of being human."

"But is it?"

"For sure," said Pygmalion. "We've reached an exciting and pivotal stage in our evolution, Galatea. We can breed, genetically modify living organisms or their essential parts, clone almost anything, and cure ailments. Recently, geneticists discovered that DNA survived intact and unaltered for very long periods in eggshells. Soon it will be possible to bring back animals like the elephant bird and the dodo from extinction."

"But none of that involves creating an original article," said Galatea. "The endeavors you describe all act upon a preexisting natural model. You multiply and divide, modify and alter, subtract, and add, mimic and mend. But never create. I'm sorry to burst your bubble but poking and prodding about a DNA double helix is not creating. You're simply working with what's already there."

"So, what you're essentially telling me is that humans and their mimetic arts are completely inferior to the forces of nature which create these models and articles," said Pygmalion. "Right?"

"That's exactly what I'm saying."

"But what is *nature* exactly?"

"That's for me to know and for you to find out. What do you think it is? What do you think the purpose of all this is?" asked Galatea, gesturing toward the moon and the grove of giant cypress trees outside.

"How am I supposed to know?" said Pygmalion sarcastically. "I'm not a god. I'm just a lonely sculptor who tries to make a living by ripping off copyrighted material from Mother Nature and selling it to the bourgeoisie for a modest price."

'You're not wrong there," said Galatea. "It's all a matter of faith in the end, isn't it?"

"You mean with respect to the nature of being?"

"Yeah."

"I sometimes resign myself to the idea that it was just a chance accident," said Pygmalion, folding his hands into his lap. "There was no plan. Just spontaneous generation. Things just happened. The universe happened. Life happened. Evolution happened. People happened."

"Darwinism?"

"Yeah, you know, survival of the fittest. Favorable

mutations are selected for survival and so forth. That's the aim."

Galatea laughed.

"What's so funny?"

"Nothing," she said. "I'm just a little surprised is all. There's an obvious incongruity between your semi-established beliefs and your actions. You don't honestly believe that bedtime story, do you?"

Pygmalion shrugged his shoulders.

"Let me tell you that chance played no role in anything," Galatea said.

"What do you mean?"

"There is a grand purpose," she said. "Everything was planned out. Everything was meticulously planned out."

"If I'm to believe anything, I have to see proof," he said. "Evidence!"

"And you will," she said. "If you're nice to me, I'll tell you things that will make your hair stand straight."

"Riveting," said Pygmalion. "Not only is my newfound lover agonizingly beautiful, but she's also a pathological creationist."

Pygmalion had to pull Galatea's body through a subterranean crouch way to reach their intended destination; a sea cave with a collapsed roof. Throughout the abbreviated journey, he was forced to lay her down on the bare ground for the sake of clearing away a recent breakdown or simply wiping away beads of sweat from his forehead. It was uncharacteristically warm for a midwinter's day, muggy even. He could feel the thickness and humidity which pervaded the air as it filtered through his lungs, sapping his reserves of strength and warping a modestly difficult task until it appeared Herculean. The sudden incline in the terrain was bothersome, but in no way was it insuperable. Grunting like an Olympic competitor going through the motions of a difficult clean and press, Pygmalion pulled Galatea through the crouch way and into the canyon with one fluid motion. He managed to stand her up against the flowstone without scraping her against any brittle rocks and issued an extended sigh of relief. Exhausted by his overland and subterranean excursion, he dropped to his knees near the cave mouth and splashed seawater onto his face.

"This better be worth it," he gasped. "For your sake."

"It will be."

"Did you see everyone gawking back at the beach?" asked Pygmalion.

"Well, it's not as if you're a food wholesaler wheeling cheese and eggs into a retail store," said Galatea. "What you just did is quite left of the middle. People are going to stare."

"I should have at least covered you with a cloth."

"If you did, I wouldn't have been able to see where I was going," said Galatea. "You keep forgetting that the simulacrum enables my physical senses."

"Right," said Pygmalion. "What's in here that I just had to see?"

"Look to my right," said Galatea. "Can you see the fossilized clams on the floor near the crouch way?"

"Yes."

"Test them for vibratory rates," said Galatea, "with the pendulum."

Pygmalion withdrew the brass pendulum from his pocket and held it over each of the fossils, adjusting the length of the string until it began gyrating. Then he counted the number of revolutions.

"What do you have?" asked Galatea.

"They all react to the fourteen-inch rate," said Pygmalion. "Some also respond to the twenty-four-inch and twenty-nine-inch rates."

"Fourteen is silica so that's to be expected," said Galatea. "The other two denote male and female."

"That's odd."

"Why?"

"Well, the animals that lived in these shells have been dead for thousands if not millions of years, haven't they?"

"More like a hundred million," said Galatea. "So, yeah."

"How does it know what sex these organisms were when they died?" asked Pygmalion. "That shouldn't be possible, right?"

"Not according to contemporary science, it shouldn't," said Galatea. "Yet here it is."

"So, correct me if I'm wrong," said Pygmalion, "but the pendulum actually reacts to an energy or radiation of some sort that has survived beyond death, or beyond the organism's physical death, and exists independent of time."

"That's right," said Galatea. "The field continues to exist as long as the matter does, quite literally in fact. Didn't the ancient Egyptians believe that the soul could only return to the corporeal plane if the physical shell remained intact? The history of each object or substance is literally transcribed in the field around it."

"I know we tested heaps of things yesterday in the yard. I mean, we have individual rates for plants, metals, substances, foods, vegetables, and animals. We even have rates for thoughts, qualities, and intangible principles."

"Go on…"

"I'm not going to deny that there's a congruent pattern in the rates. I think that's clearer than glass acrylic."

"Yet you don't believe what it's telling you about survival?"

"Well, no... I mean, yes, I do," said Pygmalion, staring at the clam shells. "I just can't seem to jettison the absurdity of the implications."

"You're definitely a conservative," said Galatea. "Isn't all science supposed to be based on observation, Pygmalion?"

"Yeah, but..."

Galatea chuckled. "Only when it sugar-coats the existing theories, huh?"

"I didn't say that."

"You don't agree with it because it seriously challenges the established conventions," she said. "That's all."

"No, Galatea..."

"I think we're living, or you're living I should say, in an age where science has usurped the antipathies of dogmatic religion."

"We've come a long way since the days of bonfires and mud huts," said Pygmalion. "Give us some credit."

"It's true but there's no shortage of theories that presume to measure and reflect the nature of being," said Galatea.

"They do."

"No, they don't," she rebutted. "A correct theory prompts new insights and truths and attracts to itself supporting evidence with the passage of time, in the manner that a credible academic authority will eventually gain the respect, admiration, and support of the general public, does it not?"

"Sure," Pygmalion nodded. "Theories are like snowballs that increase in size by rolling down the slope of a snow-capped mountain."

"Great analogy," said Galatea, "but that's definitely not the case with what is learned about the nature of being at schools and universities today. Take psychiatry, for instance. It's a science, a medical specialty, no more than about two hundred years of age that pigeonholes bundled-up psychological impulses under the aegis of mental illness, stripping people of dignity and self-respect in the process. It keeps categorizing, putting names and labels on emerging so-called mental disorders without the slightest idea of how it might cure them. What does that tell you about psychiatry, Pygmalion? You can pretty much put your precious Darwinism in the same boat."

"Well, like it or not, that's where we're at."

"That's where you shouldn't be at," Galatea pushed on. "It's like you're being led astray by medieval demons masquerading as angels. For a while now, scientists have been coming to the table with one-dimensional paradigms, perimeters, and programs which they strap to the limbs of the planet in the hope of satisfactorily answering the eternal questions of 'how' and 'why'. Then, when things don't go quite the way they expected or don't work out at all, they either blame their instruments or go on scratching the scalp of their heads until the skin flakes off. It will never ever occur to most of them that the founding principles on which the skeletal framework of their science rests is an illusion, a desert mirage."

"That would be too much of an ego bruiser," said Pygmalion.

"Exactly the root of the problem, I say," said Galatea. "Heaven forbid if someone else stole the spotlight, or sat on the throne of egotistical posterity, or came up with a viable theory that could be validated. That would be a complete disaster for the competing ego. Could you imagine?"

"Most people are wired that way," said Pygmalion. "It can't be helped, I'm afraid."

"You mean most guys are wired that way!" exclaimed Galatea. "Get over it, I say. The cosmos is far more majestic than the monocular self-importance and righteousness indigenous to the pea-sized, pea-headed human ego."

"I don't disagree with you," said Pygmalion. "But fighting the oscillations of human nature is like paddling against a very powerful current. Sadly, the courageous few that have dared to do so didn't get all that far."

"All I'm saying is that people are simply not looking at life as it should, must, and deserves to be looked at," said Galatea.

"Probably."

"Look, I'll show you something."

Galatea stepped out of her clay shell and dropped to her knees. She aligned the palms vertically with the ground.

"What on earth are you doing?" asked Pygmalion.

"Just watch."

A silvery jelly began to ooze from her hands onto the ground. It wasn't long before the earth beneath them lost its opaqueness and became clear and translucent, revealing the layers of sediment arranged in tiers beneath their feet. By looking down, it became painstakingly obvious that in some areas, sedimentation had failed to transpire. The strata appeared to extend to an abyssal depth in the earth, yet Pygmalion noticed that, in several pockets, it had been anomalously inverted, twisted, or folded. Hundreds of thousands of large and hard-bodied vertebrates had been fossilized in these rocky blankets. There were both marine and terrestrial animals; a vast majority of them were prehistoric, belonging to bygone ages that were now extinct. Some were clearly recognizable, whilst others looked like creatures that grace the annals of modern cryptozoology. The manner of their fossilization in the strata fostered the illusion that they had perished whilst being hurled around in a giant washing machine.

Pygmalion gasped. "How did you do that?"

"I have a way of making people see things," said Galatea. "Especially things directly under them."

"No doubt," said Pygmalion, getting on his knees. "Wow, look here. I can see all sorts of animals–coelacanth, trilobites, shrimp, frogs, birds, dolphins, mammoths, giant arachnids, bats, monkeys, prehistoric humans."

"A thick slice of the paleontological record right before your very eyes," said Galatea. "Undisturbed, I might add."

"No, kidding," said Pygmalion. "What's that weird-looking one that's very deep? It looks like a pregnant lizard."

"That's an archaeopteryx."

"The first bird?"

"That's what paleontologists think," said Galatea. "What do you see?"

"Fossils."

"What I meant to say is, what do you notice about the paleontological record?"

Pygmalion stared at the natural museum, examining the strata, the positioning of the fossils within the strata, and the fossils themselves.

"There's no continuity," he said. "I understand that there are gaps in evolutionary sequences but seeing the whole thing up close and personal brings with it an undeniable conviction. There's no continuity between any of the great orders, at least, none between the ones I can see."

"Exactly," said Galatea. "Each order springs up out of the blue with no lasting or detectable prelude."

"Hmm... the animals don't appear to evolve into other animals, do they?" asked Pygmalion. "Their physical features don't change; they only get bigger. Either that or they disappear altogether."

"You're reading me," said Galatea. "Take a look at that cartilaginous fish from the Devonian Period over there. That's roughly the time that amphibians are thought to have evolved. How is it possible for the amphibian to evolve from a fish? Did the fish all of a sudden realize that the seas had become overpopulated or hostile and decided it was time to seek out roads less travelled? Highly unlikely, I say, not unless it spontaneously acquired the sentience of a shrewder life form."

"Maybe it was an unconscious will," said Pygmalion. "An unconscious urge, an impulse devoid of any intelligence that drove it onto land."

"Even if what you say is true, how does a cartilaginous arch become a pelvic girdle? How does a jointed leg with four or five digits form from pectoral fins? Do you see the problem now?"

"Yeah, kind of," said Pygmalion. "Their anatomy is somewhat irreconcilable."

"How did scales turn into feathers?" Galatea went on, pointing to the fossil of archaeopteryx. "According to paleontologists, that's supposed to be the first bird, right?"

"Yes, an intermediary of dinosaurs and birds that supported the evolutionary link between them."

"Did the predecessor of archaeopteryx all of a sudden wake up one morning and think to itself, 'You know what guys, there's too much danger and competition down here on the rainforest floor so I'm going to grow me some wings and fly off into the sunset?' How would the idea of flying occur to a little reptile that had spent its entire life completely grounded?"

Pygmalion shrugged. "Maybe it borrowed the idea from the pterosaurs, how should I know? What are you getting at anyway?"

"The only way any of this is possible is if it were premeditated, thought out, meticulously planned," said Galatea.

"What was?"

"The life forms."

"By whom?" asked Pygmalion.

"The disembodied intelligence that deemed them necessary," said Galatea. "The fact that certain anatomical features appear and disappear from the paleontological record without an evolutionary prologue is evidence of their existence. Scales, feathers, fins, flight, warm-blooded and cold-blooded animals, and a host of other innovations are all trails, experiments if you like, pioneered by a peripheral mind, or minds I should say. There's a host of them working under the authority of a single auto generator."

"But how can we be certain, Galatea?"

"Does an adventure novel have an author?"

"Obviously."

"Then why should the book of life be any different?" asked Galatea. "Just a few days ago, we came to the conclusion that everything in existence had a rate that could be transcribed by the pendulum."

"That's right. It formed a spiral pattern."

"If everything has a number and is ordered according to a harmonious mathematical plan, then somebody or something must have enumerated them. Just because humans can't as yet detect these forces and entities with their primitive senses and instruments, doesn't mean they're not there."

"If, and when, we do reach that level of development, remind me to seek out and interview the intelligence that planned and executed the dinosaurs."

"You're a bit too much sometimes," said Galatea. "We arrived here through sound observation and reasoning, the two most important tools of critical inquiry, and still, you remain incredulous. What hope can there be for all the others who have to do it without any external assistance whatsoever?"

"Oh, trust me, Galatea, there's no shortage of pathological creationists on the earth claiming there's a master plan behind the shadow play of the universe."

"There is a master plan, Pygmalion."

"Next thing I'll be hearing about is how you're one of the divine auto generator's subcontractors," said Pygmalion. "Am I right?"

"What if I am?"

Pygmalion smiled wryly. "Then you're my ticket to fame, my dear. Fame, fortune, and life eternal."

In the weeks that followed, the inwardly-turned and brazen Galatea tried to overturn Pygmalion's narrow little residential cove around. She would always strike and sound many intuitive notes that had lain dormant within him since childhood, but after a brief chime of revelation had sounded, he would always slump back into the slime and mud of his unoriginal and orthodox ways. After some time, he found himself agreeing with her for the sake of contentment. At night they would both lie in bed, kept awake by each other's brain noise; she would embark on soulful soliloquies which sought to convince him of master plans and predetermination, and he would secretly scratch at his flesh under the bedcovers as if her words were healed scabs that could readily be picked off and discarded. Her steadfast voice became the echo of his trials and tribulations.

One morning, the brain noise overwhelmed him in quite the same way that a violent cascade might override and silence fluttering sounds issuing from more tranquil modes of being in a tropical rainforest. He had to put an end to the noise, the chaos, the warped visions, the madness that was Galatea. He had to finish what he had started, unravel what he had knotted, and destroy what he had created for it threatened to overhaul his entire universe. He had to commit a sacrilegious act of uncreation. He hadn't the slightest notion of what the consequences might be, but the mental pain had become so excruciatingly unbearable that he hardly cared anymore.

Pygmalion wheeled the clay statue to a rocky precipice in graveyard silence. He was fearful and excited at the same time. He thrust his hand inside his Calvin Klein undies and squeezed his prick which inflated rapidly like a life raft. If it were pitch dark, he would have flung her to the ground and raped her to relieve the trauma and anguish forced upon him by her antics, but he didn't dare. There was no telling what prying eyes might suddenly veer out from a sharp corner or a grove of trees and stun him. Instead, he rubbed himself against her backside and expressed regret for what he was about to do. He quickly surveyed the steep drop and set Galatea directly in the line of fire, but before he could incite the fateful shove over the edge, she stepped out from her lifelike shell, glaring at him with scorn.

"So, this is what it's come to. I thought you loved me."

"Trust me, I don't want to, but you leave me no choice!" he

yelled, spittle flying from his mouth. "It's either you or sanity, and I'd rather have my sanity."

"Do you think getting rid of me will solve your problem?" asked Galatea. "Your problems have only just started."

"You'll destroy me if I let you live."

"I'll come back and haunt you," she said. "I'll drive you insane, Pygmalion."

"You can't," he said. "You'll die the moment your body shatters at the foot of this cliff."

"You're a feeble and weak man," she barked back. "You're unreasonable."

"The word is sensible."

"Not quite sensible enough to listen to the truth."

"It's madness."

"It's the future," she said. "It's fate. Destiny. Call it what you will."

"Yours ends here."

"I am without past, present, future, or destiny," she said.

"Oh, really?"

"You drew me to yourself of your own accord and now you're spitting me back into the whirlpool," she said. "You can't handle me. You can't handle my words because they strike too close to home, too sharp a chord in your intuition. You're a coward, Pygmalion."

"Bitch."

"You're gutless."

"Whore."

"You're a pathetic excuse for a man."

"Demon."

"You're as good as dead."

"Say goodbye, Galatea."

"Say goodbye, Pygmalion," she said, "because you're coming with me."

"You think so, do you?"

"Heed my words and you will be rewarded. Love me, listen to me, and you will be honored. Shatter me and you will destroy yourself."

Pygmalion stepped forward and drove a kick into the wax statue but found that he couldn't retract his foot. The frantic attempts to free his limb from his forsaken companion were futile. There was an undetectable force connecting the two together like a giant magnet. Sensing his urgency, it tightened its hold further. Pygmalion was flung along the gravel like a ragged doll, gaining momentum until he was airborne. He anticipated hearing his own screams as they tumbled through the air. They never came. The fall was like a muted scene, ear-splitting within his head and dead silent outside it.

He was startled awake milliseconds before they hit the ground. The disparate setting threw him into a forest of thorny confusion for some while and he wanted to scream. He was lying on an uninspiring hospital bed, sweating profusely. He couldn't wipe himself because he was heavily strapped down. He stared at the ceiling fan, pondering whether Galatea would ever come back from the dead to haunt him. The noise hadn't quite disappeared. Perhaps it was an omen. It was so noisy that he didn't really notice the warm hand on his naked shoulder.

"Bad dreams?"

Pygmalion winced. "Yeah."

"Would you like something to help you sleep?"

"No thanks, nurse."

"You've been waking every half hour," she said. "If not

every quarter."

"I'd rather not sleep."

"That bad, huh?" she said, staring into his eyes.

"Yeah."

"Things will get better," she said. "I'm sure of it."

Pygmalion turned toward a flat panel T.V. mounted on the wall of his room and caught sight of someone he knew quite well. She was elegant and beautiful, bedecked in a red satin dress and an extravagant Greek hairstyle. For a few seconds, he shook his head from side to side to make sure he wasn't still dreaming.

"Can you turn the volume up please?"

"Sure, I just need to give you this injection first," she said, pivoting toward the T.V. "Oh, it's Professor Christou."

"Who's Professor Christou?"

"An incredible woman," said the nurse. "She's a cosmologist from what I understand. She's been on the news all morning."

"Why?"

"She and her team have developed a machine which isolates an organism's life force," she said. "You know, the spark that animates you. There's word that it's identical in all members of one species. This is the start of a scientific revolution; an era, they say, that will re-enchant and spiritualize science."

"Well, she's got you all fooled."

"Why?" asked the nurse.

"She's just a demon trying to lead everyone astray with her creationist bullshit," said Pygmalion. "I know her, I know her very well. Her real name is Galatea. She's tried to convince me with these lies too, back when she was trapped in a statue."

"She has?"

"Yeah, that there's a master plan to everything and so forth," he said. "I didn't really believe any of it. For many weeks, all she did was try to drive me insane, so I killed her, threw her from a cliff. She's obviously a demon. She knew how to come back."

The nurse bit her lower lip. "Have you taken your Clozapine?"

"Are you talking about the pills?" he asked.

"Yeah."

"Nope and I won't be taking them anymore," he said.

"Why not? They're for your own good."

"'Cause I saw the way you reacted when I told you she was a demon," he said. "You're one of her minions, aren't you?"

"Pygmalion…."

"You are," he said, "and you're growing bolder now that you know that she's human. I need to kill her again, but that might not solve anything. She'll probably just come back as something even more powerful."

The nurse smiled sheepishly. "You know, you're probably right about that."

"About what?"

"About her being a demon," said the nurse.

"I know I am," he said. "I've witnessed her magical powers first-hand."

"Well, then, she must be a demon."

"She is."

"But if there are demons there must be angels, right?"

"Yes."

"Which means that God must exist, since it is God who creates them."

"Yup."

"If God exists, then everything must be built to a plan and predetermined."

"Hmm...."

"She must be telling the truth then," the nurse said. "I don't think it matters, though."

"Why not?"

"She'll end up burning in hell either way."

Pygmalion smiled at her. "That's more like it."

Eros and Psyche

The story of Eros (Cupid) and Psyche is a second-century mythologem told by the Latin writer Apuleius. It appears nowhere else in classical literature.

People usually attain worldwide fame for exhibiting exceptional skill in a sporting activity or for being adroit in a particular avenue of intellectual inquiry, but in a time before this one mortal woman, the daughter of a very prosperous king, acquired the former as the epitome of cosmopolitan femininity and beauty. Hers was a supernal physiognomy that beguiled even the most asexual of individuals. She possessed a divinely proportioned figure that was immensely easy on the eyes and would disarm even the most astute of male intellects. Her face was like the humidity one experiences on a warm, moon-lit, tropical summer's night, making all who saw it suffer instant bouts of perspiration. Imagine a hybrid woman sporting physical traits taken from our world-famous supermodels— Adriana Lima, Tyra Banks, Kate Moss, Cindy Crawford, Naomi Campbell, Elle McPherson, Linda Evangelista, Eva Hertzigova, and Helena Christensen. No, imagine the single best feature of each of these painted onto a clay-laden prototype of Eve and then magically animated to life. That was, or is, I should say, *Psyche*.

It would not be incorrect to say that the gorgeous Psyche was more popular than Disneyland or Hollywood during peak holiday season; the single men of this world would all undertake pilgrimages to the walls of the royal palace in hopes of catching glimpses of this divine creature as a photographer might travel to the African wilderness seeking that lucrative snapshot of Mother Nature at her most furious and unforgiving.

There was even hearsay that Psyche, a mere mortal, was lovelier and far more desirable than the divine frontrunner of beauty and love, the goddess Aphrodite herself. Save for being oversaturated with narcissism and egoism, the gorgeous Olympian would act as if she was the executive editor of Cosmopolitan Magazine, concerning herself with all matters relating to love, beauty, sex, and relationships. She would often spy on human beings with Earth-vision goggles and she was especially tailored to tuning into any conversations in which her name, or the names of her associative qualities, might be mentioned. Aphrodite had been keeping a close watch on Psyche for some time, growing incalculably jealous of the attention and adoration which should have been reserved for her alone.

Realizing that it wouldn't be long before she was supplanted as the quintessence of beauty by a mere mortal, Aphrodite decided that the most pertinent course of action would be to consult her own son, Eros, whose arrows could aptly incite personal ruin. She found him rummaging inside one of her personal drawers in her private rumpus room:

"What are you doing in here?"

Eros pivoted to face her. "Oops… busted."

"You know you're not allowed to look at my personal belongings, Eros," she gasped. "I've made that clear to you time and time again. Get away from there."

"I know, Mom," he said. "That's why I do it."

"Not funny," she said. "You need to help me."

"'What's this supposed to be?" he said, lifting a black vibrator toward the light.

Her face went scarlet. "Put that back where you found it right now, young man."

"I think you're getting way too obsessed with human past times and preoccupations," he said. "You tune into their channel way too often. You even copy their ridiculous inventions."

"Mine are superior," Aphrodite said. "They work without batteries."

"I'm really worried about you, Mom," Eros said. "I think you're starting to become one."

"Nonsense," Aphrodite rebutted.

"You subconsciously even want to be one…"

"Whatever, Eros," she said. "Look, I really need you to do something."

"I'm not helping you pull the wool over Zeus's eyes again," Eros told her. "Next time, I don't think he'll be as forgiving."

"No, it's got nothing to do with Zeus," said Aphrodite. "There's this girl, a princess, that everyone thinks is gorgeous."

"Who's everyone?"

"The humans, who else?" said Aphrodite. "She's got all the guys pining after her. It's pukeworthy."

Eros smiled. "She must be hot."

"What makes you say that?" Aphrodite asked.

"Well, you wouldn't be reacting this way if she wasn't," Eros reasoned. "Would you, mother dearest?"

"Look, just help me screw her over already," said Aphrodite. "I'm not letting some cheap tart stuff things up for me. There's too much at stake."

Eros sighed. "So, what exactly do you want me to do?"

"Hmm…" Aphrodite sniggered. "I want you to find this bitch and pierce her heart with your deadliest arrow; one that will make her fall madly in love with the ugliest man alive."

"Sure," said Eros. "Anything for you, mother dearest."

Aphrodite grinned.

"So, where is she?" Eros asked. "What does she look like?"

"Look into my eyes," Aphrodite said, concurrently facilitating an electrochemical cable between heaven and the ley lines that crisscross the Earth. "Can you see her? She's the girl crossing the ley connecting Delphi and Olympia right this minute."

Eros didn't as much as utter a word.

"Can you see?" Aphrodite asked.

"Yes, I see her," Eros answered.

"You will do my bidding tonight," Aphrodite told him.

"Hmm…"

"You've got her location?" Aphrodite asked.

"Yes," Eros murmured.

"Good," Aphrodite said, smiling. "I'm so going to enjoy this."

"Hmm…"

Aphrodite severed the connection mentally and picked up two glasses of nectar, handing one to her son.

"Cheers."

"Cheers," said Eros, lifting his glass toward the direction of the Olympian throne. All the while, his heart raced like a runaway horse.

The state of affairs on planet Earth was somewhat preposterous. Why? Well, Psyche was indeed characterized by supernal beauty, charm, and purity of soul; in fact, anyone who'd ever journeyed to the royal palace and parked outside its gargantuan walls in hope of catching a glimpse of the princess, had obviously been motivated by the aforementioned factors. But despite these physical virtues that gleamed brilliantly like Jupiter in the night skies and separated her from all other women, it was these same traits that kept all possible suitors anchored a safe distance away from her. In other words, her beauty resembled a double-edged blade, able to confer both contentment and desolation. Many handsome gentlemen would tussle with the thought of courting her before resigning themselves to the logic that anyone who radiated such divine beauty was bound to be as dangerous as a rumbling super volcano and as wily as a snake. What was even more disconcerting for Psyche was that her two older sisters, deemed less fair, gifted, and intellectual than herself, were both happily wed to kings of neighboring states and had become supreme mistresses of their own palaces. This weighed heavy on Psyche's heart like half a tonne of bricks. Why wasn't any man interested in her as a prospective partner? Why? The same question troubled her parents, especially her father, who temporarily relinquished his divine duties for the sake of travelling all the way to the Delphic Oracle to receive an honest and divinely-inspired answer.

The Pythia, sitting atop a three-legged tripod, breathed in noxious gases rising from the subterranean chasm.

"Speak," she prompted.

"I have come about my daughter," the king said.

"Is she ailing?" the Pythia asked.

"Nobody will wed her."

"Her name…"

"Psyche."

After a few seconds of silence, the Pythia blurted out, "The Melian is displeased."

"Who?"

"The Cytherian, the Cyprian, the foam-born—"

"Aphrodite?" the king asked.

Her voice deepened. "Psyche is the Chosen One."

"Why?"

"She has been chosen by a divine being of the highest order, even higher than the dimension in which the Olympians reside, to be his wife and mistress."

"Who is this being?"

She winced as if an invisible hand was prodding her face. "I see a winged serpent with reptilian skin and the fangs of the African lion. This is one of his many guises."

The king was mortified. "My beautiful daughter has been chosen by a beast?"

"Yes, oh king…"

"I can't give my daughter away to a monstrosity."

The Pythia ignored him. "After dressing your daughter in the dark veil of mourning, you will deliver her to the high peak near the palace, after which she shall be received by her ethereal suitor."

"But—"

"Do exactly as I say," said a deep, masculine voice issuing from the delicate mouth of the Pythia.

The king broke out in gooseflesh. "I will do as you say."

Disquieting anxiety, and a sense of foreboding, had gripped the poor Psyche from the time her love life had gone preternaturally silent, but to hear her of own fate as it had been spelt out by the most reputable oracle in the Hellenic lands was too much, even for such a courageous and stoic woman as her. Psyche locked herself in her quarters for days on end and might have cried enough tears to fill up the mighty Kourtaliotis river in south-western Crete had it not been for two songbirds which flew onto her windowsill one night and belted out a mystical chorus, reminding her of the possibility of life after death. Armed with this newfound faith and hope, she dressed accordingly, kissed her family and friends farewell, and then began walking toward the only place near the palace she knew of that could be described as a high peak. The walk was long and strenuous and before long, Psyche was wiping eternally forming beads of sweat from her brow. Exhausted, she stumbled toward a natural edifice likely to offer temporary respite—a boulder which resembled a stone table. Psyche climbed atop and curled into a fetal position, resting her face against its cool surface. A few seconds had barely elapsed, and she was sound asleep.

What happened next was eerie, celestial, mystifying, and miraculous. The lips of Zephyr, the god of the west wind, formed into the shape of an 'O' and he began to blow; he blew hard, harder, and harder still until Psyche split into two beings in the manner that animal cells divine during cellular mitosis. One part of her was liberated from the corporeal plane, then lifted above her own indisposed body and diffused through the corpuscular membrane which separated vibrations of differing frequencies, and hence different realms of existence.

"Can you hear me, Psyche?" a voice echoed. "Can you hear me?"

"I hear you," she said.

"You hear me?" the voice said.

"Yes."

"Wonderful," the voice said. "It worked, just as I thought it would."

"I'm confused," said Psyche.

"I am the only being that exists here."

"You are the only being that exists here," Psyche repeated.

"I will lead," the voice said, "and you will follow."

"I will follow," said Psyche.

"Follow the light of my voice, Psyche," the voice continued. "I am the light at the end of the tunnel, and you must follow me."

"But I can't see," said Psyche.

"Don't try to see with your eyes," the voice said. "Eyes are instruments that channel a sense of the physical plane, and you no longer have use of them because you're no longer on it. Try to see with your unconscious mind, Psyche, your unconscious will."

"I'll try."

"Come deeper into the plenitude and the stillness with me. Psyche," the voice said. "Deeper and deeper with every breath."

"I'm going deeper and deeper…"

"Follow me," said the voice. "Deeper and deeper into the abyss."

"I'm following you…"

"Do you see anything?"

"Yes…"

"What do you see?" the voice asked.

"I see a golden meadow," Psyche said. "There are many beautiful flowers; bees are pollinating them. There are towering mountains in the background, an alpenglow…"

"Good," the voice said. "Can you see anything else?"

"Not really."

"Concentrate on the horizon," the voice prompted.

"Oh, yes."

"What can you see?"

"Oh, it's a pearl-colored palace gilded with silver, gold, rubies, emeralds and every precious stone imaginable," Psyche said. "There are mighty citadels, and spacious courtyards, and running fountains, and freshwater springs, and aquamarine pools, and lush gardens, and…"

"Go on…"

"It's all mine," Psyche continued. "I can feel that it's mine."

"How did you know?" the voice asked.

"Intuition," Psyche said. "I felt it."

"You learn fast," the voice said. "Intuition is the most powerful sense of all."

"How do I get closer?" Psyche asked.

"Will yourself there."

Psyche concentrated on the palace, urging herself toward it. "I'm there."

"It's easy, isn't it?" the voice asked.

"You sound much closer to me now," said Psyche. "Almost within arm's reach."

"I'm right beside you."

"Really?"

"Yes," the voice said. "Don't you believe me?"

"I believe you," Psyche said. "I can feel the radiation of your voice, its warmth, its vigor. I believe you."

"Do you know who I am?"

"The beast?"

"You'd better believe it."

"You don't sound like a beast," Psyche said. "Or feel like one, for that matter."

"I am, occasionally," the voice chuckled.

"And you're so warm," Psyche said. "I can feel the radiation of your voice burning me. It's the most intense, most powerful, most erotic, most passionate and quixotic thing I've ever felt against the skin of my being."

"Oh, Psyche," the voice said. "I've been burning feverishly for you from the minute I laid eyes upon you."

Many months passed before the two elder grief-stricken daughters of the king decided to embark on a commemorative journey to honor their sister who'd been lost to the corporeal world. As they trudged uphill, a thick mist descended from the heavens and coiled itself around the mountain like an anaconda about to asphyxiate its prey. They had barely made it to the monolith that resembled a stone table when a languorous sleep overcame the two of them. Then a violent schism, a crackling, cacophonous noise, issued from beneath their indisposed bodies and ripped through the confines of their inner beings. It spawned a subtle division of consciousness to which they were completely unaware, sweeping their ethereal doubles into a whirling vortex and consequently flushing them into a higher dimension of existence. They awoke on a cosmic shore in which sounds, colors, textures, emotions and feelings, and landscapes were infinitely more beautiful and vibrant, more meaningful, and more titillating than those to which they were accustomed. Everything here was intimately connected to and dependent on everything else, and it was impossible to comprehend or understand anything unless one adopted a bird's-eye view of creation. This world was a benthic zone in which the weight of any penetrating foreign entity caused ripples that resonated outward in concentric circles and rendered the autochthonous inhabitants cognizant of its whereabouts.

"Sisters, is that you?" Psyche asked.

"Psyche?" they called out in unison.

"Yes, it's me," Psyche said. "How in Zeus's name did you find me?"

"We just went to the peak where you disappeared," one of them said. "And then—"

"And then what?" Psyche asked.

"Umm... I can't really remember. The last thing I remember is this thick mist," one said.

"Yeah, and the tiredness," said the other. "How does one climb such a scoundrel of a peak? I got bitten by so many mosquitoes."

"It doesn't really matter. You're here now," Psyche said. "Can you girls see me yet?"

"Hold on," said the eldest sister. "For a while, my vision was really blurry as if I was swimming underwater, but now everything is coming to."

"Can you see me?" Psyche resounded.

"Oh, my gods," said the eldest sister. "I do see you. You look, umm..."

"Like a goddess," said the other.

"What's that massive thing around your neck?" the eldest inquired.

"It's called the Heart of Time," Psyche said.

"It looks like one hell of a giant pearl," said the younger sister. "The most gorgeous thing I've ever seen."

"It was a gift from my husband when we exchanged vows," said Psyche. "A testament of his love for me, as he himself declares. I watched him skin-dive in one of the deepest parts of the sea to retrieve it from the lips of a giant clam. He had to hold his breath for quite a while. When my husband holds his breath, time actually stops."

"Yeah, right," the younger sister said. "Do you really expect us to believe that? No human can do that."

"You forget that I'm not married to a human," said Psyche. "My husband is superhuman. He has risked a great deal for me in the time we've been together, including the safety and harmony of the Earth itself."

"Is that why you named the pearl the Heart of Time?" the eldest asked. "Because time actually stopped?"

"Yes, literally," said Psyche.

"What about the splendid palace I see surrounded by stone fountains, and that mountain of riches beyond it, and the gold-ridden land, and the pastures and animals?" asked the eldest sister. "Are they all yours too?"

"Yes," said Psyche. "This is our home."

"Where is your husband?" asked the younger sister. "I don't see... sense him anywhere."

"He has an infinite number of pastimes, my dear husband," said Psyche. "He left this morning to hunt deer, and probably won't be back until dusk."

"So, you've hit the jackpot then," said the older sister.

"Excuse me?"

"What I mean is that you've married someone rich, multi-talented, down-to-earth, and genuine, and very loving. What more could a girl want? And if what I've seen already is anything to go by, he must be very handsome too. Am I right, Psyche?"

"Umm... he has a chiseled jaw, aquiline nose, with blue-green eyes and locks of hair that are the color of the aurora. He is olive-skinned, broad-shouldered, and very muscular; we're about the same height."

"He sounds like a god," said the younger sister.

"I bet he feels very nice too, doesn't he?" said the elder one. "Just the thought of squirming against a physical specimen like that makes my heart race."

"Which heart are you talking about, sister?" asked the other. "The one down there?"

"Come on, girls," said Psyche. "You're getting a bit crass."

"Stop being so prissy, Psyche!" exclaimed the eldest sister. "We used to talk about this kind of stuff all the time back when we were all living at Dad's palace. Since when did you become so proper?"

"Well, that was then," said Psyche. "You're talking about my husband. You need to be more respectful."

"Is he good in bed?" the eldest sister pushed on. "He must have great sexual prowess?"

"Well, anyone who can make time stand still can probably make eternity feel like an orgasm," said the younger one. "I'm sure Psyche would agree."

"He's the most sensual and intimate being," Psyche said. "He cuddles me like no other has before, as if embrace was a matter of life and death."

"Nice," they both said.

"It's a bit difficult sometimes because he's much taller than me," said Psyche, "but we find ways around it."

"Wait a second," said the eldest sister. "Didn't you say before that you were the same height?"

"Yeah, you did," said the younger. "You lied to us. What in Zeus's name is going on Psyche?"

"Well…"

"Well, what?" said the eldest sister. "Do you even know what he looks like? Have you even seen him before? Does he even exist? Or is he a ghost husband, existing only in your own imagination?"

"He exists," Psyche said. "You can be sure of that."

"Then why don't you know what he looks like?" asked the younger sister.

Psyche sighed. "He only comes to me after dusk."

"So, you've never seen him in the light of day?" asked the oldest sister.

"Nope."

"And you've never asked yourself why he won't let you see him?"

"Why should I?" asked Psyche. "I trust him."

"A great quality to have," the eldest sister said, "but I wouldn't be so trustworthy and credulous if I were you. Nobody ever hides without a reason."

"Yeah," said the younger sister. "There must be something horribly wrong with him. He might be physically scarred or disfigured."

"Or a snake in the grass…"

"Pretending to be someone or something that he isn't," said the eldest sister. "He'll be really, really nice to you until your blind trust and faith in him become second nature."

"And then he'll strike," said the younger sister, "sinking his sharp fangs into your throat while you sleep."

"Exactly," said the eldest sister. "That's what the Delphic oracle told Dad. Have you forgotten already?"

"No, I haven't," said Psyche. "I think about it every day."

"Don't just think, Psyche," said the younger sister. "Act."

"Exactly," said the eldest one. "You must expose this fraud

for what it is."

"What are you implying?" asked Psyche.

"Kill him," she went on. "Kill the worn-out pretender. Tonight, when he returns from his noonday hunt, have a hand-held butane blow torch and an ice pick under the bed. When he's cuddling you, get on top of him. Straddle him."

"Do it when you're having sex," suggested the younger one. "He'll be disarmed by the pleasure you're giving him and so acutely focused on getting off that he won't see it coming."

"Bend sideways and pull the items out from beneath the bed when you're riding him," said the eldest sister. "Make sure you've tied his hands to the bedposts first so that he can't harm or stop you. Use a white silk scarf or something. You would have plenty of those. It will be really kinky and lull him into a false sense of security as if you were trying to spice up your sex life by engaging in something completely different. When that's all done, steadfastly light the small butane blow torch so that you can see the monster who has embroiled you for so long. Then plunge the ice pick into his neck and chest repeatedly without remorse."

"The new blow torches create their own spark at the push of a button and ignite quite easily," said the younger one. "It'll be a piece of cake for you. Rid yourself of the monstrosity and return to us, your family, who love you so dearly."

"Burn his face with the blow-torch if you have to," said the eldest sister. "Just get away from him as quickly as you can."

"But I love him," said Psyche. "I can't just kill him."

"Yes, you can," said the eldest sister. "If only for your own sanity and peace of mind."

"He loves me too," Psyche blurted out.

"Love hurts," said the eldest sister.

Before Psyche could respond, Zephyr, the west wind, incited a furious tempest which dissipated their contact and sucked her sisters' etheric doubles back into their vacant bodies which were still slumbered near the stone table. Both awoke after their prolonged sleep feeling befuddled, nauseous, and saturated in a spray of perspiration; in a preternatural ocean which had been churned into a psychic battleground by a host of disembodied wills and egos, neither remembered their encounter with Psyche.

That afternoon, Psyche sat near a rock pool and recollected all the times she and her husband had conversed. She pried the depository of her memories in search of any clues that might reveal sinister intent on his part and rescind his integrity. She couldn't find any, not one. Nevertheless, the seed of doubt planted by her sisters would rear its ugly head from time to time. Just when she thought she'd jettisoned the avenue of possible treachery, it would climb up and out from the viscous swamps of her personal unconscious. It made her stomach lurch, her heart race, and a snake of a chill would coil along the back of her spine. It spun cobwebs around her judgment and induced temporary dementia. Bewitched by the idea of finally attaining closure, she hurried about the palace collecting implements that would set in motion this unprecedented conspiracy. Once everything was in place, she bathed in a freshwater spring within the palace and doused herself in rose perfume so as to make herself especially salacious and enticing. Then she crept into her corner of the bed and pulled the covers up, waiting anxiously for his appearance.

She didn't feel his hands curl around her waist because she had fallen into a light sleep, dreaming of the deceitfulness she was about to endorse. However, she was jolted awake once his hands began poking and prodding about her navel. Giggling like a shy schoolgirl, Psyche turned to face him. Sweaty heat emanated from his face and body.

"Did you miss me?" he asked, kissing her shoulders.

"I always miss you, my love," she said, sighing. "There are never enough hours in the night."

"Mmm... you smell amazing," he said. "What are you wearing?"

"Rose perfume."

"You don't really need to wear anything, Psyche," he told her. "You have the best natural scent."

Psyche tittered nervously.

"The best natural scent on the most gorgeous girl in the universe," he said.

"Did you catch anything today?" Psyche asked.

"A wild deer!" he said proudly. "Took a while, but I got him by the lake when he stopped to drink water. Did you speak with your sisters?"

"Yeah," said Psyche. "It was quite emotional for all three of us. We hadn't spoken in a long time."

"I know," he said, squeezing her breasts. "That's exactly why I opened up the conduit."

"Mmm…"

"I did it for you, Psyche," he said. "Only you. I actually don't trust your sisters as far as I could throw them."

Psyche put her hand on his chest. "Why not?"

"Because they're envious types," he said. "I've known plenty of girls like them. They see what you have, and they want it for themselves."

"They were just concerned for my wellbeing," said Psyche.

"Or made it seem like they were," he pointed out.

"Come on," Psyche said, pulling away from him. "They love me; they wouldn't try to hurt me."

"I've been around for a while, Psyche," he said, "and let me tell you, my love, that jealousy abounds in all hearts; a little in some, more profusely in others."

"I'm not naïve," said Psyche.

"Oh, that I know," he said, kissing her breasts. "Did they ask anything about me?"

"No."

"Did they say anything against me?"

"No."

"Good," he said. "I would sever the connection permanently if I ever found out that they've been trying to drive a wedge between us."

"They would never do that," Psyche said, grabbing his wrists and mounting him.

"What's going on here?" he said.

"I'm in charge of proceedings tonight, soldier."

"Oh, I see," he chuckled.

Psyche kissed his chest, taking each nipple into her mouth separately and teasing it with her tongue. Then she pulled the covers over them and began flicking her tongue about his thick shaft which began to inflate rapidly like a helium balloon. Pinning his hands down with her own, she milked him vigorously like a powerful vacuum cleaner.

"Oh…" he gasped aloud. "What happened to you?"

Psyche ran her right hand along the side of the king-size bed and pulled out a silk scarf from beneath it as she swirled her tongue around his manhood. His breath hitched, getting heavier and heavier as she bopped up and down on him. Knowing at once that he was harder than a ten-meter long wooden telephone pole, Psyche pushed herself up and aligned their bodies for consummation. Spreading her legs wide open, she impaled herself on her husband's phallus which was now pointing proudly upward. She started grinding her body against his, rhythmically, whilst concurrently running the scarf over his face.

"Oh... that feels so good."

"Yeah, baby," she said, grinding her pelvis against him. "Give it to me, my man."

"Where in Zeus's name has this Psyche been hiding?" he asked. "Where has she been, huh? You're driving me crazy, babe."

"She's come to you expecting a big night out like a jack-in-the-box," said Psyche, gasping.

"Oh, yeah..."

Psyche stretched the scarf out, wrapping either end around his wrists and binding them securely to the bedpost. He gestured his approval by taking each of her wholesome breasts into his mouth as she keeled over to do so, biting them lightly with his teeth. His incessant thrusting generated tremors of titillation which coursed through her body, incapacitated her, and had the adverse effect of momentarily overriding the higher purpose of the venture. Nonetheless, it wasn't long before the seed of doubt regarding his true identity sprouted like a thorny weed in her consciousness once more. Acting somewhat mechanically, she rested the side of her face against his powerful chest and continued grinding against him while her hands scuttled beneath the bed in search of her two inert co-conspirators. Once she had the ice pick firmly in her right hand and the blow torch in her left, she lifted herself vertically and kept riding with both arms stretched upward toward the ceiling.

"The kinky you are mind-blowing my love," he panted.

"Yeah?"

"Aha," he said. "If you actually knew my mother, I would have guessed that she'd been giving tips on how to...."

"Spice things up?"

"Aha..." he huffed. "Oh, the gods... Oh no—"

"What's wrong?"

"Oh, Psyche... I'm going... to cum," he gasped. "I'm going to cum... deep inside you..."

"Cum in me," Psyche cried, bouncing up and down on him.

"Ohh..." he screamed. "Ohh... Ohh...."

Psyche waited until the second his baby-maker started to spurt inside her like a geyser. Then she lit the blow torch and drew the ice pick backwards, ready to strike the dishonest monstrosity that was orgasming beneath her. What her prying eyes gazed upon during that split second of a moment left her gobsmacked and breathless; the husband who had fallen madly in love with her wasn't the vicious beast her sisters had intimated he'd be, but the fairest man she'd ever laid eyes upon. The depth and scope of his beauty made her ache inside; Psyche ached from the shame which came from having erroneously misjudged and doubted her husband, as well as from the lasciviousness that erupts from making love to such a stunning creature. Inexplicable that he should look exactly the way she described him to her sisters, too, as if the fact had been unconsciously known to her from the minute they'd met.

Lost in the vortex of his own orgasm, her husband's eyes remained closed. But the emanation of sudden light snapped him from his erotic reverie, and within seconds, the sheer delight transcribed all over his face transfigured into an expression of pure horror.

"What are you doing?" he cried out.

Psyche screamed, dropping the ice pick on the floor and the blowtorch onto his chest.

"Ahh… I'm burning."

"Oh no!" Psyche knocked the blowtorch onto the floor.

"Do you know what you've just done, Psyche?"

"I'm so sorry, my love," she sobbed. "I didn't mean to…."

"You betrayed me," he said. "I loved you. I believed in you. I had faith in you. I trusted you unconditionally…"

"It was my sisters," Psyche revealed. "They planted the seed."

"… and all the while you have merely pretended to reciprocate…"

"No," she sobbed. "That's not true."

"But it is, Psyche," he said. "I, Eros, the God of Love, have done everything in my power to move the stars so that we may be together, but you could not as much as give me the benefit of the doubt…"

"That's not true," she repeated.

"And I just cannot *be* where doubt overrides trust or faith…"

"Please," she begged. "Let me explain."

"You explained with your actions."

Before she could utter as much as a word, Eros dematerialized into thin air. Hence, Psyche was left to ponder the ensuing consequences of the tragic mistake just made in cacophonous solitude. As it was, her husband was no monster or beast but the God of Love himself. How was it that she had attracted the fidelity of the Love itself, only to be cast down from its starry and melodious heavens by the doubt imparted to her by two jealous, resentful sisters? The realization that her sisters' primary concern had been to hasten her downfall was too great a burden to carry and she cussed them repeatedly. Then, exhausted by the trauma and lamentable outcome of the ordeal, she slumped against the empty bed and cried herself to sleep.

Aphrodite lay on the ground, perusing the movement of individual stars in the constellation of her birth. They teased her, blowing clouds of confusion about her intellect one minute and delivering blinding sparks of vision and insight the next. The sudden disintegration of her soul relationships with her mortal lovers had been reason to panic, but the stars assured her that a sabbatical was on the horizon, through which her yearning for romantic love would finally be realized. There was also a significant celestial event about to transpire like a sunflower coming into bloom; a total lunar eclipse. As she already knew, eclipses almost always signaled a significant change. When Aphrodite concentrated on the impending image, the stars articulated that there would be an overhaul of the feminine in the anatomy of Love. This really confused her. She couldn't quite discern whether the stars were talking about changes on a cosmic level or if they were alluding to the psyche of a human or some disembodied entity. Perhaps it was both.

Before she could make any further queries, a loud crackling noise boomed from the constellation of Sagittarius. Aphrodite swiftly changed the trajectory of her concentration to the frequency of the commotion and, using the electromagnetic sonar atop her head, calculated its overall distance. The entity, extremely luminous, was hurtling toward her at supersonic speeds like a burst of radiation from an exploding supernova. The twinkling light grew brighter and brighter, taking on multiple forms as it drew nearer and nearer. It started off as a jade-colored serpent before morphing into a scaly red gargoyle, a charred human with wings and canine teeth, and finally into a newborn, pink-lipped male cherub. The latter fashioned an archery set from the cosmic ether, adopted an aggressive stance, and proceeded to draw back on his bow.

Aphrodite screamed.

"It's only me," Eros said, poking her shoulders.

"You shit!" Aphrodite darted up from the velvet cushions she'd been lying on. "For a second, I thought it was Artemis."

"Why?"

"I think she's still angry about Hippolytus," said Aphrodite, trying not to squint. "It's so bright in here. Can you roll the shutters down for me?"

"Not that bright, Mom,' Eros said. "That's what happens when you get addicted to astral travelling. You should see—"

"What in Zeus's name happened to your chest?" Aphrodite asked. "You've been burnt."

"I um… was um…" Eros stuttered. "I was trying to steal one of those glowing plants from the Garden of the Hesperides and got burnt by Ladon on the way out."

Aphrodite laughed. "You couldn't lie to me if your life depended on it."

"Yes, I could," Eros blushed.

"Ladon's fiery breath wouldn't leave that kind of burn anyway," Aphrodite reasoned. "That burn was made with some kind of machine or mechanical device, maybe a blow torch."

"No," he persisted. "It wasn't."

"It was," she said. "Who burnt you, Eros?"

"Umm…"

"I know when you're lying," she said. "Tell me the truth or

I'll tell Zeus who was behind his less-than-noble love affairs with despicable women."

"Fine,' he said. "It was an accident."

"With a blow torch?"

"Yes."

"I was right," Aphrodite said. "Who did it?"

"A lover."

"A woman, no doubt," Aphrodite said. "So now your love life has become a secret too, has it, Eros?"

"No, I..."

"We made a pact to never keep secrets from one another!" Aphrodite exclaimed. "Especially when it comes to our love lives. Have you forgotten that?"

"No, I just didn't think..."

"That mother dearest should know, lest she put in her two cents worth," said Aphrodite in an ironic tone. "What's the girl's name?"

"Why do you want to know?" Eros asked.

"I want to know who my son is bedding or wedding," said Aphrodite. "According to the decree of Olympian Zeus, it is my divine right to know."

"Fine."

"You can't consummate the marriage without my consent either."

"Where does it say that?" Eros asked, gulping. "I've never heard that one before."

"On the tablet of divine laws in the innermost sanctuary of the Great Temple," said Aphrodite. "You obviously haven't read them."

"I didn't even know that such a thing existed."

"Because half the time you're too busy taking divine law

into your own hands," Aphrodite said. "Such impudence!"

"You're one to talk," said Eros. "Since when did you ever play by the rules, Mother?"

"Don't attempt to change the subject," said Aphrodite. "Who is your chosen one, Eros?"

"She's a stunner."

"Who is it?" Aphrodite insisted.

"She's the most gorgeous thing in the cosmos."

Aphrodite's eyes narrowed. "It better not be who I think it is."

"What do you mean?"

"I mean that girl that you were supposed to put into place some time ago," said Aphrodite. "That girl who everyone thought was the best thing since mint-flavored nectar and mousse ambrosia. Hmm… I can't quite remember her name."

"Psyche."

"Yeah, that's it. How in heaven do you—" Aphrodite's face turned a pasty white.

"What?"

"It is her, isn't it?" Aphrodite asked.

"Yeah, it is."

"You little shit!" Aphrodite exclaimed. "Not only did you not do what I asked of you, but you also went behind your own mother's back to fandango with this… this… mortal whore who has used sorcery to bewitch every single male being in heaven and on earth."

"That's not true!" Eros snapped at her. "You know it's not."

"Don't you dare raise your voice at me, young man," said Aphrodite. "You haven't done so all your life. Now's not the time or place to start."

"Then don't hurt the woman I love," he said.

"The woman you love?" Aphrodite asked, feeling the fiery anger diffuse out from her temples. "How can you love her? She's just a mortal for Zeus's sake?"

"She is all soul," said Eros. "Nothing compares to her."

"Really?"

"Yeah, really."

"Well now she'll have to deal with me," said Aphrodite. "In person."

"I won't let you—"

Aphrodite scooped up a handful of skin-rejuvenating sleeping dust from her Ourania make-up kit and threw it at Eros. The expression of angst on his face quickly transmuted into one of pure astonishment as its instantaneous effects took hold. Eros didn't have any time to react, let alone mutter another word of objection. A debilitating torpor took hold of his consciousness and he dropped to the floor like a sack of potatoes.

"Sweet dreams, my boy," Aphrodite mocked, running her hands through his golden hair. "By the time you awake, mother dearest will have disentangled the mess you've made by sending that girl Psyche to the dreaded depths of Tartarus from whence there is no return."

Psyche sat beside a stone fountain in the spacious courtyard, pondering on what course of action might win back Eros's heart. Thus far, none of her hymns or prayers to the gods and goddesses of Olympus had been addressed. At night. she'd compose masterful poems praising their omniscience and insurmountable powers in the hope of impressing and provoking communication with them through dreams or visions, but all her efforts seemed to fall on deaf ears. Was this a premonition of the calm before the storm? Perhaps she had incurred such wrath that no divine being was willing to put his or her own rumination and peace of mind on the line for the greater good of reuniting her with her estranged husband.

Lost in the eruptions of her unconsciousness, Psyche remained oblivious to a supernatural phenomenon unravelling directly beside her; emerging from the pressurized body of water which spewed forth from the gilded head of a winged griffin. It was a colorless protoplasm which congealed into an anthropomorphic being. Within seconds, the translucent characteristic of many liquids was jettisoned for an opaque, rose-tinted patina. It then differentiated into a full-fledged living form, as if it were being sculpted on a potter's wheel by an invisible hand; ridges and depressions around the nose, eyebrows, lips, chin, and cheekbones all formed, hair sprouted from the head, and the eyes phosphoresced with a deep turquoise color.

"Feeling rather depressed today, are we?" a mechanical voice asked from the stone fountain.

Psyche jumped.

"So deep in thought there…"

"Who are you?" Psyche asked, trying to mask the tremor in her voice. "What do you want here?"

"I am the mother of the husband you once had or hoped to have," it cackled.

"You are Eros's mother?"

"Yes," it said. "I am she who is known as the Melian, the Cytherean, and the Cyprian… I am the fairest in heaven and on the earth… Queen. Lady. Mistress—"

"Aphrodite?"

"In the flesh."

"Where is my husband?" asked Psyche.

"Recovering from the terrible burns you gave him," said Aphrodite, discarding her robotic vocals. "Not that you'll ever see him again."

"I love him."

"Shut up," said Aphrodite. "You hurt him. You hurt him badly."

"I know."

"I could strike you down right where you stand," said Aphrodite, "or char you alive for having done that."

"It was an accident," Psyche blurted.

"Shut up," Aphrodite repeated. "You are nothing but a witch who beguiles everyone into believing that you're the most desirable creature on the planet. You're a cock-trapping whore."

"Please—"

"Do you honestly think you could ever hold as much as a twisted candle up to my fairest beauty? Do you think that you could ever compare to me?"

"No."

"You're lying," said Aphrodite. "You're a lying, ugly mole of a witch."

"I am."

"Don't you dare patronize me," said Aphrodite.

"I'm not," said Psyche. "I am genuine."

"Then admit that you're ugly."

"I am a nobody," Psyche sniffled. "I am nothing. An insignificant speck of dust on the island shores of your divine beauty. If humans have ever thought me to be beautiful, it is because I reflect an infinitesimal shard of your infinite majesty. Attempting to draw to myself your transcendence, of which I am unworthy, makes me as ugly and miserable a creature as Medusa."

"Very good," said Aphrodite, grinning.

Psyche sighed. "Will Eros fully recover from the burns?"

"Yes," said Aphrodite. "Not that it will be of much or any help to you. Not where you're going."

"What are you going to do to me?" asked Psyche.

"You're going to a place from whence there is no return," said Aphrodite, "to fornicate with the Titans, the scum of the Underworld."

"Tartarus?"

"Yes."

"Please don't do that," Psyche begged. "I'll do anything… I'll be your servant for the rest of my days."

"I have a better idea," said Aphrodite. "Let's play Divine Game."

"What's that?"

"It's one of my favorites," Aphrodite sniggered. "I ask you five questions relating to the gods. If you answer all five correctly, you are forgiven for your treason. If not, you will be tossed to the depths of Tartarus like a purpled fruit."

"Fine, I accept your challenge."

"Let's see if you're as fair as you think you are," said Aphrodite. 'First question: what does Life wish to accomplish?"

Psyche hesitated for a while before answering, "Immortality."

Aphrodite frowned. "What is the essence of immortality then?"

"Friction, opposition, struggle, conflict…"

"Name the single most sought-after condition that is but a by-product of immortality," Aphrodite prompted.

"Um… knowle… No, wait."

"What were you about to say?"

"Wait."

"Answer the question, Psyche."

"Freedom."

Aphrodite's face reddened like a radish. "How did you know that? You're cheating."

"I'm not," said Psyche. "How does one actually cheat in this sort of game?"

"You tell me."

"I'm not," Psyche insisted.

"Liar."

Aphrodite made a swirling motion in the air with her right hand and an hourglass appeared.

"Time," said Psyche.

"That's right, ill-favored girl. You mortals measure it with clocks and hourglasses.

How do I measure it?" Aphrodite asked, fluttering her eyelids.

"You don't," said Psyche. "You live in a timeless zone."

Aphrodite grabbed the levitating hourglass with granular red sands running through it and hurled it at Psyche with all her might. Psyche possessed great reflexes and swung clear with plenty of time to spare. The instrument crash-landed on a wooden table and shattered into little pieces.

The goddess didn't look at all content with the way things were panning out. She clicked her fingers and a swinging pendulum appeared.

"What might this symbolize?"

"Eternal recurrence," Psyche blurted. "The pendulum moves back and forth, back and forth, just as everything happens over and over and over again."

"Someone is helping you," said Aphrodite. "I can sense it."

"No."

Aphrodite exhaled a cloud of dust which formed into a horse-drawn carriage mounted by two individuals: a driver and a master.

"What is this?"

"The sixth question," said Psyche. "You've already put forth five, and I believe I answered all of them correctly."

"Oh, really? Well, now it's ten."

"Why?"

"'Cause I said so," said Aphrodite, scowling. "Now answer the question."

"It's an allegory for the human being," said Psyche. "The carriage is the body, the horse is a stand-in for the person's feelings or emotions, the coachman is the intellect, and the master is the consciousness."

"You're cheating!" screamed Aphrodite, stepping toward Psyche and grabbing tufts of her hair. "Someone is telling you the answers!"

"Let go! Please!"

"Admit that you're cheating."

"I'm not."

"What's this over here?" Aphrodite yanked the chain with the giant pearl from Psyche's neck, severing it.

"No!"

She held the pearl up in the air. "I know what this is."

"The Heart of Time," said Psyche. "It's from a giant clam in the deepest part of the ocean."

"A present from Eros, no doubt."

"Give it back to me, please."

"No."

Psyche watched as Aphrodite generated an

interdimensional portal over the sea by muttering a few unintelligible words under her breath. The goddess then flung the heavy pearl with a sidereal sweeping motion that mimicked the technique of javelin throwing before breaking out in wild fits of laughter.

Listening to a goddess take pleasure from inducing misfortune upon a mere mortal was like a human taunting an animal by starving it to death. It angered Psyche beyond reckoning. It blew the fuse mediating the psychic transistor within the vehicle of her own consciousness, leaving a lesser automaton as the only driver. She had just been driven to the precipice of fatalism, enough to realize that, if she was to be swept into the infernal waters of chaos, it might as well be on her own terms. Acting partly from a bubbling rage beneath her skin and partly from a heartfelt desire to vindicate her love for Eros, she charged through the dimensional rip, screaming at the top of her lungs before Aphrodite could dematerialize it.

Everything transpired within the space of a few seconds. One minute, she was at the mercy of Aphrodite's will in the exotic gardens of her own home and the next, she was thrashing about in the middle of the ocean somewhere. Her heart thumped so loud that she thought it might burst out of her chest. She tried to scoop the pearl out of the water, but the motion of trying to ensnare it in the clasp of her hand merely pushed it further away. All she could do was watch as her most prized possession sunk deeper and deeper into the abyss.

Psyche did her best to remain afloat. She flapped her arms about, screaming for help until fatigue finally benumbed her limbs enough for the sea to swallow her whole. Even though she could hold her breath for extended periods of time, she knew that she'd have to inhale at some point. The burning sensation expanded in her lungs like helium gas, trying to enfeeble the willpower to stay alive and let natural processes take their course. For a while, there was nothing but a whirling sensation as she spun around in circles with her eyes firmly clenched. She sunk lower and lower into the infernal regions, closer and closer to death. Luckily for Psyche, the latter never came, for a pair of familiar hands fastened themselves tightly around her waist and propelled her aloft at the speed of a bullet train. She wheezed for breath as they broke the surface.

Psyche awoke to the sound of lapping waves. There was a warm hand resting on her shoulder. Acting out of pure impulse, she pivoted to see who was beside her. Psyche shuddered. She squeezed her eyes shut and opened them again, wondering whether she'd become permanently entangled in a nightmarish ordeal or whether she'd finally passed into the next world. The mirage didn't disappear.

"Yes, it's me, Psyche," said Eros.

"Dear Zeus!" Psyche exclaimed, throwing her arms around him and planting kisses on his mouth. "Is it really you?"

"From head to toe," he teased. "You ought to be a bit less impulsive and a lot more considerate of others, my love. I almost lost you back there."

"I couldn't bear the thought of losing—"

"What's wrong?"

Psyche winced. "I think I did lose it. My—"

Eros opened his clenched hand. "Is this what you thought you'd lost?"

"How did you—"

"I dived for it after bringing you back here," said Eros.

"How did you find me?"

"I followed you through the portal," said Eros, "before Mom could destroy it."

"You got through without being noticed?" Psyche asked.

"We have ways of moving undetected," said Eros, winking. "I learned from the best!"

"Your mom doesn't really like me."

"A lot of daughter-in-laws have that problem," said Eros. "She'll get over it, eventually. When it comes to the partners of her own children, my mom's painstakingly high standards are enough to scare away even the boldest of nymphs."

"She'll never accept me."

"You're wrong," said Eros. "She actually thinks very highly of you."

"That's a pretty odd way of showing approval, don't you think?" asked Psyche. "She was trying to find any excuse in the divine rulebook to kill me."

"But she didn't," Eros pointed out.

"What's your point?"

"It's her way of testing you," said Eros. "I know it's rather cruel, taunting and severe, but that's the way she measures love."

"By terrorizing them?"

"It's the only way she knows how," said Eros. "Look what she did to me. She drugged me so that I couldn't interfere with her plans or try to see you."

Psyche sighed. "I'm taking your word for it."

"Why, what's changed from before?" asked Eros.

"I trust you."

"I know," he said. "I know that you love me too."

"You do?" Her eyes were sultry.

"I do," he said. "Who would willingly go through the

motions of forfeiting their life for another, Psyche? Who?"

Psyche smiled. "A madwoman."

"A woman in love."

"I'm crazy."

"One's of love's many by-products." Eros embraced her, sliding his hand over her breast. "Another is hot sex... you know..."

"Hmm..."

His fingers orbited her nipple before they squeezed gently. "... like the good time you were showing me before you decided to break the spell with your ice pick and blowtorch...."

"Dear Zeus."

"I spoke to him via microchip earlier," said Eros.

"You did?"

"Before crossing worlds," said Eros. "He tuned into Mom's Divine Game and was quite impressed with your knowledge of divinity. He's going to make you an immortal."

Psyche's eyes widened. "Really?"

"Aha," Eros nodded. "Your baptism is tomorrow morning."

"Oh, the mighty Zeus!"

"You're going to eat ambrosia and drink nectar."

"I've heard that it tastes a bit like Lindt chocolate," said Psyche.

"The ambrosia? Yeah, it does,' said Eros. "Once you taste that, you're stuck with me forever."

Psyche smiled. "Literally, huh?"

"Yes."

"I think I can live with that," she said, running her hand against his thigh.

"Me too, my love."

"Tomorrow is still aeons away," said Psyche. "What are we

going to do to fill up the time?"

"How about some loving? Let's pick up where we left off."

"But how will we get home?" asked Psyche.

"Leave that to me!"

Psyche felt Eros's grip around her waist tighten and, in the space of a microsecond, they were back inside the comfort of their accustomed bedroom. This time around, there was no hiccup, no doubt boiling to the surface of her conscious mind and spoiling their bliss. This time, it was like one superheated jet of passion exploding from a subterranean vent somewhere; she was the progenitor of the pressurized force, he the water pumping through the vent. They interpenetrated and sublimed into one another like solute and solvent. They rode through waves of titillation like a pod of mating dolphins. They enacted acrobatic somersaults which propelled them onto unprecedented fringing reefs and left them marooned there for hours at a time. The encounter was miraculous and vigorous, fiery, and energetic, earth-shattering and blissful, impulsive and instant. It was, well, the procreation, accomplishment, and multiplication of new life.

Hence, after entwining around one another like a couple of baby lianas, Eros and Psyche, love and soul, were destined to partake of the same being, to grow toward the pocket of glorious sunlight that is that being, and to experiment together with the polychromatic and multidimensional Unity that is being.

The Magic Room

The myths associated with Narcissus appear in an early eighth-century Homeric Hymn and in Ovid's narrative poem, Metamorphoses; the latter unravels as the story of a beautiful youth who falls in love with his own likeness reflected on the surface of a pond and falls into the pond and perishes whilst trying to get up close and personal with it. Here, I have taken the fundamental concepts of the myth and infused them into a modern-day narrative.

Unable to keep his exhaustion at bay, he fell asleep on the floor. As if he were a spiraling galaxy in space, there was a prolonged darkness for a while, and then the vivid dreams unfolded like white lilies in a watery film of unconsciousness. In one, he was charging through a meadow, trying to evade an assailant whose footfalls were as loud as summertime thunderbolts. Then time stopped and the dream melded into another in which he was kneeling over a lake, trying desperately to discern his own physical features. Before the nebulous reflection began to differentiate, he was sucked out of the dream by an invisible hand and spat back into mind space.

The nightmares, themselves dispersed amongst the sinister visions, were worse than they'd ever been. In one, he stumbled through a hospital mortuary, trying desperately to find the exit as a host of eyeless corpses broke out from their refrigeration chambers. They were all duplicates of his last victim. Despite their empty eye sockets, they knew exactly where he was. That much was clear. Calling his name out loud, they stumbled toward the shadowy corner in which he was now crouched. A sinewy hand suddenly appeared out of nowhere, curling tightly around his leg.

Saturated in his own sweat, he awoke to the sound of his own garbled cries. It was pitch dark and it terrified him. Although darkness was quite indigenous to his state of being, he had not grown accustomed to it. He scampered to his feet, trying to defog the mental inertia and orient himself.

Suddenly he remembered. Some time ago, he'd been assigned a major task by the faceless men. His most recent mission had been to dispose of an intellectual nuisance, a man whose research was irreconcilable with their long-term plans. That's what they told him. To his detriment, they forgot to mention that the scientist didn't live alone. Without the aid of a firearm, the hand-to-hand combat fated to transpire was decidedly not to his advantage. He'd managed to escape unscathed, albeit without fulfilling his duty. The punishment for failure to appease the faceless men was a time in the Magic Room.

He knew exactly what that meant, for he had been in there countless times before for not conforming to collective will. Nothing in the Magic Room felt right or natural; everything was random. Sometimes it was abyssal, as dark as night, and at other times, the lights were excruciatingly bright. Sometimes the hidden speakers would belt out cacophonous, high-pitched noises. On some occasions, he heard threatening whispers and at yet other times, he still heard the screams of men, women, and children before being beheaded. Everything was translucent which made shuffling around a rather hazardous affair. Films and videos were played on a projector in reverse; animals and insects were released into the room at random, and variant drugs were slipped into anomalous-looking, unconventionally-tasting meals which spurred hallucinations, hyperactivity, languor, or deep sleep. Sometimes he awoke gagged and tied to an inclined bed and sometimes he was awakened by ice water being poured over his head. Human limbs would jut out through the walls quite suddenly and then retract again. People appeared in the room and disappeared, pausing only for a brief moment to ask irrational questions. In short, the Magic Room was a mental hell of psychic-bending lava.

"Narcissus?" boomed a robotic voice from a speaker. "Are you awake now, Narcissus?"

"Yes, Mother."

"Do you know why I put you in here, Narcissus?"

"Yes."

"Tell me."

"For not being as I should," he said. "For not thinking and acting in the manner that you instructed."

"Your aim is to kill," said the rasping, mechanical voice. "You must execute, no matter what the consequences are. Your masters will describe details of the scene to the best of their ability, but there is always the chance that things will be different. You must become more versatile so as to accommodate for that, you understand?"

"Yes, Mother."

"Why did you try to kill yourself yesterday?" asked the female automaton.

"But I didn't."

"Oh, but you did, Narcissus. You forget that I am the all-seeing eye and that nothing escapes me. Last night, after your last meal, you tried to hang yourself with a coat hanger from the back of the circular doorway."

"No, I didn't."

"You might try feeling around your neck…"

He pressed the palms of his hands up against his neck. It felt sore and tender in some spots. Strangely, he had never harbored any thoughts of suicide and had no memory of enacting such a stunt.

"See? Mother sees everything…"

"I know."

"So why did you do it?"

After a brief pause, he said, "Because I'm scared of the darkness, terrified of it."

"The darkness and the pain will all go away if you do exactly as you're told."

"Thank you, Mother."

"The Magic Room becomes kind to he who listens," said the robotic voice tauntingly.

"I understand."

"Now, take a few steps forward until I tell you to stop."

He hesitated, listening for any commotion around him before taking a wary step forward with his right. Then another with his left. Then another with his right.

"Stop right there!"

Narcissus flinched as something pricked his naked shoulder, but he didn't dare swat it away. It felt like the sting of a needle. For a brief second, he contained a build-up of rumbling tension by holding in his breath, unsure of what might transpire next. He squeezed his eyes tightly and opened them again, wishing that the darkness would just go away. Then two pairs of arms were upon him; cold brittle steel snapped around his wrists and a very thick elastic band was wrapped tightly around his head and eyes to constrict his vision. One of the hands accidentally brushed against his genitals, inciting a nervous twitch. Realizing the punishment was over, he expelled the tension through his nostrils.

"Let's go, big boy," said a male voice brusquely. "You've escaped the furnace yet again."

The hands of both his escorts were glued to his back and arms as they walked along the corridor. It was rather disquieting to walk in complete silence, something Narcissus was compelled to do frequently. Their relative size enabled him to estimate their physiognomy; without a doubt, they were nowhere near his size and stature.

"What do you think the authorities will do if they ever find out about the activities of Egregor Laboratories?" one of them asked.

"*Shhh!*" exclaimed the other. "Not in front of him, Rosie."

"We're safe, he doesn't understand a thing. He's just a puppet."

"Things might get out."

"Trust me, they won't, Allan," said the bold one named Rosie. "Why do you suppose they called him, Narcissus?"

"Beats me," said the one called Allan. "Isn't that the boy from the Greek myth? You know, the one who fell in love with himself?"

"Oh, yes, I remember it now," said Rosie. "I took classics as a semester-long subject when I was at university. Narcissus was a highlight. I can see how the myth might apply here and what could happen if we get careless with the set procedure, but we shouldn't forget that the real Narcissus was human."

"This one's not exactly a robot, Rosie; far from it, in fact."

"Well, anyone who sees him *knows* that he's different. And if they don't see it, they'll hear it, if you know what I mean."

"Yeah," said Allan. "It's not really a voice that you can imitate, is it?"

"Not at all," said Rosie. "Not unless you were unlucky enough to be born with a deformed voice box. The powers-that-be call him a homunculus."

"Appropriate for a human forgery."

"Indeed."

Narcissus could hear the jostling of keys as they shuffled to a halt. The familiar sound of an unlatching lock calmed him further; soon, the large, circular steel door leading to his room swung open and he was nudged along.

"Home sweet home," said Allan.

"Home sweet boring home," said Rosie. "Here, take this."

Something bumped against Narcissus's hand.

"What are you giving him there?" asked Allan.

"Just something for him to play with and pass the time," said Rosie. "No harm could ever come of it if that's what you're worried about."

"Fine."

His escorts swiftly relieved him of his temporary shackles and before long, he was alone again in the somnolent darkness. Narcissus cleared a space in the rubble and sat cross-legged on the ground, fumbling with the plastic device that he'd been gifted and rummaging through his personal memories. Long ago, the Great Mother had told him that he wasn't quite like anyone else on the planet. He had no physical father or mother because he was a son of God who had been magically teleported to the Earth at the moment of his birth to weed out and destroy all who opposed His Word. If he was, indeed, different from humans, as the Rosie-human and the Allan-human had intimated, then were humans also children of God? Or were they the spawn of the Devil, cleverly disguised as divine beings for the sake of misleading and corrupting him? But why would they employ him to annihilate evil unless they, themselves, were good? Had they been lying to him all along? Had they lied to him about his origins? What about their true identities, purpose, and the nature of the world at large? What was the magnitude of their treachery? Were they little white lies or earth-shattering ones full of venomous acid? Was his name really Narcissus? What was he exactly? The incongruities comprising what he recognized to be fact didn't really harmonize with the coherence that spells truth; some of them, if not all, must be lies. Nothing made any sense otherwise.

Troubled by this insurmountable riddle, Narcissus remained oblivious to the magnificent beam of light that emanated from the plastic tube and cut through the fabric of darkness each time he applied firm pressure to one side of it. The newfound phenomenon startled him until his light-sensitive eyes became accustomed to its fiery glow. He waved it vigorously around the empty room like a talisman, revealing a horde of hitherto unseen paraphernalia: broken bits of furniture, including chairs, wardrobes, and tables; a rusting sink cluttered by an assortment of plates and cutlery; a few dilapidated wooden shelves filled with bags of chemical powders, acids, drugs, and other tinctures and a silvery, phosphorescent-looking glass which suffused the entire wall.

Narcissus was instantly drawn to the looking glass, for he had never seen anything quite like it. He scurried right up to its reflective surface, pointing the beaming circular device down at his feet. The light revealed two powerfully built and chiseled legs. He changed the trajectory, moving it upwards to reveal a flaccid penis couched amidst a thick nest of black hairs. The sight of it excited him beyond reckoning; blood began to pump, transforming it into a purpled, angry-looking implement ready to spit its venom like a cobra on the attack. Narcissus surged forward and pressed himself onto the cold surface of the glass, grinding and rotating his pelvis against it so that his own manhood tussled with the other. When he stepped back, the being in the looking glass stepped back too. He let the light course further up to six convex-shaped plates and two powerful nipple-crowned mounds that were the masculine being's chest, and further up still to the delicate contours of his face.

For a while, Narcissus just stared into the glass, transfixed by the two turquoise orbs that sucked him through the dark veil of physical appearances and into a psychedelic, multi-themed circus of mystical beings. He was, at once, the young blooming sunflower, sentient enough to form innocent, intuitive perceptions but not yet mature enough to understand the external forces at work in the cosmos. Time jarred and everything around him fell away like shards of a broken mirror; he savored the dark ridges around the patrician nose, the almond-shaped eyes and the bulbous lips, the chiseled jawline, and the crème-colored skin. Each was a dreamy experience in its own right, a primal act of love and coming-to-be. When he smiled, the supernal being in the looking glass smiled back. He pointed a finger at the being, and the being pointed back. When he pouted and planted a kiss on the cold, brittle surface of the glass, the being on the other side reciprocated. He squirmed and writhed against it, probing the glass with his tongue; so, did the being on the other side.

Narcissus pulled back from his like-minded friend,

intending to speak. But the being in the looking glass spoke first: "How will we ever get out of this place?"

Startled by the unexpected turn of events, Narcissus pressed the nose of the plastic device directly onto the glass and tried to discern whether anything or anyone else lay beyond it. To his surprise, rows of many glasses suddenly became visible. All were attached to rooms shaped to look like rectangular prisms and subsisted an equal distance from one another. Moreover, each confined a separate being and all beings were identical. The revelation lifted a ton of weight from his broad shoulders; it made the looking glass blur.

Narcissus winked, and the others winked back approvingly.

He wasn't alone anymore.

An Encounter with the Minotaur

In classical mythology, the Minotaur was the product of an inexplicable union between Queen Pasiphae of Crete and a magnificent white bull sent as a gift to King Minos by the sea god Poseidon. It was imprisoned in a labyrinth constructed by the Athenian-born architect Daedalus beneath the Cnossian palace and was eventually slain by Theseus, the illustrious hero of Athens.

Pontinija and Talos.

The night was preternaturally silent and void of its usual disturbances. We'd walked a fair distance from Cnossos and were yet to hear the fluttering wings of an owl swooping down toward an unsuspecting rodent or the eerie cry of a jackal loitering around the desert in search of a decomposing carcass. There was no moon, so we had to make do with what little light came from the stars.

We attempted to follow the path of the most powerful electromagnetic current. At times, I felt like we were going around in circles, probably because most of the subterranean waters that mapped out magnetic lines proceeded in exaggerated zigzag courses. Every so often, I would drop to my knees and, with the aid of a pendulum, determine if we were still on course. I did this by holding the gadget directly above the path in question, waiting for the familiar gyration, and then counting the number of revolutions it traced before coming to a halt. The existence of water was marked by thirty revolutions, a milestone which was also the rate for qualities which you and your peers would consider highly disparate: the cardinal direction of the West; the color green; the marker of age; the moon; the sense of sound; and the element of hydrogen.

Speaking of elements, we had to ensure that fire, water, air and earth, and the qualities of hot, cold, wet, and dry were all present in some form or another for the experiment to have any chance at succeeding. Their rotation would be facilitated by a light source other than the sun. I say this because our sun is the motive force behind the world of matter alone. A venture of this sort called for the heat of a much more formidable planetary body, the heavenly light of Sirius. Only an ethereal body such as hers, of an ethereal kind, could accelerate the motive force behind element rotation and spark an interdimensional portal between physical and psychoneurotic matter, something which our sun cannot do.

We stopped in what we took to be a virgin cut of the desert. We marked out a circle with some pebbles and lay down to rest beside one another in the enclosed space, ensuring that our heads and outstretched hands pointed south and our feet north. Then we relaxed and entered a hypnotic trance, directing our energies toward the region of the solar plexus that so typified *ka* projection to other places and into other living things. The energy proliferated quickly, diffusing out of our limbs and gathering like a ball of wool in our abdominal regions. We had to remain in a state of heavy concentration yet resist fragmentation. It was difficult, even for two people who had experienced projection innumerable times before. We weren't allowed to push ourselves over the edge, or to let ourselves be pushed either. Only light from the star's heliacal rising could infuse us with enough power to break the interdimensional threshold.

Soon, we were floating. There was nothing but a whirling sensation as we spun in circles, going faster and faster with each revolution. We sank lower and lower into the infernal regions, closer and closer to death. A rumbling noise came from somewhere below us as the ground gave way. We were dropping, and fast. We splashed into an ocean of violent water. The current into which we fell was strong, stronger than I thought it would be. There was no way I could navigate through it, let alone garner any control over it. I wasn't even sure if Talos was still with me, or if an adverse current had carried him someplace else. The noise was now thunderous like a snow-storm, like the white noise that came through the television when an analogous receiver lost its signal. It blunted my receptive senses, my intuition. Before long, the infernal waters formed into a mouth, the mouth morphed into a set of lips, and the lips opened wide to reveal a flickering tongue. I was sucked into this gaping tear, deep into the funnel of darkness. Then there was nothing. I felt, heard and saw nothing.

The first sensation I became conscious of when I awoke was the foul smell; the air was permeated with the putrid stench of urine. There must have been a cesspit nearby. Jerking my head up, I studied my surroundings. It appeared that I was in something subterranean, probably a grotto; somebody had covered its walls with pieces of woollen cloth in an attempt to render the place homely. There were urns, jars and other utensils splayed onto the ground, some of which were engraved with beautiful geometrical motifs, including one with which I was quite familiar—the flower-of-life. Some were intact, others smashed beyond recognition. Next to those were human remains; skulls, bones, and decomposing carcasses.

Talos, I thought. Where's Talos? The last thing I remembered was our kas floating upward as we readied ourselves for projection into the psychoneurotic world. Was Talos still with me, around me? Pardon the pun, but was he in me? I couldn't sense or detect anything, within or without, inside or out.

I tried to speak. I couldn't. The most I managed was a small croak as if my vocal cords had been surgically removed with a scalpel. There was a lantern glowing in the distance, so I decided to play detective and investigate. I staggered to my feet and stumbled toward the source of light. The first thing that came to my attention was my height. I was a colossus in stature, nearly as tall as the ceiling. Strange, very strange. I peered down and that's when I nearly had a coronary. My body was scaly, covered in crumpled folds of skin and my feet terminated in serrated talons.

Perhaps the strangest thing of all was that I had a phallus. Yes, you heard it, a phallus. How could I have a phallus? It was prominent and hung quite low between my legs. Stranger still was that it was endowed with movement; I could move it and not just partially, either. I had full control of it as I did my arms or legs. My hands darted straight up and groped around my head. It was somewhat enlarged, or better to say, deformed. My snout was bulbous, much wider than what is accustomed to a human. There were small, hornlike protrusions growing out from my temples.

I screamed, but even that came out as a strange, bellowing noise. I tried to keep calm, telling myself that it was merely a *night terror, and I would soon awake drenched in my own sweat. It had to be. I could not, should not, would not have become a monster, a chance freak of the illimitable imagination. Phenomena such as this didn't just manifest from an attempt at an astral projection or even a failed one. Something far more sinister was at work here.*

Before long, I was overwhelmed with pangs of hunger which stirred deep in the pit of my stomach. The unconscious urge seemed to proliferate, to grow within me in quite the same manner that sexual tension builds up when you haven't pleasured yourself in days or weeks, even. It threatened to possess my entire being because all I could think of was eating. I needed to satisfy my carnal desire, to find my ambrosia. And I knew exactly what I wanted; human flesh.

My eyesight was extraordinarily sharp and transcended the limited spectrum of light frequencies delineating human vision. In fact, it appeared that I encompassed the ability to see in longer wavelengths, in infrared. The color red was my sincerest ally, my lifelong interpreter. I saw, felt, heard, tasted, smelled its many sides, its innumerable faces. It could be fire, heat, the east, youth, the sun, movement, violence, or anger. It could be one or two or the sum of these things, the vital force we call life. Life, or red, resonated from all living bodies.

There were two living humans, a male and a female, amongst the cadavers and other severed body parts littered and putrefying on the ground. Both had long, wavy hair and were lying huddled behind a clump of rocks, whispering to one another in a language I didn't know and couldn't understand. In one of them I made out the contours of the seat of life; the beating heart.

Both were shuddering, trying desperately to obstruct my view by hiding behind a wall of discolored, misshapen bodies. No doubt some had worms in them. I wasn't interested in those. Only warm, blood-nourished living flesh would do. Only red.

I let out a spine-chilling ululation and lunged towards the pair, clawing through the rotting heap on the ground. The humans didn't have any time to react, scream or even flinch. They didn't stand much of a chance either. I seized the male by the neck, lifting him one to two cubits off the ground. He writhed and slavered against me, swinging his legs wildly in the air. Our eyes met. His fear was intense, urgent, acute. Before I could smother him, something, or someone, crashed onto my back. A sharp pain exploded from my shoulder as nails pierced my skin. It was the young woman. Adapting an altogether more proactive approach to the situation, she was trying to play savior and heroine. I reached behind, clamped my hand around her head and squeezed. Her scream was cut short as the cranial bones snapped. I relinquished my grip and her limp body crashed onto the ground.

The struggle was beginning to excite me sexually. It suggested the manner in which the greatest African predator, the lioness, might, before strangling it to death, toy with a newborn calf separated from its mother. My phallus pointed toward the ceiling, proud and purpled. I wanted to relieve myself, to beat off with a dozen or so strokes, but any premature release would blunt the growing vortex of excitement. I tightened my grip on the man's neck. He rasped for breath, desperate to peel my fingers off his throat. His face was rapidly draining of color; his will to resist waning. In a matter of seconds, I would have my meal.

What ensued next was completely unprecedented. The man

attacked me with a weapon, a sharp rock which he'd kept well concealed in his woolen clothes. I lurched back to avoid the counter-attack but it was too late. It ended up grazing me just under the jaw. Blood welled from the searing wound. My phallus sprang into action, knocking the weapon from the man's grasp. I lunged forward and bit into his jugular vein with my serrated teeth. The saline taste of blood sent a powerful, electric shock coursing through my body.

Now was the moment of my glory—time to deliver the final blow, to severe the thinning cord still connecting this hopeless being to its life force. The moment never came. Before I could recover my wits enough to finish what I'd started, everything began to pixelate, to gyrate, to dematerialize. Through no volition of my own, I was sucked back into the whirling vortex from whence I'd come. The whirling vortex, tapered into a funnel of darkness, spat me out at the place of the infernal waters. Then I lost consciousness.

I awoke on the desert sands, shivering. Talos, curled on his side, dribbling spit out of the corner of his mouth and mumbling to himself, was still with me. How long had we been travelling? I guessed about twenty to thirty minutes, seeing that the heliacal rising of ethereal Sirius lasted no longer than that. The first light of dawn must have zapped our *kas* back into our physical bodies.

"What happened?" Talos mumbled.

"What do you think happened? We screwed it up," I said.

"Did you feel the power of its urges?" said Talos. "It had no control over its urges whatsoever."

"So, you were there," I said. "Literally there. In the flesh there."

"Yeah, I was with you the whole time," he said. "Beside you, actually."

"What was that, Talos? Call it what you will but it was anything but projection to the *materia prima*."

"It felt like we'd gone back in time."

"Nope."

"Forward in time, then?"

"Nope," I said. "How can something like that have ever existed, or come to exist in the future? How credulous of you, Talos." I was surprised at the irony in my own voice.

"Why not?" he asked. "Anything is possible, isn't it? I learnt that from you, *Potinija*."

"I don't think it's that."

"Your thoughts for a pendulum then?" Talos smiled.

"I think we tapped into a fantasy of yours," I said. "One that you've been moping on for years."

"No," he said.

"Definitely, something a man like you would think about, Talos."

His face went scarlet. "You're wrong."

"Colors don't lie."

"Don't know what you're talking about," he insisted.

"Well, I think you do," I said, scrambling to my feet. "I'm just glad that I came out of that before the big crunch. That was awful."

Phantasia

In the mythic Grecian landscape, Proteus, a minor sea god, could alter his shape at will and predict the future. Some classicists hold him to be Poseidon's son. No known cycle of myths features this fascinating, mysterious god.

21ˢᵗ December 2012

Sara Li wasn't one to tempt the gods. When a stroke of gold-laden serendipity came her way, she always attributed it to the moral and social values instilled in her by her late mother.

Nobody, not even the savviest businessman who had climbed to the capstone of society, should ever forget that we're born into the world completely naked, she could hear her mother saying. Not even the cotton fabric of your underwear or the democratic right to self-determination is yours. Everything that may pass into your small hands is loaned to you, my Sara, sometimes under the pretense of a gift. If you use these gifts to the best of your ability in spreading cosmic love and enacting virtuous deeds, karma will handle you sympathetically in your subsequent incarnations. If, though, you go against the providential will of humility and self-sacrifice in prioritizing your own egotistical needs to the detriment of the greater community, you will be cast down like a rag doll and subjected to physical laws that further tighten the reigns on your personal freedom.

Even though she wasn't a practising Buddhist, the great

wisdom bubbling beneath this timeless philosophy strongly resonated with her. Sara mulled these words over and over as she intermittently took sips of her soda and lime and savored delicious pieces of her chicken Kiev. Her recent successes in being promoted to a more senior position as Manager of Research and Development at Roseneath Laboratories, Inc., as well as another government grant for recombinant DNA research, was no doubt the result of tireless dedication and striving for these moral codes. So, too, she supposed, was the instant rapport she'd struck up with Dr. Jonathan Garner, a geneticist working under the same umbrella whose primary interest lay in the application of newly developed genetic manipulation technologies to the reproductive cloning of entire animals.

In their first few months of working together, she'd carelessly assumed that Jonathan was a timid, gentle, shy man who grew nervous around women and was severely limited when it came to social awareness and breadth. But to assume was a dangerous liaison and she'd been proven wrong, very wrong, in fact. As soon as he'd discovered that they shared many of the same interests, he'd bloomed to life like a sunflower. He'd even been quite flippant in the way he'd gone about organizing the rendezvous; he'd marched onto the front porch, knocked on her door, and asked a ceramic frog if it approved of his advances as soon as she'd swung the door ajar. That had instantly won her over. For the first time in years, she dared to wonder if the charming and attractive scientist sitting opposite her would eventually weave himself into her lonely life. Was Jonathan the gift of her karmic energy, or was he merely a contingency of chance? Only time would tell.

A plump waitress suddenly jolted her from her thoughts.

"Water?"

"No, thanks," said Sara. "There'll be enough water after twelve."

The waitress had a blank stare on her face as if she couldn't quite understand what Sarah had told her. Then she laughed. "Had to think about that for a second. You know, if I knew for a fact that the end of the world was just around the corner, then I'd be doing exactly what you two are doing." She knelt down beside Sara and whispered into her ear, "Intimacy over hysteria any day of the week, sweetie."

Sara smiled at her. "Definitely."

After the waitress had ventured onto the next table, Jonathan said, "Care to tell me what that was all about?"

"Women's work."

"Oh, I see," said Jonathan. "Now we're keeping secrets, are we?"

"How's the cannelloni?"

"Don't change the subject."

"I'm just asking how your dinner is," said Sara. "Are you going to start being cruel to me?"

"Even the most heartless tyrant would find it exceedingly hard to be cruel to you, sweet Sara."

Sara blushed. "What were we saying before the waitress interrupted us?"

"You're trying to change the subject again," said Jonathan.

"Wiseass."

"We were talking about the human imagination," said Jonathan, impaling pieces of tubular pasta with his fork. "We were talking about its inclination to create false beliefs like what's supposed to be happening tonight."

Sara took another sip of her soda and lime. "Looking

around the restaurant tonight, there seems to be, like, a nervous tension in the air. Don't you think? People know nothing's going to happen but there's still that superstitious part of the soul that keeps the door of feasibility slightly ajar."

"What makes you say that?"

"Well, for starters there are more people out and about for a Friday night than usual," she said. "There's that one in a quadrillion chance that the romanticists are right, and so they're out to enjoy themselves before the Big Bang."

"The romanticists will be severely hung-over tomorrow morning," said Jonathan, "because the only Big Bang that's going to be happening will be a sudden thunderbolt of revelation followed by heavy showers of disappointment. Those who've sold all their belongings in readying themselves for Armageddon will be most affected by the tempest."

Sara nearly choked on her drink. "You can be so entertaining, Jonathan. It's a side of you none of us have ever had the pleasure of seeing at work. In all seriousness, though, I think phenomena like this are detrimental to our cause."

"How so?"

"Well, they deflect attention away from the issues that we should be addressing, such as global warming and world hunger. Westerners tend to get caught up in things like that."

Jonathan, cocking his eyebrows, checked his wristwatch. "What? Procrastinating?"

"No imagination," said Sara. "They imagine far too much, often to the detriment of the entire human race. They search for meanings that aren't there."

"Hey, don't knock it," said Jonathan. "You realize that to imagine is to create, right?"

Sara frowned. "How's that?"

"It generates images which drive thought and memory," said Jonathan. "And thought and memory are fundamental to recognition and identification of self."

"This is deep," said Sara, shoving another piece of chicken Kiev into her mouth.

"Plato and Aristotle both called imagination *'phantasia'*, a faculty of knowing between the physical senses and the crowning intellect."

"*Phantasia*," said Sara, musing over the syllables. "It's a beautiful word. It sounds so exotic."

"Its original meaning is to make visible or reveal," said Jonathan. "The ancient philosophers believed the invisible, eternal realm could only be accessed through the form conferred to them by *phantasia*, the imagination. It was an intuitive faculty and expressed itself through dreams, fantasies, visions, prophecies, and any other altered state of consciousness. In contemplating these forms or images, we give them life."

"Hmm... are you saying that when we imagine we're kind of creating our future, our destiny?" Sara asked.

"You could say that," said Jonathan. "Images of the *phantasia* are created by people, but these phantasmagorias also exist independently. The possibility of images is infinite. We know this because people have been able to pry into them and see the future."

"Wait a second," said Sara, taking a deep breath. "Are you saying that imagination is kind of like an all-seeing eye of the soul?"

"Exactly," said Jonathan. "Our recorded history offers overwhelming proof of this. Things that our predecessors imagined have, eventually, come to pass. Ancient and medieval alchemists wished to make gold of lead. Nowadays, nuclear fission has made that endeavor a reality. The Franciscan philosopher, Roger Bacon, was talking about automobiles, flying machines, submarines, and suspended bridges a great many centuries before they finally became a reality."

"Leonardo Da Vinci, too," Sara added.

"Absolutely," said Jonathan. "What about the Renaissance physician, Paracelsus? He spoke widely of artificial generation during his time. He believed it was possible to create a homunculus, an artificial human grown inside an alembic."

"Cloning."

"Correct," said Jonathan. "You see, Sara, the imaginings of science fiction first become possible, then probable, then fact. Think of a *Brave New World*, the novel by Aldous Huxley. You and I both know that science has decreed that foresight a reality and the only thing separating us from it is the disputation of ethics. Think of our own progress in genetic engineering and how it has been sealing the gap between the fiction of Michael Crichton's *Jurassic Park* and scientific feasibility. The images all start out as invisible possibilities in the unconscious. Once they are ensouled and made visible by the human imagination, they eventually become fact."

Sara was genuinely shocked by the depth of his thought. She gazed into his almond-shaped grey eyes, shaking her head from side to side in sheer admiration.

"Don't you agree?" he asked.

"I see you've been mulling this over for a while," she said. "Time for a career change?"

"Me, a philosopher?" he asked, pointing to himself. "I'm too much of a hands-on kinda guy. I'd miss the lab and microscope. In any case, didn't the great Paracelsus say that the true philosopher comes to know the cosmos through his own observations, and not what has been learned from books? We're philosophers too, Sara."

"I suppose the line between the two isn't really clear-cut, is it?" she asked. "The two are partners in crime."

Jonathan smiled at her before glancing at his folded hands again.

"What's wrong?"

"Oh, nothing," he said, looking up like a child caught in the act of doing something it shouldn't have. He proceeded to clear his throat. "So, first, we tap into the unconscious, or whatever you want to call it, then we bring forth the image by imagining, and when the right milieu finally comes along, it incarnates."

"We incarnate the ghost," said Sara. "It sounds kind of Messianic, even."

"It is Messianic, even," he mimicked her. "It's like a fear that's been lingering for ages, deep in the abyss of your subconscious. You know it's there. You feel it, you hear it, you see it in your dreams. You know it's there, but you won't dare acknowledge it because by acknowledging or naming it, you give it existence and admit that it's a potential threat. One day, it finally materializes, and before you know it, you're living out your worst nightmare, trapped in a projection that is itself your own creation."

"You're starting to sound like the Dalai Lama," said Sara. "He says that we Westerners are victims of a nightmare that we ourselves created."

"He's right, Sara," Jonathan agreed. "We Westerners imagined the world this way a long time ago, and now it's materializing, spewing itself forth from our collective imagination. We exist in a cosmos which is itself a strange and odd contradiction. On the one hand, we encompass free will and actively pave our future; on the other, we're subject to the will of some higher force of which we're generally unaware and cannot fully comprehend. The latter means that we're also passive participants, like pawns being shuffled around a chessboard by an invisible hand, a hand whose movements we're largely unaware of and don't quite understand. My best guess is, we'll understand when we're meant to."

"Perhaps," said Sara, looking down at the remaining scraps of her dinner. "Surely not everything that we imagine has the potential to become reality."

"Says who?"

"Oh, Jonathan!" Sara exclaimed. "Now you're sounding like the lab technician, Frank, with his, 'Everything's possible when one's will is as strong as a diamond necklace' motto."

"Well, it's true."

"Diamond might be strong but, if stressed enough, it still fractures," said Sara. "One's will can be broken."

"All science must be based on observation," said Jonathan, ignoring her comment and glancing at his lap again. "Come on, Sara, you know that as well as I. And what observation has shown us is that our imaginings, the science fiction and magic of today, become the worlds of tomorrow. As eerie and strange as it might sound, it's true."

Sara finished the last of her diet coke. "Maybe you're right, and maybe you're wrong, Dr. Garner. In fact, in this world of strange contradictions, maybe you're both right and wrong."

"I have a hunch that you may be right."

"So," she said, licking her lips suggestively. "In all the time you've had to ruminate about the significance and role of human imagination in the evolution of our species lately, what have you imagined about me?"

Sara sensed that the question made him somewhat uneasy. He fidgeted nervously with his hands and smiled sheepishly at her.

"Well, Sara, when I first met you, I imagined you were damn good at what you did," he said.

"What made you think that?" she asked.

"Your workmates spoke very highly of you," he said. "I also imagined that you were a very dedicated and honorable person. I mean, anyone who can juggle a research position that involves long, tedious hours in the lab and also raise a child deserves a medal. The responsibility that comes—"

"How did you know I had a kid?" she interrupted.

"Oh, there's a picture of you in the tearoom with a little boy," said Jonathan. "I just assumed that he was—"

"Yes, of course," she nodded. "Foolish me. I'd completely forgotten that I'd brought a picture of the two of us into work."

"Cute little kid."

"Thanks," she said. "So, the first impressions were good, hey?"

"Definitely," he said. "I also felt a sense of kinship with you. Call it a sixth sense or whatever, but from the moment we'd had that conversation about reproductive cloning in the staff room, I intuitively felt that we were on the same wavelength with many things, both professional and personal. I also knew you were completely trustworthy, otherwise, I wouldn't have brought you here tonight."

"I so knew it!" she exclaimed. "I knew there was a reason you asked me out on a date!"

"There is."

She winked at him. "I think you should spill the beans,

then, Dr. Garner. You know I'm not psychic!"

He took a deep breath, exhaling slowly. "I wanted to share something with you that I haven't yet shared with anyone else."

Sara's heart began thumping so loudly that she was sure it would come smashing out through her ribcage at any minute. Her palms had become so sweaty that she had to brush them against her black denim jeans. She looked across to him anxiously, wondering if this was the night, he'd chosen to profess his love for her.

Then he checked the time on his wristwatch again.

"Are we double-parked?" she asked.

"What?"

"You keep checking the time," she said. "You've been doing it for the last hour or so."

"You don't miss a thing, do you?"

"It helps when you've got two sets of everything."

He frowned. "Excuse me?"

"I'm a Gemini."

He laughed. "You're too much sometimes, Sara."

"That's me."

"Well, I'd like us to be back before midnight," he said.

"I see," she said. "The breathless kiss before midnight Armageddon, hey?"

"You'll have to wait and see," he said. "It's a surprise."

"I like surprises."

"You do?"

"Yeah, especially when they're from philosopher-scientists who know so much about the art of imagination."

"Can you imagine what the surprise might be?" he asked. "I've given you a few clues already."

"I have a rough idea," she said. "I'll need to fine-tune my

faculty of imagination on the way back to your place. That way, I'll be better able to recreate the events due to unfold there between the two of us."

Sara was horrified at the insinuation she'd just given voice to. She wondered if it was the alcohol talking. It had to be. She never overstepped the implicit boundaries of first-date etiquette, no matter how attracted she was to a man. But the ethereal fences that kept her bubbling emotions and feelings from transmuting into spoken words weren't quite there anymore. It was as if some madman had charged into her inner space with a bulldozer, knocking them down like a set of dominoes. She couldn't quite remember how many martinis she'd had at the bar earlier whilst waiting for him. One, two, three, four, even?

Jonathan winked at her. "It will be great."

Sara purposefully knocked her keys from the table and keeled over to pick them up.

"What on earth are you—"

"Don't look now," she whispered, "but there are two guys sitting a few tables away that keep looking our way."

"Where?"

"To our right," she said. "I get a funny sense that they've been trying to tune into our conversation."

Jonathan turned to his right, thrusting his arm up into the air and waving it about to grab the attention of the waitress. After a few seconds, he said, "Do you smell what I smell?"

Sara fiddled with her keys. "I don't think they're private investigators."

"Federal police?" Jonathan asked.

"Doubt it," said Sara.

"CIA?"

"We're government-funded," Sara pointed out. "They'd be

able to tap into all our records electronically. Why would they waste time spying on employees of Roseneath Laboratories?"

"Maybe they're working for Roseneath Laboratories," Jonathan suggested

Sara frowned. "Why would Roseneath hire private investigators to spy on its own employees? It doesn't make any sense. Unless... umm—"

"Unless what?"

"They might do it if they had reason to suspect that an employee was engaged in suspicious behavior," she said. "Something unlawful."

"Like, leaking files and selling secrets maybe?"

"Yeah," she nodded. "Something like that."

The same waitress was suddenly at the table, forcing a smile that revealed stumps of broken teeth. "Would you like coffee and cake? The tiramisu and mango cheesecake are absolutely scrumptious."

"No thanks, we'll just have the bill," said Jonathan.

"No problem."

Jonathan waited until she was out of vocal range before whispering, "Do you think they've tapped our phones?"

Sara stood up, seizing her jacket from around the chair. "I think that maybe our imaginations are getting the better of us tonight, Dr. Garner."

"Maybe."

"Any more clues?" she prompted. "Or do I have to keep imagining what this surprise might be all the way to your home?"

"No more clues," he said candidly. "Not here, anyway."

Sara tried to look over and see if the couple in question was staring at them as they walked over to the counter, but her view was obscured by a clump of indoor plants. She kept glancing back as they walked to the car park from the restaurant, though nobody seemed to be following them. Perhaps she'd misread the visual cues and the whole thing had merely been a figment of her vivid imagination.

As they drove back to Jonathan's house, she attempted to distract herself from the disconcerting experience by perusing the beautiful Christmas decorations that adorned the power poles at this time of the year. The atmosphere was kindred and electrical: children chased one another on the pathway, attempting to steal each other's candy; couples walked hand-in-hand along the promenade, sometimes halting to engage in public affection, sometimes to peruse nature's nocturnal miracles and wonders; and upbeat, chilled-out music blared from the internet cafes lining the main road. A profound tranquility and bliss preponderated, yet Sara couldn't quite shake a sense of foreboding that had wiggled itself into her consciousness at the tail end of her dinner date.

Uncomfortable with where her mind was taking her, she changed the trajectory of her thoughts again. Jonathan's impending surprise was mystifying; what did he have in store for her? Why didn't he just spill the beans at the restaurant? Why did he deem it necessary to return to his home before he unveiled it? Was it so dark and personal that he just couldn't risk another human being overhearing? Perhaps it was about the combined efforts of their government-classified research at Roseneath, a project that had proliferated from right under the public nose faster than the damaged cells of virulent cancers could multiply. Was Jonathan having second thoughts about his involvement in such an explosive and controversial field, potentially one that could damage his reputation? Sara didn't think so; they weren't really doing anything wrong. On the contrary, his whole appeal to the realm of imagination and to esoteric philosophies was unprecedented and unnerving. Sara couldn't quite put a finger on it, but at times, it had felt as though he was priming her for something. Maybe she was just overanalyzing everything, as she had a tendency to do. It often got her into trouble and now, at this time, she could do with less trouble in her life. Tossing and turning the possibilities in her head like hot stones and pancakes, she fell asleep.

Lying unconscious on the passenger seat, she dreamt that she was pregnant with a being that wasn't human. It was large, grossly out of proportion, and telepathic. Sara didn't really know how it had gotten inside her. It wasn't human and did not belong to this world. She sensed and feared its powers. The only viable explanation was that extra-terrestrials had used her as a surrogate mother. As soon as she gave birth, they would return steadfastly to collect their progeny.

Still wiping sleep from her eyes, Sara followed Jonathan down a flight of steps leading to the basement of the three-bedroom house. What lay at the very bottom exceeded her wildest expectations. Instead of workbenches brimming with tools like buzz saws, rakes, drills, blow torches, as well as screws and nails and a busted tyre or two, the space had been meticulously arranged into a rectangular slice of biotechnological microminiaturization.

Sara found that her eyes had suddenly acquired a mind of their own. They explored every corner of the narrow space in the manner that a small child saturated itself in the floral sights, multi-colored sounds, and ambrosial tastes of Luna Park, without ever pausing to ponder the potential risks of oversaturation. All scientists became wonder-filled children when dropped into a kingdom of advanced scientific equipment, and Sara was no exception.

There were two stainless steel benches propped up against the brick wall to her right. One supported a comprehensive, state-of-the-art, self-contained computer system with the kind of unlimited data storage capacity available only to government agencies and laboratories. Many pathology departments of renowned universities could not afford these. They usually came equipped with software programs associated with genetic manipulation technologies that displayed and analyzed gene editing, targeted gene knockouts, and genomic insertions in complex organisms. In layman's terms, the programs transposed the elaborate theories and practices of cloning to an intelligible level, thus enabling the aspiring scientist to meddle with God's creation. These systems also encompassed the ability to give detailed transcriptions of the molecular composition of chemical and metal samples, human blood, tissues, and other bodily fluids.

The adjoining bench held machines and devices of a more diagnostic nature: a centrifuge whose primary purpose was to separate the vital components of blood; a Soxhlet extraction apparatus used for chemical processes like distillation, maceration, and decoction; two electron microscopes used to scrupulously pick apart the anatomy of living cells and their structures; an assortment of beakers, flasks, test tubes, pipettes, metal stirring rods, crucibles, along with glass phials containing gels, buffers, and reagents; steel racks to hold lab utensils upright; a distillation train; a large refrigeration unit; a dozen or so notebooks on laboratory procedure and safety; a yellow safety bin for biohazardous waste; and a lot, lot more.

"Talk about Aladdin's Cave," said Sara, turning to face Jonathan. "This is a scientist's dream."

"Just wait until you see the magic lamp," he said. "Or better still, the genie."

Sara put her hands on her hips, smiling. "Where's the genie?"

He motioned toward his micro-marvel, speaking with a tone of frivolity. "Welcome to Jonathan's magic cave of wonders, little lady. Don't be shy! Step right up here, beside the centrifuge, and taste this newly fomented nectar which will strengthen your immune system and make you immortal."

"I like the sound of that."

"And here," he said, "besides the red elixir, we have the frozen embryos of the meat-eating savages Phorusrhacos and Smilodon…"

His words were suddenly like little fists punching her in the gut.

"These little beasties were erased from the book of life by Mother Nature but now they're back in full force, ready to embark on an unrelenting assault against the Soviet and Middle Eastern terrorists. And watch out, folks, cause they're a hell of a lot smarter and nastier than they used to be—"

"Jonathan!"

"Yeah?"

"How can you joke about this?" Sara said. "That's supposed to be classified research, remember?"

He scowled. "I was just trying to entertain you."

"Where did you get all this stuff, anyway?" she asked.

She could instantly see that the question bothered him. He loosened the buttons around his shirt and cleared his throat. "Most of the stuff I bought myself."

"What about the computers?"

"They're gifts from a close friend who works for a government agency."

"They look very cutting edge," she said. "Similar to the ones we have at Roseneath."

"Same brand."

Sara watched Jonathan walk up to the drawer of a cabinet and retrieve a pair of eyeshades. He held them out for her to see.

"What are they for?" she asked.

"They're for you," he said.

"You want me to wear them?"

"Just until I wheel the surprise out," he said, checking the time on his wristwatch again. "Sheesh, it's ten to twelve already."

"Nearly midnight," she said.

"Nearly time for the fireworks, pretty lady."

Sara rubbed her hands together in anticipation. "So, this is my long-awaited surprise, I take it? About friggin' time, Dr. Garner!"

He danced merrily around her, sliding the eyeshades over her head and adjusting the band so that they fit snugly around her eyes.

"Besides myself, you have been chosen to witness the ensoulment," Jonathan told her.

"What ensoulment?"

"You'll see in a second."

Sara didn't quite know quite what to make of Jonathan's banter. There was something hysterical about it. In her experience of the world, there was a fine line between the controlled flame of ingenuity and the unharnessed fireball of madness. It appeared that Jonathan was straddling the two. Even though she wasn't any closer to guessing what his big secret actually was, she'd experienced enough to understand that something uncanny was unfolding right before her very eyes. What was ensoulment? Who, or what, was going to be ensouled? She didn't have the slightest clue as to what the word actually meant, but it had gone a long way in ruffling her feathers. It had immobilized her mercurial thermostat, leaving the expanding air of anxiety to rise unchecked and throttle her inner amity.

She stood there in silence, listening to an array of sounds unravelling only a few feet away: first, the clink of a dial being turned and a combination lock coming undone; then the groaning of two doors being pulled open; and finally, the cluttering of a portable table being wheeled out of the hidden space. She took deep breaths, trying to stay calm.

Jonathan's big hands were suddenly around her head, yanking the eyeshades away. "Feast your eyes on this, baby."

For a moment, Sara stared at the object, confused. Then flecks of horror began to collect in the pit of her stomach as she realized what she was looking at. She squeezed her eyes shut and opened them, hoping the act might banish the apparition from her mind's eye. It didn't.

When she'd finally mustered up the courage to look again, she allowed her gaze to travel along the length of the steel table and back up to the flat-bottomed glass flask resting on top of it. The latter was about the size of a water filter and contained a clear solution of reagent. Suspended inside was something that could only be described as a fetal mannequin. Although the being was still in a preliminary phase of development, Sara could discern many anthropomorphic features. What would eventually crystallize into a mature human face—two jet black buttons, a jutting bump, and a small slit—adorned an abnormally elongated and bulbous head. She also determined that the four limbs, as well as the twenty subanatomical parts that would become toes and fingers, had differentiated clearly from the trunk of its torso. In fact, the tiny thumb and forefinger of one hand touched in such a way that suggested the mannequin had been striking up mantras and poses. Its chalk-white skin reminded Sara of albino troglobites which lived out their entire lives in the darkness of the subterranean. If appearances were anything to go by, then this creature was surely descended from the same Stygian sludge pile. The degree of its strangeness was such that Sara could not stop ogling it.

"God almighty," she whispered. "What is this?"

"This, my dear, Sara," said Jonathan, "is where our destiny lies."

"Our destiny?" she heard herself whisper.

"Yes," said Jonathan, urging her toward the glass for a closer look. "Call it a forward leap on the evolutionary ladder."

"What is it?"

"The genie."

"Are you pulling my leg again, Jonathan?"

"Not at all," he said. "What you see in the glass is quite an upgrade to the human condition, a much-needed improvement. It is part human and part god; not mortal, but not wholly divine either."

Sara opened her mouth to respond but her vocal cords failed her.

"Meet Proteus," said Jonathan. "A dream of our future."

It was an efflux of mercurial power which had existed for time immemorial on a plane unencumbered by space and time. Some time ago, an ambient explosion came to pass which killed off half of its ethereal tissue. The consequences had been colossal. It could no longer remember the exact nature of its being or ponder its own reflection. The concept of amnesia and the loss of knowledge pertaining to its own physiognomy was so disorientating that it never quite readjusted to this newfound reality. Everything about its condition indicated that it inhabited an impersonal dimension of non-identity and obscurity, though, somewhere within the recesses of its own mind, it knew that the condition was non-indigenous and that it had been cast down there like a purpled fruit when one half of its amorphous body had mysteriously died.

To relearn its own inner workings and to eventually remember what it was, it had to find a viable entry point into its necrotic tissue, explore the connections therein, and push the inert and detrital matter toward a state corresponding to that of its living, functioning half—a condition of total freedom. The endeavor was taking a lot longer than originally anticipated because once the projections of its own vital force had diffused into the inanimate half via an interdimensional membrane, their strong sense of purpose waned, became distorted, or blurred. Further, its sentient half would frequently decelerate its mental processes and enter prolonged periods of inactivity. These unconscious states of blissful rumination were known as nirvana and facilitated the rejuvenation of its creative energies. As beneficial as they might have been, the dreamlike episodes also solicited an undesirable side-effect by halting the spiritual teleology of the necrotic portion of itself and driving it toward the precipice of devolution.

Thankfully, the rudimentary faculties of thought and

memory in consort with its inherent tendency for linear progression through learning had remained unaffected by the spontaneous detonation. Hence it was acutely aware that its brain, the supporting nervous tissues, and its mind had all survived the disaster intact. The ambition to reconcile its living and dead hemispheres through the evolutionary ascension of the latter had originated in the green slime of the earth's ancient seabed. Deep inside those superheated layers of subterranean darkness, it toyed with rays of light and drops of water, inveigling them into chemical reactions which erupted and destroyed many elementary limitations. It couldn't remember how to surmount the laws that would lead to freedom, and so it employed methods of experimentation like trial-and-error that ingeniously aligned it with corporeal permanence one minute and brought it perilously close to perpetual expulsion the next. At times, it would speed back and forth between hard and soft-bodied organisms, unsure as to which medium might hasten its transcendence of physical laws. Once it had travelled a few nautical miles and steadied the corporeal ship, it used every increment of consciousness it had attained to swim, crawl, stand, and fly. Its first breath was a liberating revelation that still burns brightly in its memory and will never be forsaken.

Sex was also an unprecedented and welcomed affair, partly because it offered titillation and partly because it opened up the gates to a kaleidoscopic world of variant tastes, habits, lifestyles, and modes of being. With carnal love came war and predatory instinct, the latter a phenomenon which inaugurated the Age of Transmutation. This was a time of upheaval, uncertainty, and fierce competition; which life form would be most receptive to developing suitable armor which preserved the life force from the infernal dangers that each transitory *epoch posed? As it became more conscious, freakish errors in the anatomical and physiological design of life forms tapered down considerably. On the odd occasion, unforeseeable events would modify environmental conditions to such an extent that it seemed as though the mercurial being might be pinched out of its own creation, however, just before this came to pass, the former balance would miraculously be restored again and its vital force would go on breaking the weighty bonds that kept freedom imprisoned.*

Regardless of whether or not it would eventually end up remembering what it was, nobody could deny that it had come far—very far. Now, it was possible to interact across multiple dimensions including time and space. It could transmute electrochemical signals into a conscious stream of thoughts and feelings inside the prevailing organism of the current epoch; subsequently, it would cleave influential paths along the material plane to inspire a surmounting of cosmic laws, previously thought permanent, without being changed. When the conditions for infiltration were ripe, the mercurial power would inject a small portion of its being into the dense, grey matter of the animate vessel and let it thrive there until the physical agglomeration suffered so much wear and tear that it could no longer contain it. Contrary to what had been written about it, it didn't so much care for the vessels it inhabited, how it probed and manipulated their DNA, or when their use-by dates would expire. There was an impartial temperament to its impervious investigations. It wasn't malevolent in its dealings with the realm of matter but wasn't benevolent, either. Its sole objective was to raise its necrotic half to a state of disembodied freedom that would harmonize the two corresponding hemispheres and lead to a rediscovery of self; nothing more, nothing less.

Jonathan stared at the fetal mannequin with awe and admiration.

"Finally, all those decades of research into the genetics of higher intelligence and eternal youth have come to fruition," he said. "Proteus over here is evidence of that."

"Proteus is evidence of impudence," Sara whispered.

Jonathan ignored her snide remark. "He'll live for at least two hundred years or so, thanks to a radical modification of DAF-16 and SIRT1."

"Did you tamper with the genes for ageing?"

"Sure did,' said Jonathan. "He will also be significantly smarter than humans, thanks to the ground-breaking research of the Darwin Project."

"What?" Sara gawked at him in disbelief. "You used the combined efforts of our team to engineer this... this... monstrosity."

"This monstrosity, as you call it, is going to revolutionize the world, my dear Sara," said Jonathan. "Nothing will ever be the same again."

"Are you even listening to yourself, Jonathan? You sound like a fucking maniac."

"A sane maniac."

Sara lowered her head and sighed. "What possessed you to name it? It's still a developing fetus, isn't it? Couldn't be more than nine or ten weeks old."

"Forty-nine days, to be exact."

"Proteus? Isn't that a Greek god?"

"There's the reason I've called him that."

"Why, Jonathan?"

"He'll be able to enact god-like feats."

"What do you mean?"

"Proteus was a shape-shifter," said Jonathan. "He could change form at will."

Sara grinned ironically. "How's a human going to shape-shift?"

Jonathan scuttled around the portable unit holding the monstrosity and stopped a few feet away from her. He entwined his hands behind his back and proceeded to shuffle back and forth as if he were a college professor giving a lecture on biotechnology to a class of first-year medical students.

"A team of scientists in Russia recently made a causal link between intelligence and the powers of the unconscious," he said. "They examined a group of twenty to thirty-year-old men and women with an IQ of one hundred and eighty or over and what they found was truly mystifying. When the subjects were put in hypnotic trances and forced to endure highly stressful conditions simulated through guided visualization, their unconscious willpower manifested paranormal powers like telepathy, psychokinesis, and even the ability to vacate their own bodies and possess another living being."

"Bullshit."

"I basically activated all the dormant genes that the scientists causally linked to brain capacity and intelligence," said Jonathan, looking more than pleased with himself. "Proteus is bound to add a whole new dimension to the axiom, mind over matter."

"You did all that here?"

"All from the comfort of my own home," he said. "I wanted you to be the first to see him. I thought that you and I might be his parents. You know, raise him and everything. I know it's come as a huge shock to you and there's still a lot to take in, but Proteus won't be like any normal infant. He won't cry or wet his diapers or misbehave. Somebody born with the kind of intelligence that I'm anticipating will surely be different. He'll be like a full-grown adult trapped in the body of a baby. There's no doubt that he'll be one hell of a whiz kid. Hell, he'll probably have more things to teach us about the world than what we can teach him! The three of us would make one hell of a team. What do you think?"

Sara shook her head. "You know what?"

"What?"

"You're crazy, Jonathan," she said. "Do you know that?"

"You're funny, Sara." He tapped his watch. "Three minutes to twelve."

Sara rolled her eyes. "For Christ's sake, Jonathan."

"Nobody has to see him," he said. "We can hide him here until he's old enough to—"

"No!" she exclaimed. "You're not listening to me!"

Jonathan seemed genuinely shocked by her sudden outburst.

"If the authorities get as much as a whiff of what you've been doing in here," she said, pointing a finger at him, "you'll be stripped of your title and blacklisted. You'll also do quite a bit of time in prison, and you'll never be able to work in this field ever again."

"There's no way that they know."

"I'd rethink that if I were you," she said. "Have you forgotten our inconspicuous friends back at the restaurant? Who's to say they didn't follow us back here? Who's to say they're not at the front door right this very minute with a search warrant, getting ready to ring the doorbell?"

"I don't think they were spies," said Jonathan.

"What if they were?" she asked, tapping her foot on the ground. "Is that what you want? To go to prison?"

"It will never come to that."

"You think?"

"They'll see evidence of its brilliance," he said in defiance. "They'll realize how beneficial my creation can be in advancing their interests and the interests of society at large."

"Are you listening to yourself?" Sara asked. "You're speaking as if the gene sequences we identified as markers for intelligence are definite. They're not."

"It worked for the two children of the Darwin Project," said Jonathan. "My sabre-toothed cat and your elephant bird were a success."

"That was after two hundred trials," she said, "and millions of dollars of government revenue squandered. What's the success rate for clones, Jonathan? It's something like one in every a hundred, isn't it? That's not including physiological and psychological complications that may arise later in life due to the incorrect expression of genomic sequences. Do you remember the deformities? The mortalities? Some went of pneumonia, some from liver failure, some from obesity, some from premature birth. How many of ours died in such a manner before a healthy one was finally born? In any case, you know what I'm getting at. Sometimes you put in a superhuman effort and it's all for nothing."

"It won't be."

"So, Proteus over here is the one-hundredth experiment of his kind, is he?" Sara asked.

"Why are you being a bitch when it's not in your nature to be," said Jonathan.

"I'm not being a bitch," she said. "I'm just being a realist who is desperately trying to make a romanticist like you see the light."

"I have this feeling that it's going to be a success," he said. "I can feel it."

"Scientists never ever leave things to faith," she said. "You know it, and I know it, Jonathan. The genomes that we've tampered with thus far belong to animals that are below us on the evolutionary ladder."

"Extinct animals."

"That has no bearing on the point I'm trying to make." Sara stepped toward Jonathan and tapped him on his shoulder as if the physical act might somehow knock some sense into him. "Whatever else they may be, they're much less complex than human beings. Using recombinant DNA techniques to alter the genomes of extinct animals and clone them may be controversial to a general public long kept in the dark, but that doesn't as much as hold up a candle to the sheer outrage that attempting to modify the human genome would spark. The complex relationships between genes involved in higher faculties like intelligence are not as black and white as those involved in, say, eye color or body type. You wouldn't have a chance in hell of predicting any complications or unwanted by-products which might arise throughout its development. I'm afraid that your Proteus over here was doomed before his artificial conception."

"No," said Jonathan, shaking his head. "I know for a fact that there's nothing wrong with Proteus."

"Yes, you know," said Sara, "like all the conspiracy theorists today knew that the world would end when the clock struck twelve midnight."

"Only two minutes away now," said Jonathan. "It's coming."

"A scientist of your caliber rarely considers the socio-political ramifications that an investigation of this kind might incur before *he* hits the railroad with a project that *he* thinks is the best thing since sliced bread," said Sara. "I mean, how will a society with clones operate? How can it operate? If they've been artificially created, who gets to be a parent? Will it even have a parent or legal guardian? Will clones have the same right to self-determination and free will as people born via natural means do? Will clones have legal rights? These are only a few of a million possible questions that would need to be addressed before the production of clones commenced. Who's going to do that, Jonathan, you? Oh, hold on a second, you're the wacky scientist riddled by a grandiose sense of self-righteousness. You only make them, that's right."

"We've been edging toward that direction for some time Sara," said Jonathan. "We've been imagining it for some time. Remember what we were saying before about imagining?"

"I'm imagining that, if it does happen, then many of the books would have to be rewritten," said Sara. "And I'm not talking about the Bible, either. I imagine that a *Clones for Dummies* book would have to be on the shelves of all libraries and bookstores; terms in the English dictionary would have to be modified, changed and added; legislative procedures would have to expand to accommodate for a newly created subdivision of human beings, and specialized medical clinics would have to be set up to deal with some of the more complex issues a clone would inevitably face during his or her lifetime. I also imagine that the world is not quite ready for that degree of change yet. People are receptive to change when it comes bit by bit, but a change that involves the introduction of clones to society would be akin to a massive leap over quicksand, one that may end up falling way short of the safety mark. I imagine that we're not quite ready for all that, Jonathan."

"It might be too late," he said.

"No, it's not."

It took Sara no more than a few seconds to identify an implement which might easily smash the glass. She darted toward the steel table closest to her, retrieved a small mallet that rested against one of the supports and offered it to Jonathan.

"What's this for?" he asked.

"You know what it's for," she said. "You need to end this, now."

"You want me to kill Proteus?"

She bumped the weapon against his hand. "I want you to put an end to what you started, Jonathan. It was a tragic mistake, a fleeting weakness of the heart. You need to exorcise yourself of the hold it has on you, Jonathan. You've become way too attached; don't you see that? You've lost your sense and sensibility. You've let it consume your life for so long that you can no longer think objectively, and a scientist who loses his or her objective orientation to the world has ceased to be one. Come on now. Do the world and yourself a favor and finish this atrocity. It does not belong, not yet anyway."

His eyes were empty. "One-minute left."

"Jonathan, break the glass."

"I can't," he said. "It's a living being."

"Does it even have a soul?"

"It will in a minute."

"Jonathan," she said, gripping him by the shoulders. "What if this Proteus of yours is much more powerful than we? Did you think of that? What if its intelligence and ability are such that we can't control it? What if it turns on us? What if our differences far outweigh our similarities? What if, somewhere along the line, it starts to think of itself as not only separate from the human race but superior to it? Not part of us, but above us."

Jonathan pursed his lips.

"You know what would happen, right? We'd slowly but surely lose our privileged place at the top of the animal totem pole. You'd be relegated to the dustbin of human traitors and heretics—an aspiring Matthew turned Judas. Who's to say that, in a hundred years or so, we won't be the ones being poked and prodded at in cages?"

For quite some time, Jonathan had been mentally distant, not wanting to acknowledge and deal with Sara's concerns. But now she could see that something inside him had finally clicked and an understanding that had hitherto been stifled by the running faucets of passion and emotion had begun pummeling through him like a hailstorm. Within the space of a millisecond, his funneling perceptions were miraculously inverted and his aura had changed to reflect this new telescopic coordination. He had just grasped the sheer magnitude of the bigger picture. The overwhelming evidence for it was those grey-specked eyes which shimmered with ethereal light and revelation.

An urgent eruption spiraled up from the abyssal depths of its own being. It knew what that meant. The most complex collection of animated matter that co-existed with other disembodied creations in its necrotic hemisphere had been manipulated to such a degree that a greater projection of vital energy could now be sent across to possess it without the risk that the vessel might suffer spontaneous combustion. The new incarnation would drive it farther up along the vertical trunk of final causes, away from the gravitational pull of deathliness and closer to the star-speckled skies of weightless freedom and immortality.

All reactions of this nature were homologous and simulated mental orgasms. They always started off as unusual tingling sensations that escalated into burning aches and culminated as excruciating titillations which could only be relieved by firing an infernal ball of self-awareness toward the revolutionized, yet inert, grey matter that had just formed in the realm of its numb half.

Now the cosmic being was compelled to surrender to a much-desired bout of euphoria yet again, as a jet of searing energy coursed out of its own body. Life on earth was about to get very interesting.

Without as much as uttering a word, Jonathan seized the mallet from Sara and stepped toward the fetal mannequin. Then he shook his hand and shoulders in a bid to jettison the mounting tension from his body. Sara could see that he had purposefully averted his eyes from the glass flask, afraid, perhaps, that the sight might stir emotion and incur another change of heart. He closed his eyes and took a few deep breaths to compose himself. When he finally came to, he turned to his side so that his shoulders were parallel with the glass flask and drew the weapon back like an archer preparing to prematurely end the life of a fleeing forest animal.

"Come on, smash it," Sara prompted him.

Jonathan's arms sparked to life but the curved trajectory of a mallet hurtling through the air and the sound of glass shattering never came to pass. Instead, he yelped out in pain and dropped the mullet to the ground.

"What the hell are you doing?"

"Proteus bit me." Jonathan drew his sleeves up, revealing a set of little red indentations on his forearm that looked like teeth marks.

"What's that?"

"He just grabbed my arm and bit me."

Sara knelt beside Jonathan and scooped the weapon up, intending to take matters into her own hands. However, before she could enact any violence upon Jonathan's creation, she was stopped dead in her tracks by the laughter of a child. It wasn't anything that had sounded on the physical plane, but rather an internal projection emanating from the direction of the fetal mannequin itself. She hadn't the slightest idea who or what it was and where it had come from, but it made her skin crawl.

Holding the mallet tightly in one hand, she stood up and started to back away. Jonathan followed in her stead. They got no further than the steel table when the jovial and light-hearted tone of a child's voice punctured the graveyard silence:

"*Hi, mommy and daddy.*"

The voice had unmistakably come from the mannequin. They both pivoted on their heels and stared at it, transfixed by the phrase it had just broadcasted. There was something distinctly different about it now. It was nothing that Sara could put a finger on, but the fetus looked Aeolian and alive as if the mouth of an invisible god had just breathed life force into it. Is this what Jonathan had meant by ensoulment?

Sara checked her watch. It was a minute past twelve.

Mind Games

*This narrative tells the story of the Theban Sphinx, a creature
which features in Sophocles' play, Oedipus, as an antagonist.
The standardized version of the riddle posed by the Sphinx
wasn't an original component of the play; it was amalgamated
into the story by the poets and playwrights of the late
Hellenistic period.*

Alex knew the suggestion had been a mistake as soon as it had
left his mouth. What idiocy had possessed him to suggest
meddling with something that had terrified him out of his wits
only a few weeks ago? He slouched back on his chair, tapping
his knee, and biting his lower lip. The screeching of chairs
being arranged around the kitchen table didn't do much to
placate his mounting anxiety.

He attempted to take his mind off the Ouija board by letting
his eyes wander about the large room. Slouched opposite him
on the sofa was Jason, a law graduate whose overall
musculature suggested he'd be just as comfortable on a football
field as he was in his daytime office job. Jason's life resumé
was impressive, however, his integrity was questionable. He
wasn't the most sensible or insightful of people, either, and for
that reason, Alex didn't much associate with him or his circle of
friends.

Splayed out next to him was Kristen, another law graduate.
She was a conventionally attractive girl and of an intellectual

breadth that pleasantly surprised her acquaintances. Some of the things that spiraled out of her mouth were brilliant, though she was rarely reflective and, like all youth, she was bound up in an intricate web of superficiality. Alex didn't particular like girls like her; in the presence of decent-looking guys, they often regressed into shy, adolescent schoolgirls whose sole purpose in life was to woo the most popular jocks in their class. Alex noticed her close proximity to Jason; the position of her hand atop his vindicated they were something more than friends.

Then of course there was Sergio, a phlegmatic, stoic middle-class scientist who thought his newly acquired doctorate in biology automatically elevated him to a privileged class above that of the average mortal. He'd recently been offered a prominent position at Peter MacCallum's Cancer Centre in Parkville and had spent the last three hours deafening everyone with egotistical ramblings and emotive soliloquies of self-importance. Sergio found it hard to interact with others because anything that didn't revolve around him wasn't really worthy of his attention. His propensity for shyness seemed rather odd and unprecedented for someone who big-noted himself every chance he got. Alex saw traces of the latter in the manner that he fumbled with his watch, trying to deflect boredom without drawing attention to himself.

The other person who'd joined Inara's festivities that evening was Jemima or Dolly. The latter was a derogatory epithet conferred upon her by Jason. Alex thought that her eccentricity was delightful and refreshing; she liked to gather bits and pieces of litter—cloth, buttons, beads, string, rubber, and rock—and fashion them into occult marvels. Alex had perused some of the little devils, witches, vampires, evil clowns, and other dolls she'd made on the internet. From what he'd seen, there was no doubt that she was a very talented woman. She even went so far as to dress like her creations. But in a contemporary culture which placed enormous pressure on individuals to conform to standard behaviors and values, her peculiarity prevented others from seeing through the generalized veneer to the deep, benevolent, and selfless individual that she was. It could also be said that what, others perceived as a horde of irreconcilable differences, spurred by her external appearance had the adverse effect of evoking mistrust and suspicion. Hence the vast majority inadvertently judged her without entering into social intercourse. Alex watched her as she swayed back and forth on a cushioned rocking chair, staring into space.

Inara's head suddenly popped through the doorway. "All set folks."

"Way to go!" Jason yelled.

"I need to know who's playing, guys," said Inara, looking at Jason.

"I'll play if Jason does," said Kristen.

"If Jason jumps off a cliff, would you follow in his stead?" asked Alex.

"Shut the fuck up, Alex," said Jason.

"Can you not speak like that while you're in this house, Jason?" Inara told him.

"Relax."

"I am when you're not swearing."

"I'm in," said Jason, slapping Kristen on the knee.

"Me too," said Kristen.

"Sergio?" asked Inara. "What about you?"

"Sure," he said. "Why not?"

Alex swung around and gaped at him in disbelief. "I

thought you didn't believe in it."

"It's purely for entertainment reasons," he said, adjusting his shirt. "Anyhow, I need to witness its many shortcomings first-hand so I can debunk it properly."

Inara rolled her eyes. "Alex?"

"Thanks, but no thanks."

"Why the hell not, poster boy?" asked Jason. "What are you afraid of?"

"Nothing, I've done it heaps of times before."

"I'll bet," said Kristen, smiling at him.

Alex ignored the comment and pushed on, "I'm just not in the right frame of mind for it, that's all."

"And what frame of mind does one have to be in to play this game?" asked Sergio.

"Definitely not a negative one," said Alex. "You don't want to attract negative energy."

"There won't be any of that here," said Inara. "We're going to say a prayer."

"Oh, that will definitely help," said Alex ironically.

"Since when did you become a critic?" asked Inara, looking into his eyes. "You're the one who used to go on and on about how wonderful it was."

"And you're the one who suggested we play with the Ouija board, or have you forgotten?" Jason added.

Alex remained silent.

"Jemima, you've been rather quiet over there," said Inara. "Would you like to play?"

"Of course, Dolly will play," said Jason. "She's a witch, she gets off on it."

"Shut it, Jason," said Inara.

"Sure," said Jemima, her lips curling up into a smile. "As if

184

a witch like me would turn down the opportunity to commune with denizens of the other world."

Alex could feel the anger bubbling in the pit of his stomach. If Jason didn't stop with his senseless and callous provocations, an eruption would ensue and the consequences would be dire.

"Can we turn the lights off?" asked Jemima.

"Yeah," said Kristen. "We definitely want the appropriate atmosphere."

"Sure," said Inara. "I've got some rose-scented candles and holders in the bathroom drawer."

"Great, I'll get them," said Jemima.

"Dolly will get them," said Jason, taking a sip of his beer. "She's got ones exactly like that at home. She collects bits of hair or nails from those she hates, attaches them to the candles and burns them after midnight."

After watching Jemima disappear down the hallway, Alex turned toward Jason. "Where in the Australian constitution does it say that you have to be a first-degree arsehole all the time?"

"You're the one who thought she was odd," he said. "Now we're all, of a sudden, her protector, are we? Her dazzling knight in shining armor."

"Better than being an invisible coward dressed in water-filled muscles to hide your lack of depth and your insecurities," said Alex.

"Oh, really?" Jason arched forward as if getting ready to stand.

Sensing that a fight was on the horizon, Kristen grabbed hold of Jason's hand and turned to Inara.

"So how is this thing supposed to work?"

"Um… well, we all just sit around the board and each of us

puts a finger on the pointer. One of us calls forth a spirit from the light and starts asking questions. If a spirit is present, it will spell out messages using letters, numbers, and the indicators for 'Yes' and 'No' on the Ouija board," said Inara.

"Yeah, but it's not a spirit moving the pointer, it's your mind that moves it," said Sergio, tapping his forehead.

"Ignorance is a terrible thing," said Alex.

"Exactly," Inara agreed.

"Do you two think that spirits, disembodied entities, earth-bound spirits, lost souls—call them what you will—are behind the whole thing? Do you realize that the spirit hypothesis has been debunked countless times by scientists? Blindfold the participants and the Ouija board loses its supernatural ability to produce messages, it's that simple," Sergio said with an expression of triumph on his face.

"What does that mean?" asked Jason.

"It means that the unconscious will of the participants controls it," Sergio explained. "Or the person who has the strongest will."

"It helps to keep an open mind," Alex pointed out.

"There's a marked difference between open and gaping open."

"Yeah, you two are out of your minds," said Jason, winking at Sergio.

Alex caught sight of the gesture and issued a pretend cough so that he wouldn't break out in fits of laughter; their newfound alliance amused him greatly.

"From what I've experienced, I have reason to doubt Jungian analysis," said Alex. "If you fool around with the thing for long enough, you might have a change of mind."

"Or heart," Inara added.

"Does anyone remember that girl from *The Exorcist*?" asked Kristen. "What was her name again?"

"Reagan," said Alex.

"Yeah, her," said Kristen. "Didn't she get possessed by fooling around with it?"

"That was just a movie," Jason told her.

"Fiction," Sergio agreed.

"We're all set to rumble!" Jemima called out from the kitchen.

"All right!" yelled Jason.

"Here, hun," said Inara, dropping a ballpoint pen and notebook onto Alex's lap. "You can take the messages."

"Poster boy is going to be the messenger between worlds," said Jason, slapping Alex across the shoulder. "Make sure your satellite dish is tuned into the right channel—*Looney Tunes*!"

"You're hysterically funny, Jason," said Alex.

"That I am."

"Everyone inside, folks," Inara ordered.

As Alex started to rise off the couch, Inara reached for the light switch to the sitting room. Soon, they were enveloped in darkness.

After ensuring that the hands of all the participants were interlinked, Inara spoke with a soft, sensual voice: *"Universe, hear our plea. Earth, open. Let the waters open for us. Trees, do not tremble. Let the heavens open and the winds be silent. Let all our faculties celebrate in us the All and One!"*

"Very dramatic performance," said Sergio. "A-plus."

"Cut it out, Sergio," said Alex. "Who wants to be the conduit?"

"What are you talking about?" asked Jason.

"Who is going to talk and ask the questions?" Alex

187

elucidated.

"You do it."

"I can't. I'm not playing," said Alex. "Inara?"

"Sure thing," she said.

Alex watched as a troop of fingers came to rest on the plastic pointer. The shadows they cast onto the Ouija board formed the impression of a giant arachnid. He obviated his gaze, hoping the frightening mirage would disappear.

All attention was now firmly on Inara. She cleared her throat before going on to speak in a strong and steady voice. "We, the occupants of this circle, welcome all spirits of love and light into this space. If there is a spirit in the room, please indicate by moving the pointer."

Jason chuckled. "Earth to Mars, calling all the spirits and denizens, extra-terrestrials and…"

Alex powered a kick in Jason's direction from beneath the table. "Stop it."

"If there's a spirit in the room, please indicate by moving the pointer," echoed Inara.

Everyone's eyes were fixated on the pointer. It suddenly slithered across the board, following a zigzag course. At first, the movement was slow and steady, but it gradually worked itself into a much more vigorous motion. It traced out half a dozen concentric circles before coming to a stop near the smiling sun.

"It's thinking," said Inara.

"Bullshit," said Jason.

"Who did that?" asked Kristen.

"Jason's pushing it," said Sergio.

"No way, man," Jason blurted out. "I'm not."

"Jemima?" asked Sergio.

"Not me," she said.

Sergio knocked Inara with his elbow. "It's you, aren't it?"

The pointer was jolted into action again, sliding across the board in a way that was markedly different. The motion didn't look airy and fluid anymore; it was jagged, lethargic, and discontinuous.

"That was me just now," said Inara. 'Did you feel the difference?"

"Shit," said Jason, retracting his finger.

"Revelation?" Inara mocked.

"You know, I'm not so sure about this anymore. Is it too late to suggest Monopoly or Scrabble?"

Alex pivoted to look at Jemima. He could almost sense her smiling in the darkness, secretly chastising both Jason and Sergio, whose flippant attitudes had now evaporated fully. In light of what had transpired in the last minute or so, their initial disbelief was sheer sacrilege.

"Come on, don't be a wuss," Alex told him.

Jason hesitated before placing his finger back on the pointer. "Okay, go ahead."

"If there's a spirit in the room, please indicate by spelling out your first name," Inara prompted.

The pointer moved to the letter 'J', pausing for a second or two before moving on to another. Its movements were orderly, slow, and precise, enabling Alex to transcribe the letters onto the notepad without any problems.

"J-I-M-M-Y-D," said Alex.

"James Dean?" asked Kristen, smiling nervously.

"Hardly," said Inara. "Hello there, Jimmy. We welcome you to this space of warmth and light. Do you have any messages for anyone in the circle tonight?"

"If it spells out my name, I'm going to scream," said Kristen.

The pointer shot up diagonally and came to rest on the crescent moon.

"No," said Alex.

"To what though?" asked Jemima. "Does it mean no to messages or no to spelling out Kristen's name?"

"I'd say the first," said Alex.

"Is there anything else you'd like to tell us?" asked Inara.

"H-E-Y-Y-A-L-L-N-I-G-G-E-R-I-F-U-C-K-U," said Alex.

"Wow," said Jason. "I think we've got a white trash American."

"And a horn bag," added Sergio.

"Okay, we've got one of those," said Inara. "Jimmy, your presence is no longer required. We thank you for your visitation and will you to return to the light. Go with peace and love."

Kristen was the first to pull her finger away from the pointer. "I don't want to play this anymore."

"Why not, Kris?" asked Jason. "It's just a game."

"Gambling is also a game," said Kristen. "Some of its players end up losing a small fortune and then hurl themselves off the West Gate Bridge."

"It's funny how a few minutes is all it takes for the wind to blow the other way," said Alex.

"Do you mind if I switch places with you?" Kristen asked Alex.

"Come on, poster boy, it will be fun," said Jason. "Be a gentleman and relieve a damsel in distress, will you?"

Alex was highly resistant to the idea at first but crumbled when he saw the anguish painted all over Kristen's face. He gestured his approval by standing up and walking around the circular table to where she was seated between Jason and Jemima. She, in turn, thanked him and vacated her chair. Once Alex had assumed her position, he let out a groan and placed his right index finger on the pointer. "I really am crazy for doing this."

"Is there another spirit in the room with us tonight?" asked Inara.

The pointer rocketed up to the smiling sun.

"Yes," said Kristen.

Inara smiled. "Wonderful. Who are you?"

"S-P-H-I-N-X."

"Does it mean that literally?" asked Jemima. "Or is it trying to be funny?"

"Maybe it's an Egyptian sphinx," said Jason. "Like that big ol' stone beast that guards the pyramids."

The pointer hurtled towards the crescent moon and came to rest on 'No'.

"I guess that answers that question," said Inara. "Are you male or female?"

Alex's finger nearly lost contact with the pointer as it took off swiftly to the right, pausing briefly over a selection of letters on the curved alphabet before coming to a complete halt in the middle of the board. He watched Kristen frown as she read each of the letters out aloud, "I-A-M-C-O-M-P-O-S-I-T-E-P-A-R-T-L-I-O-N-P-A-R-T-B-I-R-D-P-A-R-T-W-O-M-A-N." After a brief pause, she said, "I think it's pulling our leg."

"No shit, Sherlock," said Jason.

"They do lie," Inara pointed out. "They're mischievous and enjoy playing games with the living. Maybe it's having a few cheap laughs at our expense."

"Or maybe it's telling the truth," said Jemima.

Sergio looked toward Jemima. "What, that it's a sphinx?"

"Yeah."

Sergio snorted. "Right, maybe it's the Theban Sphinx."

The pointer took off toward the smiling sun as if having picked up his proposition telepathically.

"Yes," said Kristen.

Sergio rubbed the back of his neck. "Well, then, it appears our friend, the would-be sphinx, is about as crazy as all of you."

"Maybe it just identifies with the Theban Sphinx," said Alex.

Sergio gawked at Alex. "Didn't you just see the message? It didn't imply anything of the sort. It actually thinks it's the Theban Sphinx."

"Does anyone here know anything about Greek mythology?" asked Inara.

Jemima squeezed Alex's shoulder. "Alex, you're Greek, yeah?"

Alex nodded

"Do you know anything about the Theban Sphinx?" asked Jemima.

"Yup," said Alex, fiddling with his shirt. "It was a ravenous beast that stood on the Theban acropolis asking passers-by the same riddle."

"What kind of riddle?"

"It was something along the lines of, 'What creature goes on four legs in the morning, two at noon, and three in the evening…'"

The pointer began gliding across the three rows of the curved alphabet.

"… to which the answer, of course, is…"

"M-A-N."

Everybody stared at the three letters on the notebook that encompassed the whole human race, its evolutionary path, its gargantuan ambitions, and its tireless search for divinity. Nobody uttered a word.

"Those who gave the wrong answer were eaten alive," said Alex. "The Theban Sphinx had a field trip because nobody had the intellectual aptitude to figure it out. Nobody until Oedipus, that is, the ill-fated Oedipus. The Sphinx couldn't quite handle the fact that a mere mortal had solved her riddle, so she threw herself from the cliffs and died."

"She killed herself?" asked Jemima.

"Yup."

"Maybe it's a spirit with a gender complex," Jemima suggested. "Either that or a woman who committed suicide after a revelation of some kind."

The pointer crept towards the crescent moon, paused for a few moments, and then traced out another message. "M-U-R-D-E-R-E-D."

"Let's just take what it's saying at face value and see where that leads us," said Inara. "Where were you murdered?"

"C-A-D-M-E-A-5-2-0."

"Cadmea," said Inara. "Does anyone know where that is?"

"Sounds like a place in Greece." Alex pulled out his iPhone and did a quick web search for the just-mentioned name. He scanned the results and proceeded to open the first link. "It says here that Cadmea was a fortress of ancient Thebes."

"Really?" Inara lurched over and peered at the screen.

"The primary one, it seems."

"Jesus," whispered Inara. "What about the numbers at the end?"

"The five hundred and twenty?"

"Yeah, what's that supposed to mean?"

"Maybe that's the date it died," Jemima proposed. "520BC."

Their outstretched fingers slid diagonally towards the left-hand corner of the Ouija board and came to a halt near the smiling sun.

"Bingo," said Inara. "Who murdered you, Sphinx?"

"O-E-D-I-P-U-S."

"Why did he do that?"

"S-O-T-H-A-T-I-C-O-U-L-D-N-O-T-T-E-L-L-A-N-Y-O-N-E-E-L-S-E-T-H-E-S-E-C-R-E-T."

"I don't get it," said Inara. "What secret is it talking about? I thought it committed suicide because it couldn't handle the fact that Oedipus solved the riddle."

"That's what the myths say," said Alex, "but perhaps what has come down to us is only a small fragment of the original story."

"What are you thinking?" Inara smiled at him. "I know when there's something on your mind."

Alex tapped his free hand on the table. "I'm thinking that the Sphinx was supposed to divulge some grandiose secret about the cosmos to the person who solved her riddle. Perhaps the secret was of such a profound and explosive nature that it would have turned the world upside-down once unveiled to the public. Oedipus, the first man entrusted with this information, probably felt that the only way that these catastrophic consequences could be avoided was to ensure the secret never got out. The only other being that knew the secret was the Sphinx, and so he killed her."

The plastic pointer suddenly sparked to life, weaving an invisible web through the alphabet. Kristen's eyes latched onto the letters singled out by a brief pause in its motion and transcribed them onto the notepad. At first, she seemed genuinely perplexed by the message, as if she was having trouble comprehending it. But then the clouds lifted, and the confusion morphed into a genuine smile. "Y-O-U-A-R-E-I-N-G-E-N-I-O-U-S."

"Woohoo!" exclaimed Jason as he slapped Alex across the back. "Looks like you've got yourself an admirer, poster boy."

Everyone laughed.

Suddenly Sergio, who'd been looking rather discontented in the last few minutes, jerked his chair backwards, folded his hands across his chest and glared at everyone around the kitchen table. "Everything about this game stinks. Why is everyone all of a sudden acting like it's the Theban Sphinx that's controlling the Ouija board when it's not? All it's done is thrown around a few crummy facts that could have easily been obtained online and you've all taken and run with it at a hundred miles per second. Even you two are entertaining this fantasy," he said, pointing at Jason and Kristen. "You know for a fact that no sensible person would swallow this crap. The Theban Sphinx is part of myth and folklore, not history. The keyword here is 'myth'—it's a made-up story, guys! Wake up and smell the roses. A creature like that could never have existed. It's far more likely to be a mentally ill patient who died in a room at La Rundel Mental Asylum than the Sphinx of Thebes."

"And why all of a sudden are you acting like it's a disembodied entity?" asked Alex. "I thought you didn't believe in ghosts."

"I don't," said Sergio. "All I'm doing is offering a much more plausible explanation to what is being implied by everyone around this table tonight."

"So, what, are you calling it the quits?" asked Alex.

"As a matter of fact, I am," said Sergio. "Unless it proves to us that it's the Theban Sphinx."

"No," said Inara.

"Why not?" asked Sergio. "You want to know who or what you're dealing with Inara, don't you?"

"I'm not asking for a materialization," said Inara.

"Of course, you wouldn't because you know it would never happen. And that would shatter your illusory looking glass which would then come raining down around you—all of you—I should say," said Sergio, getting on his hands and knees and peering under the table. "Are you sure you haven't got magnets under here, Inara?"

"What's gotten into you Sergio?" asked Inara.

"Ask for proof, otherwise I'm leaving," said Sergio from beneath the table.

"This is my domain, Sergio," said Inara. "It's my house and if you're not happy with what goes on here, you're free to go."

"I don't think it would hurt if we asked," said Jemima. "It seems friendly enough."

"'Till you start to doubt its integrity," said Alex.

"Just ask it," said Jason. "Let's see what it comes up with."

Kristen nodded. "Yeah, ask."

Alex locked gazes with Inara. He indicated his preference by shaking his head.

"So?" asked Sergio. "Are you going to do it?"

Inara let out a long sigh and dropped her head down in defeat. "Fine, but don't say I didn't warn you."

"Great."

As soon as everyone's fingers were back on the pointer, she

cleared her throat and spoke loudly: "We want you to prove to us that you're the Theban Sphinx. We want you to prove that you're telling the truth. Are you telling the truth about your identity?"

The solemnity that pervaded the room coagulated into a thick tension which appeared to bounce off the floorboards, the walls, the ceiling, and the participants themselves. It shrank the room to half its size and turned the space of a few seconds into an eternity. It immobilized everyone completely.

"Are you telling us the truth about your identity?" Inara repeated.

"Told you it was all bull," Sergio said, laughing. "The Ouija board—"

Sergio was cut off mid-sentence as a clap of thunder ripped through the skies, causing everyone to jump from their seats. As it wallowed down to a distant rumble, the television in the adjoining sitting room began to switch on and off. An electrical storm was wreaking havoc with the transmission signal; everyone watched as innumerable greyish, white, and black dots flickered on the screen and a portentous hissing blared out from the speakers.

Then the unthinkable happened. The pattern of dots formed into a discernible figure, a deformed woman with the teeth of a dog, the wings of an eagle, and the hind legs of a lion. She scampered up to the screen like a cat, probing the world beyond with her large, beady eyes. Her feline nature was mesmerizing; she sniffed and licked at the screen, no doubt trying to ascertain whether her mortal acquaintances lay beyond it. Suddenly her swollen mouth yawned open.

"Yesss…" the television speakers whispered.

Kristen screamed.

For a while, they just sat slumped over the table, musing over what had transpired. The uncanny animation had lasted for all but a few seconds, but it was enough to incite profound fear and distress into their psyches. It had also reoriented them away from Jungian analysis, toward a primitive vision of the world familiar to our ancient ancestors. Alex cast a brief glance at the others. Sergio and Jason, epitomes of masculinity and brute force, had lost the rosy hue from their cheeks and were now clad in perspiration. Kristen was huddled against Jason, grappling with a ring around her middle finger. She held onto it as if it were an ancient prophylactic whose sole purpose was to stave off the supernatural forces of evil. The two least visibly affected were Inara and Jemima; being occult dabblers, they had probably experienced phenomena like this before.

Inara was the first to break the silence: "Alex and I told you it wasn't a good idea."

Sergio nodded in a way that implied regret on his part. "No, it really wasn't."

"Do you guys want to call it quits?" she asked.

Jason thrust an arm around Kristen's shoulder. "We don't want anything more to do with this Inara. We're out."

"Maybe now's not the best time to call it quits," said Jemima. "After all, we now know that it's real."

"I'm with Jemima," said Sergio. "The Theban Sphinx might have some pretty interesting things to tell us, folks."

"As long as she keeps her paws out of our hair," said Jemima.

"Literally."

Inara looked at Alex. "I guess it won't hurt to go on."

"Well, we've come along this far," said Alex. "Might as

well go all the way in, hey?"

"Sure," said Inara. "We'll continue but if she starts acting up or trying out any funny business, I'm pulling the plug on her."

"Sounds good," said Alex. "Who wants to take the messages now?"

Sergio grabbed the pen and notepad. "I'll do it."

Inara extended her arm out and placed her finger on the plastic pointer. Alex, Jemima, and Sergio followed suit.

"We would like to thank you for your cooperation," said Inara, trying to maintain a tone of authority. "Do you have a message for anyone present tonight?"

"M-E-S-S-A-G-E-F-O-R-A-P."

"Who is AP?" asked Inara.

"Maybe they're someone's initials," suggested Jemima.

"Hey," blurted Alex. "AP is me. Alex Pappas."

"Do you have a message for Alex?" asked Inara.

The pointer traced a diagonal line all the way up to the smiling sun.

"That's a yes," said Inara. "Sphinx, please spell out your message on the board."

Sergio's hands both had minds of their own. One was gliding over the board, spelling out letters, and the other was copying them onto the lined notepad. Once the pointer stopped moving, he recited them out aloud. "Y-O-U-C-A-N-B-E-O-E-D-I-P-U-S."

"Alex is Oedipus?" Jemima looked perplexed.

"I think she wants Alex to assume the role of Oedipus," said Inara.

Their conjoined fingers darted off toward the smiling sun again.

Alex laughed. "History repeats itself."

"O-V-E-R-A-N-D-O-V-E-R."

Inara glanced over at Alex. "I imagine she wants you to answer a riddle."

The plastic pointer remained pinned on the indicator for 'Yes' on the Ouija board before weeding out a long message from the labyrinth of curved letters.

"I-F-Y-O-U-A-N-S-W-E-R-C-O-R-R-E-C-T-L-Y-I-W-I-L-L-C-O-M-E-A-N-D-G-I-V-E."

Inara frowned. "What will you give, Sphinx?"

"T-H-E-S-E-C-R-E-T-O-F-C-R-E-A-T-I-O-N."

"This is heavy stuff," said Jemima. "She basically agreed to tell us what it told Oedipus before he killed her."

"Why should she entrust the secret to us?" asked Alex.

"Who knows?" said Sergio. "Maybe she just wants to... get it off her chest."

"Yeah, it's not as if she's at risk of dying either. Someone can only die once. Here's your chance to extricate us from our middle-class misery," said Inara, turning to face Alex. "Our ticket to fame and fortune."

"Posterity," added Jemima.

"Contracts, book deals, the annals of history!" exclaimed Sergio. "The world is our oyster."

The platform on which their fingers rested sparked into motion again, tracing out asymmetrical routes over the board. Sergio laughed as soon as he realized what had been written. "O-P-R-A-H-W-I-N-F-R-E-Y-S-H-O-W."

Jemima cocked her eyebrows. "Hmm... she has a sense of humor too."

"Too right." Inara smiled. "You ready for it, Alex? All psyched up?"

"I'll never be more ready than what I am now," said Alex.

"Sphinx," said Inara, "go ahead and spell out your riddle."

The plastic indicator vacillated on the letter 'W' for a short while and then began tracing out its message at a supersonic speed. The movements were relatively curbed and short, though it felt as though they might drag on forever. Sergio handed the notebook to Alex as soon as the message was transcribed onto the notebook in its entirety.

"What does it say?" asked Inara.

Alex held the notebook up beside a candle. His heart started racing like the rhythmic trotting of a runaway horse as he tried to make sense of it.

"Well?"

"I-T-I-N-F-U-S-E-S-W-I-T-H-L-I-F-E-I-T-I-S-H-E-A-T-I-T-I-S-M-O-V-E-M-E-N-T-I-T-I-S-F-U-E-L-T-H-A-T-T-R-A-N-S-F-O-R-M-S-E-L-E-C-T-R-O-C-H-E-M-I-C-A-L-I-M-P-U-L-S-E-S-I-N-T-O-T-H-O-U-G-H-T-S-A-N-D-F-E-E-L-I-N-G-S-I-T-A-L-L-O-W-S-F-O-R-I-N-T-E-R-A-C-T-I-O-N-W-I-T-H-T-I-M-E-A-N-D-S-P-A-C-E-I-F-I-T-L-E-A-V-E-S-A-L-L-T-H-I-N-G-S-E-N-D-W-H-A-T-A-M-I."

Inara glanced at the message. "Can anyone make any sense out of that?"

After a brief pause, Alex said, "I think I've got it."

"Well, don't leave us in the dark!" Inara exclaimed. "Tell us!"

"It infuses with life," he said. "It is heat; it is movement; it is the fuel that transforms electrochemical impulses into thoughts and feelings. It allows for interaction with time and space; if it leaves, all things end. What am I?"

"Deep," Inara whispered.

Sergio nodded. "Looks like you drew the short end of the

straw, Alex."

'Yeah," said Jemima. "She's cracking it up a notch in terms of cerebral depth. The one Oedipus got was cushy compared to this whopping brain teaser."

"Relative to the times, I would say," said Sergio.

"Any ideas?" Inara asked Alex.

Alex let his mind wander; examining each of the clauses, he superimposed them onto an intellectual looking glass, comprising everything he'd ever learnt and all that he'd intuitively felt to be true about reality and cosmology. Each affirmation was a vital piece of information which fit snugly into one another like the bits of a jigsaw puzzle and formed a holistic picture whose significance rose tiers above the significance of the individual mechanistic parts themselves.

"Come on, you must know something," Inara prompted him.

"Yeah."

Inara's eyes lit up like a firestorm. "So, you know it?"

"Yeah."

Inara motioned for him to address the Ouija board. "Go on."

"The answer to your riddle," said Alex hesitantly, "is the soul, and specifically the human soul. It is the soul that infuses the body with life; it betrays its presence through heat and through movement and works as an intermediary between the physical and psycho-spiritual worlds. In enabling interdimensional transmission, the human spirit can work in time and space. When it finally deserts its post, the body dies and corrupts."

The pointer swooped about the board for a few seconds, coming to a halt near the smiling sun.

"S-P-O-T-O-N-A-L-E-X-R-E-A-D-Y-O-R-N-O-T-H-E-R-E-I-C-O-M-E."

Alex had barely finished reading the message when his vision blurred. Everything began to distort and shape-shift; animate and inanimate objects either deflated, inflated, or melted into one another like an assemblage of acrylic paints being squeezed through the same metal tubing and transmuted into fleur-de-lis-type mandalas. Then a bee-like entity the size of a shoe swarmed into the room and circled about the chandeliers before finally settling atop his head. Alex felt it crawl onto his face and pry his mouth open with its mandibles. He tried to scream but nothing came out. Instead, the bee-like entity sucked the procession of thoughts and ideas that were his consciousness from the cavity in his skull and regurgitated them somewhere in outer space.

His consciousness was now without a body, free from mathematical and physical laws imposed by the shackles of incarnation. Was he dead? He didn't think so. What he knew for sure was that he was now *free* to expand, contract, or move in any direction he so desired. He was free to influence and to be influenced, to control and be controlled, to impinge and be impinged upon. Limitations collapsed around him like a concentric row of dominos.

Then, he blanked out.

Alex heard his own whimpering as he came to. He was on his side, arms folded across his stomach and spit drooling from his mouth. Something about the bed felt odd. He tilted his head up and realized that he was no longer resting on a pillow but on his mother's lap. Her hand was caressing the top of his head.

"Are you okay, Alex?" she asked.

"Yeah," he mumbled. "Just a bad dream."

"I heard you all the way from the hall," she said. "You were saying something in your sleep, but I couldn't make out the words. Must've been some nightmare."

"Yeah, it was sort of jumbled," he said, scratching his head. "I was at Inara's house. We were playing this game and things got out of hand."

"What game?"

"Umm... never mind. What time is it?"

"Eleven-thirty," she said, darting to her feet. "I've got a lengthy list of things to do today—market, yoga, and Sara's kitchen tea—so I won't be back until this evening. There's moussaka and salad in the fridge if you get hungry."

"Cheers."

"Oh, yeah, before I forget," she said, pivoting near the door to face him. "There was a package left out the front for you today."

"From whom?"

"I don't know," she said. "The sender's details were left blank. There wasn't any name on it."

"Oh."

She gestured towards the cabinet. "I put it in there for you."

"Thanks, Mom."

"See you later, honey."

When the sound of the front door slamming shut finally came, Alex threw the covers off his bed and scurried to the drawer. He yanked it open and searched its contents. The mysterious arrival, a rectangular box swathed in plain-colored wrapping paper, lay atop a clump of university textbooks. Alex eased it out gently, pushed the drawer shut, and sat cross-legged on the floor to examine its contents. A single lining of sticky tape held the package together. He used the thumb and index finger of his right hand to peel it off and then tugged with his left at the white-colored wrapping paper until it fell away.

"Ouija, Mystifying Oracle," he read out in disbelief.

This can't be happening to me, Alex thought. He pondered whether he'd awakened from one dream sequence only to fall into another. Was he still complacent in his bed, dreaming that an Ouija board had mysteriously turned up at his house, or was he actually awake? As irrational as it was, he knew the answer.

The Gorgon

In the Greek myth, the Gorgons were three fearsome sisters with a perturbing physiognomy that could turn anyone to stone. Traditionally, there were three. The first two, Stheno and Euryale, were immortal whilst the third, Medusa, was mortal and suffered decapitation at the hands of the mythic hero Perseus. The gorgon was a widespread and popular image during the classical era and many people used their images as prophylactics against evil and other unsolicited influences.

Stheno had been loitering aimlessly about the wooded alpine forest for weeks on end before finally stumbling upon the perfect hiding place. The entrance was by a tubular crouch way, two feet wide by two and a half feet long, no more than about thirteen steps from a subterranean pool of water in the deepest part of a breathing cave hewn from the face of a striated cliff. One of the first things she'd come to notice about her newfound home was that a mildly unpleasant odor, akin to ozone, hovered in the air and that the prevailing temperature was at least five degrees cooler than outside. However, these were only minor and trivial discomforts to contend with compared to the valuable seclusion and protection the grotto offered from the natural elements and from the fearsome Others.

Further, if outward appearances were anything to go by, it was unlikely that she would be discovered any time soon. The trajectory of what little sunlight penetrated the three-meter long entrance was confined to the shallowest parts of the cave before the ground steepened dramatically to form a magnificent, marbled canyon. The small orifice that might betray the location of her cozy lair was tucked away in a yawning spot that was constantly soaked in darkness, and so an intruder's chances of finding it were precariously hinged on the sonic radar of touch alone. Thankfully, touch wasn't at its sharpest or most acute in the arsenal of sense weaponry belonging to the Others.

It had been only a few days or so since she'd discovered the dark, musty pit at the end of the orifice, yet Stheno had already done much to render the place homely. First, she'd begun by stacking clumps of litter, shrubs, bark, and other long grasses in one corner of the limestone floor, spreading them out evenly so as to create something analogous to a bed. To keep herself warm, she'd arranged a hoard of small rocks she'd collected into a circle and attempted to light a fire by furiously grinding two pieces of pinewood together. Stheno had succeeded in starting it and had even managed to keep it going long enough to roast a few rabbits she'd slain out in the wild, though a lack of sufficient fuel had caused it to pinch out shortly afterward and she was without the gusto or energy to venture out and collect more. Last, during the nocturnal hours, a time when she knew the Others were reposing and would not get in her way, she'd gone to great pains to haul a plastic bucket full of fresh water into the pit from a nearby stream. She needed to have a supply of clean water beside her at all times, for periodic sips helped alleviate the nascent, primitive flushes of savagery that would possess, overcome, and compel her to commit murderous acts from time to time.

Last night, the trajectory of her fate had taken a fortuitous turn because she'd managed to break into a farmhouse without getting caught and stole select items that would go far in making her lonely and tortured rural life more bearable. These she arranged neatly and equidistant from one another on calcite protrusions that jutted out from the cave wall next to her bed: a ball embossed with a black and white geometrical pattern; an exquisitely crafted turquoise and gold-colored mask of a beautiful Other; a shard of broken mirror that was her best defense against the abominable Others; a much-needed flashlight to peruse the Sethian darkness; a small hourglass with red grains; a high-necked quartz crystal vase that held a bouquet of red and yellow roses; an aquamarine copper pot with flowery mauve and pink decorations; a porcelain statue of someone she intuitively recognized but couldn't quite put a face to and an intricately carved bronze statue of a cherubic boy surrendering to the orgasmic whirlwind of his own cheerfulness.

The last of these treasured items appealed to her immensely and she would often gaze at it for hours on end, wondering if it was an image that existed somewhere in the world or if it was merely a figment of someone's imagination. She had wanted nothing more than to believe in it, to see it materialize right before her very eyes. She clung to it as if it were a romantic pre-waking dream with a fairy-tale ending recorded onto videotape which automatically rewound to the beginning before the last snippet of Mylar could run off the electromagnet responsible for the playback. Lying awake at night, Stheno had brimmed with hope at the thought that the bronze statue of the boy might one day come to her. In a bid to accelerate the process, she'd squeezed her eyes tightly shut and willed the image or its likeness to life, whispering the word "boy," out loud until she fell soundly asleep.

Now, having been startled awake by the sound of shuffling

feet reverberating through the subterranean quarters, Stheno wondered if someone had caught an earful of her heartfelt prayers and had aptly decided to grant them. Perhaps it was so. Without a moment to lose, she scurried to her feet and up along an old, wooden ladder she'd installed inside the shaft, connecting her lair to the rest of the cavern to make travel to and fro easier. Crouching just beneath the mouth of the crouch way, Stheno probed the cave with her voluminous eyes. She wasn't the least bit worried about being seen or heard. That was nearly impossible. The folds of darkness were all-encompassing and she was able to move through it with feline furtiveness, like a new strain of virus unknown to the cells of the immune system or like a stealth aircraft, able to evade detection by an adversary's sonic radar. She turned her attention toward the pinprick of light funneling through the entrance and that's when she saw it.

The shadowy figure was illuminated against the morning light. It flitted about the entrance for a while, undecided whether or not it was safe to proceed. After a few seconds, the vacillation ceased, replaced by a complacent boldness as it clambered down the stone steps, passing through a timeworn Gnostic chapel which had been cleaved from the wall of the chamber and came to rest near the subterranean lake, no more than a dozen or so steps from where she stood, watching. When she realized what the figure actually was, Stheno had to rub her eyes for a few seconds. It wasn't the shadow of an Other. It wasn't a spirit or god either. It was a lithe-bodied youth, a boy, exactly like the bronze statue which sat atop the stone ledge beside her grassy bed. Unlike the inanimate equivalent, Stheno could see that the real boy was chalk-colored, blue-eyed and black-haired, but that didn't detract from his charm. It didn't detract from his charm at all. If anything, it added to it. The boy wasn't a debased version of the statue; he was a dramatic improvement. She watched from her hiding place as he carelessly discarded his clothes on a nearby dripstone and dove into the lake's crystalline waters. Stheno just stood there, unable to blink, mesmerized by the never-before-seen physiognomy of this boy.

The boy wove his way around the circumference of the small lake at a slow, steady pace, utilizing arm and leg strokes that propelled him along whilst surfacing at regular intervals to take short breaths. Stheno had never before witnessed such strange behavior. It was a mystery as to why he would be so entrenched in such an aimless plight. What was the point of going round and round in circles without any objective? Whatever the reason, Stheno knew what was about to transpire. It always happened when somebody entered the lake and ruffled the dead calm, the doldrums. The ensuing violence caused a rip, a schism in the fabric of the multiverse, that sucked foreign entities into the corporeal dimension. Once the boy had completed a few laps around the lake, an opaque, cloud-like entity began to differentiate from the surface of the water, collecting near the dripstone and transmuting itself into a murky likeness of its initiator. Stheno realized that the boy must have been in tune with the intangible earth forces, for he swirled around in the direction of the ethereal presence as soon as the materialization was complete. There, only a few meters away, stood another lithe-bodied boy, much smaller than himself. The counterfeit seemed fascinated by the manner in which the real boy was running his hands through the shallow water and splashing it towards the Gnostic chapel. He was so captivated by these actions that a few moments had passed before he became sentient to the fact that the real boy was staring at him.

Naturally, the awe and wonder experienced by the little intruder would have been perfectly normal had he actually been a real boy. But he wasn't. He was a little demon created by the magic mirror of the subterranean lake, a phenomenon Stheno knew was unique to the waters of this particular cave. When the counterfeit realized that the real boy was eyeing him, he became startled. That's when Stheno knew she had to intervene, otherwise, the demonic being would steadfastly possess the boy and convert him into a living savage. She sparked to life before it could hover across and inflict any harm, charging toward it with a fragment of mirror in her hand. The little demon responded to the sudden commotion, pivoting on its heels to face her but her reflexes proved too swift a dagger to avert. She thrust the mirror into its face before it could swat her hand away and it caught sight of its own pathetic reflection. When a demon looked into a mirror, it suddenly realized that it was disembodied energy and didn't inhabit a physical body. The shock was so perplexing and earth-moving that it overwhelmed the being and caused it to self-destruct. By the same token, when the evil entity parading as a lithe-bodied boy laid eyes upon its own ugliness, it began to dissipate, shrinking to the size of a pinprick before blinking out completely.

As soon as she was sure the danger had passed, Stheno slumped against a monolith, wiped beads of sweat from her brow and sighed loudly. She didn't really like encounters of the third kind.

The boy stood in knee-deep water for a while, contemplating what had just happened. He was visibly shaken. The blood had drained from his face and his lower jaw was shuddering uncontrollably. Stheno wanted to get closer for a better look without startling him, but she didn't quite know how to go about doing it. Her being in water rendered her disguise useless. For a while, she just sat there, pondering whether it would be wise to reveal herself to him. She wasn't sure how he might react; would he engage with her in a friendly manner, or would he panic and flee? There was only one way to find out.

Stheno eased her way into the water, creating a rippling effect on the surface.

"Who's there?" asked the boy. "Who's there, I say?"

It took about half a minute for her to muster the courage to speak. Finally, she responded nervously and hesitantly. "M-me."

"Who are you?" asked the boy, his voice trembling.

"F-friend."

"Prove it."

Stheno continued to wade towards the boy, who was now propped up against the cave wall. She wondered what she could do or say to abate his worries.

"Stay where you are," said the boy, thrusting his arm out towards her. "My parents are just out there, beyond the little chapel. I'll scream for help if you get any closer."

"W-water is poison," she said, tapping the surface with her fingers.

"Doesn't seem poisonous to me."

"W-water makes s-spirits," she said. 'S-spirits come from w-water."

The boy regarded her in the darkness. He was obviously suspicious of her motives and no doubt apprehensive of her crackling voice and her odd gestures. What was going through his head? Was he scared of her? She didn't really think that was the case providing he had already commenced his descent back into the water.

"Was that a spirit?" he asked.

"Y-yes," she said in a slurred, raspy voice. "E-evil spirit."

"You mean a ghost, don't you? This cave is haunted, isn't it?"

"Y-yes." Stheno lifted the fragment of the broken mirror up above her head.

"What's that for?"

"H-hurt."

"Did you hurt yourself with it?"

Stheno pursed her lips, thinking about how to best convey what she meant with her limited vocabulary. "K-kill spirit."

"Oh, I get it," he said. "You used the mirror to kill the spirit."

"Y-yes."

"I knew that," he said, smiling sheepishly. "I saw the mirror come up when the ghost looked at you."

She threw a punch into the water. "K-kill ghost."

"You're weird," said the boy. "You don't really get out all that much, do you?"

"N-no."

"You don't have many friends either, do you?"

"N-no."

"I can tell," he said. "Your English is atrocious."

Stheno giggled and offered him the mirror. "Look."

"You want me to have it?" he asked.

"Look."

He took it from her and peered at his reflection. "It's a bit dirty."

"Pretty," she said admiringly.

"Who, me?"

"Y-yes."

"Nah," he said. "Girls are pretty, not boys."

"Much pretty."

"Here," he said, turning the mirror toward her. "Your turn."

Stheno reacted violently to his suggestion. She cried out in surprise and averted her eyes. Her left hand then curled around the boy's wrist and shoved it away.

The boy relinquished his grip on the mirror and pulled away from her. "What are you doing? Are you crazy?" he asked, cupping his arm. He must've been in some degree of discomfort, for he quickly thrust his arm into an arch of misty light that passed directly above them to examine his wrist. After a second or two, he said, "You cut me. Don't you ever cut your nails?"

"S-sorry."

Stheno watched the boy crouch down and grope around for the mirror on the pearly bottom of the lake.

"Here's your mirror," he said, handing it back to her with caution. "What is it with you?"

"C-can't look."

"Why not? It's just a reflection."

"N-no."

"Yeah, it is."

"Go b-blind," she said.

"Who'll go blind?"

"All Others."

The boy had a perplexed look on his face. "Why?"

"Ugly."

"You're not ugly."

"Much ugly."

"You're weird," he said. "Weird but funny."

214

"Know."

"What? That you're ugly?"

"Y-yes."

He laughed. "How? You won't even look at yourself in the mirror."

"S-scared."

"Are you scared of your own reflection?"

"Y-yes."

"Well, if you ask me, you don't have anything to worry about," he said.

"Others."

'What about others?"

"S-see me ugly. S-scared."

"But how do you know that?"

"J-just know."

"How?" the boy insisted.

"Know," she said, slapping the palm of her hand into the water.

"Okay, relax," he said. "Geez."

"B-blind."

"Who is blind?"

"Others."

"Why are they blind?"

"W-when see me," she said.

"They go blind when they see you?"

"Y-yes," she nodded vigorously.

"Well, I don't think you're ugly," he said.

"No?"

"Not at all," he said. "You're just... different. You're not ugly, you're just different."

Stheno stared at him, considering the implications of what

he'd just said. "M-me di-different?"

He nodded. "Sure."

"Di-different."

"Different is good. Different is cool."

'C-cool?"

"You got it!' he exclaimed. "Different is cool but it can scare people."

"Di-different."

Stheno repeated the word after the boy. It was longwinded and difficult to pronounce; however, she really liked the way it sounded. Moreover, there was an affirmative quality attached to it and rarely, if ever, were words of such a cheerful disposition used by others to characterize beings like her. She couldn't have been any happier.

"Others not s-scared?" she asked him.

"Not all of them. Some people don't understand what being different is all about and that's why they're scared of you. But there are many others that understand you as well," he said. "Like me."

"Like boy."

"I'm Percy," he said, offering his hand.

Stheno glanced at it, cackled loudly, and then said, "Boy Percy."

"You're not your typical kinda gal, are you?" he asked. "You're so... different."

"Y-yes."

"Have you ever gone to school?"

"S-school?"

"Yeah, school, to learn with others and stuff."

"N-no."

"Thought so," he said. "Do you live in here?"

"Here."

"Where?"

She motioned towards the gaping hole at the back of the cave. "Th-there."

"I can't see where you're pointing at."

Stheno grabbed Percy by the arm in such a way as to avoid brushing her talons up against his bare skin. "Sh-show boy Percy."

"Well, okay," he said. "But I can't stay too long cause my folks will come looking for me."

Percy followed the electromagnetic anomaly that proceeded in a zigzag course along the length of the subterranean flowstone until he was standing on the ceiling.

"This is pretty neat," he said. "So, this is what you do down here, hey? Practice walking on the ceiling."

"Up-upside-down!" Stheno exclaimed. "Upside-down!"

"It's awesome."

She watched him trace out a horizontal line from the corner of the cave to a ceiling pocket, an area in which the space between the limestone floor and roof dramatically narrowed and, given a million or so years, would probably form into a calcite column. Stheno realized that their heads were almost touching.

"What the hell was that?" Percy asked.

"W-what?"

"I don't know, it felt like something cold and slippery."

She lifted up her hands and brushed them against his shoulders.

"Mud," he said. "That's always fun."

"F-fun."

Stheno watched Percy circumnavigate the ceiling before

descending laterally along the canyon wall and stepping onto the ground.

He smiled at her. "Too cool."

"C-cool?"

"Yeah, fun," he said. "Can I bring my friends here one day? Your home is really, really cool."

"H-home is c-cool," she said, walking over to the cache of stolen items on the ledge and picking up her favorite porcelain statue. She spoke in the same raspy voice with a warm, inner glee. "You! You! You!"

"That's Cupid."

"Boy."

"I suppose so."

"Boy Percy."

"Who's that?" he asked, pointing to a porcelain head of a snake-headed woman. "Is that one you?"

"No! No! No!" Stheno took off at lightning speed, running around the room like somebody who had just been doused with petrol and set alight. She stopped at regular intervals, slammed her fists into the limestone wall, and then returned to face Percy.

"What's gotten into you? Are you crazy?'

"N-need water."

She ran to the plastic bucket beside her bed, dropped to the floor, and began lapping up water with her tongue.

"Are you all right?"

"H-heating," she gasped, fanning her face. "H-heating."

"You're just flushed," he said. "Did I say something to upset you?"

"D-don't want to be h-heating."

"You mean you don't want to be angry, right?"

"D-don't want to be evil."

Percy laughed. "You're hilarious. You're the farthest thing from evil. I don't think you could ever be evil."

"N-not want evil."

"You're not evil," he assured her. "You are really weird, though."

Stheno didn't respond. She finished gulping down water, scuttled over to her grassy bed and slumped onto it. "Sit!"

"I should get going," he said. "My parents might start getting worried and come looking for me."

"No, sit."

"But they'll…"

"Sit," she said sternly.

"Okay," he said. "Five more minutes and then I have to go."

She reached up and snatched the turquoise and gold colored mask from the ledge, passing it to Percy. "Is pretty."

"It's a Venetian mask," he said. "My mom has one exactly like it. Where did you get this?"

"Make p-pretty."

"You want me to make you pretty?"

"Y-yes."

"But, how can I?"

Stheno ruffled the black ribbons on the back of the mask.

"Oh, I get you," he said. "You want me to put it on you?"

"Y-yes."

"Awesome."

She pivoted and lurched backward, guiding his hands so that they wouldn't veer anywhere near her hair. She laughed as the cool ribbons of the mask coiled over her ears and tightened around her head.

"All done," he said.

"D-done."

Without a moment to lose, Stheno thrust an arm over the side of the grassy bed and retrieved a crumpled, glossy magazine which had probably been looked at a thousand times. She leafed through to a particular page and handed it over to Percy, whose face proceeded to turn a bright red.

"Ah," he said. "I've seen a few of these. Some of my friends bring them to school and we look at them during recess."

"N-need."

"What do you need?"

"N-Need," she repeated. "N-need l-lots."

Percy looked from the fornicating couple to Stheno, not quite understanding what she might be insinuating.

"W-want," she said, tapping the page.

"What do you want?"

Stheno was now tapping on the area of the man's penis.

Suddenly, the revelation came to him like the blinding flash of a Nikon camera because he blurted out, "But I'm still a virgin and I…"

Before he could complete his phrase, Stheno grabbed him by his black tresses of hair and forced him onto the sandstone floor. They began rolling around like two Olympic wrestlers thirsting for overnight glory, or two virile Spanish bulls contesting for exclusive courtship rights to a receptive cow, knocking over the plastic bucket that contained freshwater as they writhed and squirmed against one another. Stheno was suddenly on top, straddling him as her large breasts slapped against his face. He squeezed them, teasing each of her nipples with his flickering tongue.

She pulled her kilt up to her waist, letting out a shrill cry and then ripped it from her body in exactly the same way that dishevelled mourners rip tufts of hair from their heads whilst lamenting the deceased. Stheno could feel his throbbing manhood against her stomach as she straddled him, her hands pressed tightly against his hairless chest. She slithered lower and lower and lower with every prod.

Laughing hysterically, Stheno tugged the flimsy shorts down his waist. His boyhood sprung up thick and hard, like the main root of a cedar tree. She fondled it, using her fingers to stimulate the tip. The jerking motion made him twitch with delight. Then Stheno did something unprecedented; she took his member into her mouth, tightened her lips around it and rammed the shaft down her throat. There was a garbling sound as it sank deeper and deeper toward the base of her throat. His moaning went up a few decibels as her tongue swirled and flickered around the bulbous head. She could sense his breath getting shorter and shorter. Soon, he would be aching for release.

They rolled about on the ground, and she somehow ended up with her rear propped up in the air. Stheno closed her eyes in anticipation of what was coming. Bolts of titillating thunder and electricity radiated out to other parts of her body as Percy's warm, wet tongue brushed and nibbled around her pudendum.

"H-heating," she gasped, pulling his hair. "H-heating."

The ache and pang intensified as he probed deeper and deeper. It wasn't long until the titillation became all but unbearable; so unbearable, in fact, that she began to jerk her pelvis in order to dodge the mini sexual assault brought on by his young tongue. Before she could not stop him, he spread her legs apart and plunged all the way in. Stheno screamed as if she was being beaten to death with a stick, digging her talons into the limestone floor as he stabbed her repeatedly with his shaft. She responded to his act, raising her pelvis to meet his thrusts which were slow, shallow, and gentle at first, and then faster, deeper, and harder in an attempt to push the two of them over the edge.

With one violent thrust, Percy began to flower inside her, his warm seed pumping into her hugging depths with a force which may have blown the top of a volcanic cone into the stratosphere. He cried out with a double dose of pleasure and pain as her talons dug into his back, tearing flesh and her coils of serpent hair sunk their fangs into his head.

Stheno slumped against the limestone wall. She whined and hugged Percy's body with her elongated and powerful arms, both of which terminated in razor-sharp talons. Blood was smeared all over the walls and on the ground everywhere.

"Percy, are you down here?" reverberated an Other's voice.

Nothing.

"Percy, we need to go."

By lowering her head onto Percy's chest, Stheno had temporary jettisoned the greatest of her physical senses, her nocturnal feline vision, however, she could still hear movement from the direction of the lair's entrance as the Other descended cautiously along the rungs of the wooden ladder, calling the boy's name out again and again. The Other drifted about the ladder for a while, perusing the Hadean shadows which paraded in the darkness of a preternatural Underworld. Then the flicking of a switch sounded, and a beam of light tore through the somnolent blackness like a blade slicing through brittle bone. It illuminated a pile of bones and rotting carcasses at the back of the cave, before moving slowly along its fringes to reveal a canyon full of beautiful cave pearls, past a middle area brimming with angel's hair and milky flowstones and coming to rest on the ledge that proudly exhibited her most treasured items. The light dithered there for about a minute or two and then shot downwards. Stheno couldn't feel it, yet she knew it was there, projecting upon an eyeless and disembodied corpse that was reclined on her grassy bed.

"Oh, God," the Other gasped.

Stheno responded by raising her head, turning toward the beam of light, and speaking with a guttural, garbled tone that would have disturbed a pathological murderer: "K-kill Percy."

The Other continued to shine the light on the bed and stumbled toward her until it was only a few feet away. "Who's there?"

"M-me."

"Who are you?"

"Di-different."

"Where the hell are you? I don't see you."

"M-me di-different."

"Come out of your hiding place! Come out of your hiding place now, you scumbag!"

"P-Percy."

"What did you do with my boy?"

"K-kill boy," she wheezed. "K-Kill boy Percy."

"Show yourself now, you murderer!" screamed the Other, his eyes darting around the region of the boy's body. "Show yourself right this instant!"

"K-kill Percy, kill!"

Stheno's hoarse and slurred ramblings escalated into cacophonous sobs which echoed through the cavern-like claps of thunder. The heart-wrenching cries lasted for no more than a few seconds before giving way to histrionic laughter.

"What's so funny, you crazy bastard?" the Other screamed.

"Up-ipside down! Upside-down!"

As the noise died down, the Other became aware of movement behind him. He rotated on his heels to the sight of an axe hurtling through folds of darkness toward the area of his throat.

The Other didn't scream. There wasn't any time to.

Entrapment

This tale contemporizes the idea of the Trojan horse as explicated in the Iliad. In the classical myth, Odysseus' idea to build a horse containing an army of Achaean soldiers and offer it up to the Trojans under the pretense of a gift was a pivotal point in a far-famed war that lasted ten years.

The sound of rain pelting against the roof of the car had an entrancing effect on Natasha. She closed her eyes and took a deep breath to calm her nerves. She tried to clear her thoughts and enter a state of psychic repose, but the mercurial nature of her mind wouldn't allow for it.

A few nights ago, she'd received a call from her aunt Helen beseeching her to agree to a rendezvous for the sake of clarifying a few things about Geronda Demetrios. Natasha remembered her aunt's solemn tone as she had narrated the grand dream which had instigated a change of heart regarding his integrity as a monk and confirmed the divinely inspired role to which he'd been appointed. Her auntie had claimed that she'd seen the Geronda floating on an ethereal carpet of cumulonimbus clouds beside a rotating sphere that represented the Earth.

The sphere proceeded to increase slightly before decreasing to the shape and size of an egg. Then, the archangel Michael spontaneously materialized, snatched it from the cosmic ether and handed it to the Geronda. When he, in turn, asked what he should do with the world, the angel aptly responded, "Why, eat it, wise man!" The dream had signaled such a compelling revelation for her aunt that she'd immediately rung the Saint Anne Monastery and asked the phone operator if she could speak with her niece. Following an emotional appeal, peppered by heartfelt apologies and nostalgic memories of the past, Natasha had crumbled emotionally and hereafter yielded to her request.

As of late, Natasha had found herself disliking the thought of leaving the convent; she felt uneasy with the senseless modes of operation utilized by the outside world and preferred to stay well within the confines of her heavenly sanctuary where she could pray, read, engage the Gerondas with discussions pertaining to God, and ponder theosophical questions in the company of her fellow sisters. She found that monastic life was really tailored to the needs of her soul. Why had it taken her a whole thirty-seven years to come to terms with this?

In attempting to answer the question, Natasha hadn't realized that the car had come to a complete stop and that the driver, a middle-aged priest named Jacob, had turned to face her.

"We're here."

"That was quick," she said, scooping up the umbrella, her carrier bag, and a bouquet of dandelions she'd brought at a nearby florist shop for her auntie. "Thanks for bringing me."

He smiled. "You know how it works."

"I do."

"Do you want me to accompany you to the front door?"

She hesitated for a while before responding. "No."

The priest checked his watch. "Well, I'll just go sit at a café somewhere and read the paper. I'll be back in a few hours from now, say about eightish?"

"Sounds great."

"See you then."

Natasha got out of the car and slammed the door shut. Her hand fumbled for the knob along the steel trunk of the umbrella. It didn't take long to find it. She jabbed it with her thumb and the waterproof fabric along its bat like protrusions yawned open. With flowers and handbag in one hand and her physical force-field against the storm in the other, she ran along the stone-cobbled driveway, past a set of red-tinted iron gates flanked by stone lions, onto a timber patio, and came to a halt before a set of wooden doors which had been inlaid with semi-translucent glass patterned to look like a variegated collection of geometrical shapes. A green woollen mat splayed on the ground in front of the entrance read, 'Welcome.'

Fond memories of her time here erupted into consciousness as she gazed at the doormat. The same one had been greeting her for a good decade or so, ever since she'd been reunited with her long-lost cousin. Some things never changed, no matter how quickly contingencies spun people off their axes or subjected them to chemical operations which altered the interior structure of their being. Time reordered and realigned the constellations of matter but it could never modify, or wipe clean, the configurations of memory. She always took solace in that.

Natasha discarded the umbrella near an evergreen pot plant. She took a few deep breaths to compose herself and jabbed the button for the doorbell. A familiar chime sounded.

The door swung open. She recognized the face instantly.

"Hi, Peter!"

"You're finally here," he said.

"I am."

227

"We thought that you might have gotten cold feet," he said. "Mom thought you were going to cancel."

"No," she said, stepping through the door to embrace him. Turning to her right, she saw her aunt waiting in the hallway. Her lips curled into a grin.

"Hi, Natasha."

"Hi, Aunt Anne," she said, holding up the flowers. "These are for you. I got them..."

Natasha had barely finished her sentence when something crashed against her shoulder. The sudden violence was unanticipated and it disorientated her completely. There wasn't any time to react, let alone retaliate, as two pairs of forceful, powerful arms wrestled her onto her back and forced her onto the ground. Shrieking like a wounded animal, Natasha tried to swat their arms away and twist her way out of their stranglehold. but it was no use. She was outnumbered two to one and they were both far quicker and stronger than she was. One knelt over her reclining body on one side, pinning her to the floor by her wrists whilst the other blindfolded her with a strip of black satin cloth. The entire affair was thunderous, transpiring within a fraction of a second, however, she'd still managed to get a good enough look at her assailants to know that they were vaguely familiar.

What stunned her was the proficiency and timeliness with which they worked. Half a minute had barely elapsed and they had already subdued her, secured her hands together with a pair of iron handcuffs, and bound her feet with a rope. Then there was a sense of weightlessness as she was hoisted up and ushered outside. Natasha knew they were no longer in her aunt's home because she could feel the subtle caresses of the breeze against her face. The thunderous footfalls coming from the men were quickly displaced by the squawk of unoiled doors opening and before long, she was being rolled full-length onto a foam rubber mattress lining a vehicle's interior, conceivably that of a divvy van. She listened as the doors slammed shut and the engine growled to life, awakening the car from its leeward slumber and initiating a movement which saw it reverse backwards faster than a bullet train.

Natasha tried to remain gritty and calm as the vehicle tore through the torpid layers of night. She wondered where she was being taken. Perhaps the beachside ranch on the peninsula which belonged to her deceptive aunt, a place where they could interrogate her, poke and prod with tweezers and forceps without the fear that an unexpected visitor might come wondering. Apparently, even members of your immediate family, people who were supposed to love you unconditionally and whom you could trust and confide in, were liable to set you up. On realizing exactly what had just transpired beneath her nose, her face flushed a scarlet red. Her aunt's urgent phone call, her so-called dream of the Gerondas, and her incessant apologies in admitting she'd been wrong in judging him negatively were all a farce, a carefully constructed plot devised to lead her here and then abduct her. She knew exactly what this was going to become: an aggressive and brutal attack on her newfound faith, the fountain of beliefs from which she took solace and heart.

Comprehending such betrayal was too bitter a pill to swallow but she had no choice. Clenching her teeth together, Natasha turned her attention inward and began to recite a silent prayer to the Blessed Virgin Mary. Deep inside, her ethereal defenses against psychic attack locked into place and she beseeched God for an energetic force-field which would protect her and ensure she would survive the physical and psychological ordeal unscathed. Her intellect and common sense were quick to blot out irrational oscillations generated by any existing emotions. There was no use in expending unnecessary energy writhing, twisting, screaming, or trying to fight her captors. That part of the scuffle was well and truly lost. Her focus now had to be on preserving her energies for what was to come; she may have lost this battle, but she was not going to lose the far-reaching war.

Natasha lay there pondering the consequences of her capture until the somnolence claimed her and she found herself spiraling down toward the irrational labyrinth of the unconscious. She wasn't sure how long she was out. It could have been twenty, thirty, or even sixty minutes. Nevertheless, she was sucked back into the conscious universe by the sound of screeching tires as the vehicle came to a complete stop. The professional kidnappers worked silently to bring their plan to fruition in the manner that the red back spider secured its food source by mutely spinning an intricate web between two branches. Everything was enacted as noiselessly as possible. The barely-audible rumble of the engine was snuffed out every so gradually and doors were opened and shut gently. Still blindfolded and handcuffed, Natasha felt herself being dragged out of the vehicle by one of the assailants. He slung her over his wide shoulders and marched some distance away, down a spiral staircase, and hurled her onto a cushioned surface, probably a bed. A pair of impersonal hands was suddenly upon her, releasing her from elemental bonds which kept her feet and hands bound tightly together and ripping off her dark veil of anonymity.

"Sorry about that," one of them said. "Odysseus requested

that we bring you to him."

"Who's Odysseus?" she asked, trying to keep her lower lip from quivering.

"A detective."

"What does he want with me?"

"He wishes to ask a few questions about your elder, your Gerondas."

"Gerondas Demetrios?"

"Yeah, him, Demetrios. Isn't he the monk in charge of the Brotherhood of Heaven's Mirror?"

"Yes."

"You're now part of that cult, are you not?"

"It's not a cult."

"But you're part of it aren't you?"

"Yes."

"Then we have the right woman."

Even now, Natasha could feel strands of dread coiling in the pit of her stomach. She'd landed herself in deep trouble.

Odysseus was a brute of a man; about six-foot and three inches tall, broad-shouldered, and built like a brick house. Natasha got a good look at him as he approached the bed. From what she could see, he must have recently partaken in some kind of violent altercation. One side of his face was peppered with bruises, the other was partly veiled by an eye patch, and surgical stitches covered the entire length of his right arm and shoulder. There was something severely unnerving about his stare as if it were that of a ravenous hyena circling its prey and waiting for the right time to strike. If external appearances were anything to judge by, this was someone who you probably didn't want to toy with, make cross, or poke fun at. Ever.

"Do you know why you're here?" he asked in a husky voice.

Natasha didn't respond but sat there like a mute, humming a senseless tune, and staring at a brick wall.

"Do you know why you're here?" he asked again, raising his voice.

Odysseus took a few steps toward a wooden table which stood directly opposite the bed and curled his fingers around the brass handle of the upper drawer. "Okay, listen up, princess. We can do this the easy way, or we can do it the hard way. It might help to know that what kind of treatment you receive here is entirely up to you," he said, pulling out a Smith & Wesson 500 Magnum Revolver from the tiny compartment and placing it on an area of the table from where it would be clearly visible.

Natasha's eyes widened at the sight of the weapon. "What do you want?"

"Your cooperation."

"That's conditional."

"What are the conditions?"

"I won't be answering any questions relating to my religious beliefs, to the Geronda, or to the brotherhood."

Odysseus bent down beside the bed and scooped her bag up.

"Give that back to me," she said.

"You're only allowed to keep three of your possessions," said Odysseus, emptying the contents onto the table. "Everything else I will hereafter confiscate and feed to the great conflagration."

Natasha's gaze hovered over her small cluster of belongings, gauging which were of deepest significance and spiritual worth. She eventually picked out a little silver figure of the Virgin with the babe Jesus, a pocket-sized, leather-bound copy of the New Testament, and a recent picture of the beloved Geronda taken on the outskirts of the monastery.

He smirked. "Give those to me."

"Why?"

"Because now they're mine."

"But you said—"

Odysseus tapped the nose of the gun against the table with his right hand and extended the open palm of his left toward her. "Come on."

Natasha hesitated at first, unsure if she could part with her keep. But the inevitable detriment of not adhering to this man's wishes spurred a dread much more consequential than the preservation of talismans connected with personal sentimentalities. She wasn't sure if this man was capable of violence, rape, or coldblooded murder; nonetheless, she wasn't keen on finding out, either. Resenting herself for the meek and submissive nature to which she often reverted in times of uncertainty, Natasha pushed the items along the bed toward her captor.

"Jesus loves you, Natasha, this I know," he said, taking them from her. "For the Bible tells me so... That rhymes, doesn't it?"

Natasha pivoted toward the wall and continued staring into space.

"Doesn't it?"

Silence.

"What does the Bible have in common with politics? They're both bullshit."

She frowned.

"Jesus was a little faggot who liked it up the arse," said

Odysseus. "Did you know that?"

Natasha could feel heat rising to the surface of her skin. Her stomach churned.

"Jesus, Mary, and God are all made-up stories, fantasies, myths. They never existed. The Greek Orthodox Church is full of lazy hypocritical child-fuckers and poofs that dress in black skirts and jewelery. The scum of the earth prey on the naive and gullible by ripping them off left, right, and center, and then condemning them for their supposed sins."

She covered her ears with her hands and screamed, "Please stop!"

"The Geronda…"

The mere mention of that name made her heart flutter.

"The Geronda is the Devil's doctor," he said. "The Geronda is the filth that sucks the devil's cock and fornicates with the demons."

Natasha spun around to face him. "No!"

"The Geronda will die from AIDS."

Her eyes blurred. "No, no, no! Stop it, please!"

"Shall we have a little chat then?" he asked.

"What do you want from me?" she sniffled, wiping tears from her eyes.

"I'll make a deal with you."

"What deal?"

"We're going to discuss our beliefs," he said. "You have yours and I have mine. And guess what, Natasha?"

"What?"

"They clash," he said. "Big time. So, to remedy the problem we're going to sit here like two philosophy students and talk about who's right and who's wrong."

"Go on…"

"Once it's all resolved, I'll let you go."

"Really?"

"Yes, really."

"How do I know that you're not lying?" Natasha asked.

"I swear to you on the life of my son."

"What if you don't have one?"

Odysseus gave a wry smile. "On the grave of my late mother, then."

She stared into his eyes, searching for visible signs of deception. She was a great reader of eyes, those luminous beads deemed, by commonly held perception, to be doors to the human soul. There wasn't anything there to implicate him as a pretender and the disputation a sham. Finally, she offered her hand to him as a gesture of consent.

"Wise move," he said.

"Let's see, Odysseus, if you're a man of your word."

Natasha scrambled to her feet the moment Odysseus left for a bathroom break and searched the entire basement for escape routes. Save for the iron door through which they'd come, there didn't seem to be any other way in or out of the place. It appeared that her muggers had anticipated everything well. Moreover, there weren't any gadgets lying around that could be used as weapons or co-conspirators to facilitate a premature getaway. The only notable items she could see were a throng of old wooden chairs and tables clustered along the eastern wall. Natasha considered setting them ablaze with the burning candle on the table, but the idea lost its appeal once she'd brooded on it. There weren't any windows or openings for the noxious fumes to escape once the fire had been lit. What if her assailants didn't become cognizant of the smoke until it was too late? The thought of death by asphyxiation didn't appeal to her; she valued her life way too much to take such a reckless gamble. But the frustration of being held captive against her will, a sentiment now further exacerbated by the inability to steer the course of her immediate fate even slightly, was too hard a doppelgänger to swallow. At last, deflated by her rejected bids for freedom, she slumped back onto the mattress and began mumbling to herself.

Later, Odysseus returned with a few plastic cups and a glass bottle of freshly squeezed orange juice. He kindly offered her a drink, but she stubbornly refused this conditional generosity.

"You'll die of dehydration if you don't have something," he said.

"I'm not thirsty."

'Why won't you speak with your mother?" he asked, helping himself to some juice.

"She put you up to this, didn't she?"

"No."

"My mother needs to apologize for the lies she's been spreading about the Geronda and the brotherhood if she wishes to ever speak with me again."

He took a sip. "She loves you. She'd never try to frame you."

"If she loves me, she'll apologize—in public."

"She'd know her own child, don't you think? She says that all the mumbo-jumbo that's been coming out of your mouth isn't a product of your own mind. They're products of your Geronda's idiotic ideology. She knows you've changed and it's not of your own volition. It really breaks her heart to see you like this, Natasha."

"I'm very happy at the moment," she said. "Why can't she just be happy for me?"

"Because she knows her only child is entrapped and imprisoned against her will."

Natasha snorted. "This is my will."

"Is that what the Geronda has programmed you to say?"

"No."

"Tell me about the Geronda," said Odysseus.

"What about him?"

"Anything you want. What's the first thing that comes to mind when you think of him?"

"He saved me."

"From whom?"

"From the world."

"How did he do that?" asked Odysseus.

"He took me under his wing and showed me the way."

"And what way was that, Natasha?"

"The way of love."

"Really?"

"Yeah. Nothing is impossible or daunting for those who encounter adversity with the sword of love. We help those in need by sending out vibrations of love."

"And how does that actually happen if you're locked up in a monastery?" asked Odysseus.

"We pray," she said. "Prayer is the answer to the invisible forces of evil around us. We pray for the sinners, the idolaters, the murderers, the despots, the liars, and the bigots. We pray for liberation from tyranny and oppression. Just as the sunflower turns to the sun, so, too, did the Geronda awaken me to this aspect of existence. I found peace in the truth of his word. I experienced a revelation."

Odysseus stood up and leaned toward her, staring into her eyes. "Do you actually believe prayer will make this world a better place?" he asked. "People have been doing it for at least two thousand years now, princess, and guess what? It isn't working. AIDS is razing hundreds of thousands to the ground in Africa and people are still dying of starvation. Mass genocide is not a thing of the past, racism and xenophobia are as rife now as they were hundreds of years ago, and the earth is on the verge of resource exhaustion. Do you know what this tells me? It tells me that your prayer is as worthless as a piece of extra-terrestrial ice from Saturn's eight or nine rings. Ideologies and philosophies sound really good on paper, but they mean nothing unless you turn them into actions. And the chance of turning them into actions when you isolate yourself in a lofty place such as a monastery and pray all day is slim to zero."

"Prayer doesn't work that way."

"Why hasn't it reached the ears of your God yet, so that he may descend to save you from your captors?"

"In the beginning was the Word and the Word was with God and the Word was God—"

"Which you equate with your Geronda," Odysseus interrupted.

"I said no such thing."

"You imply it," he said, "by keeping a photo of him in your purse. You idolize him."

"As a mark of respect."

"As a mark of worship."

"No," she said, shaking her head furiously. "Adoration is for God alone."

"Your possessions tell another story," said Odysseus. "You keep images of Christ, the Virgin Mary, and the Geronda in your bag but none of God, the Father. Where is he?"

"He is in Jesus Christ," she said. "We also offer veneration to the Saints and superior veneration to the Mother of God, the Holy Virgin."

"And to the Geronda?"

"The Geronda is worthy and ennobled in the eyes of God for bringing so many lost and frightened souls into the arms of our Holy Mother Church. He is an illumined person who commands our respect."

"So, he commands veneration."

"No."

"People illumined in your Holy Mother Church are shown with golden halos around their heads. Aside from God, the Father, the Virgin Mary and Jesus Christ, the only people who wear them are the Saints. You just said that the Geronda was illumined, did you not?

"Yes, but I…"

"Therefore, he's worthy of veneration."

She shook her head. "No, I didn't mean it like that."

"Explain what you mean then," Odysseus said.

Natasha adjusted her black blouse and said, "You're picking at straws. I only meant to say that he's an inspired person."

"Was your life all that bad that you had to go there?" he asked.

"No."

"You grew up in a warm and loving home. Your mother gave you everything you needed and wanted. From what my sources tell me, you took a university degree in theatre performance and graduated with high distinctions. You became a successful actress and acquired many faithful friends. In short, you were an intelligent woman with a very bright future. What the hell happened to change all of that, eh?"

"I may have been successful," she said, "but I wasn't happy."

'Why?"

"I just wasn't," she said. "I was financially secure, prosperous, and stable, though these things are by no means an accurate measure of one's contentment. I needed something in my life, something that was missing."

"What was missing then?"

"Spirit," she said. "Purpose, meaning, and optimism about the world."

"The spiritual path?"

"Yeah."

"So, the Geronda put you on that path. Don't you think it was something you might have figured out on your own?"

"The blind must be led," she said. "The blind must be saved."

"He saved you, then."

"Yes."

"The world is an evil and decrepit place," she said. "It's no place for a woman like me."

"Is that what the Geronda says?" Odysseus asked.

"That's right."

Odysseus laughed. "Please help me understand this absurdity which makes no sense whatsoever. Are you actually telling me that, in order to protect you from the evil of the world, the Geronda's only viable option was to lock you away inside the four walls of a medieval convent?"

"Something like that."

"What makes you think that you're so important in the

wider scheme of things that you need that kind of protection from the would-be ills of the outside world?"

"I don't know."

"You're a smart and beautiful woman," Odysseus said. "I don't know any man who wouldn't want to have you around if you were willing to—"

"You're vile!" she retorted, cutting him off before he could complete his sentence. "How dare you imply that I'm a whore."

"It's a conclusion that any logical individual might draw under the circumstances," he said. "The key word here is logical, something that eludes the vast majority of people on this planet. Have you noticed that the Geronda only recruits good-looking women into the Brotherhood of Heaven's Mirror?"

"No."

"Just thought I'd mention it."

"That's just your opinion."

"How well do you know the Geronda?" he asked.

"Quite well," she said. "We all spend time with him."

"What do all the brethren do there?" Odysseus asked. "Sing? Dance? Chant hymns? Pray for the redemption of the world? Or do they put ear mufflers on and pretend they can't hear the cries of the ill and famished?"

"We're all free to leave whenever we want," said Natasha. "We don't have to stay. We simply choose to."

"That's what he'd like you to believe," said Odysseus. "The minute you show signs of discontent and attempt to leave, he'll change his tempo. I'd bet my life on that."

"No, not the Geronda."

"What he's selling you, my dear Natasha, is the illusion of free will."

"No, I don't accept that."

Odysseus trudged back to the little antique desk, pulled the drawer open, and withdrew something that one might find at a toy store. It was a diminutive wooden horse with a red ribbon around its neck and limbs that terminated in wheels. He slammed the drawer shut and leaned over the table, offering it to her with an urgency that made her nervous.

"What's that?" she asked.

"A present."

"What is it?"

"What does it look like?" he asked.

"A horse."

"It's a hollow horse," he said. "Your present is waiting inside."

For a moment, she just sat there, gawping at it. She couldn't bring herself to accept it. Had she been a child, she would have welcomed the anticipation that comes when the chief surprise is shrouded and rendered anonymous by a larger and less consequential gift. Deplorably, however, the existing circumstances were anything but jovial or genuine and the present waiting to pop out from inside like some jack-in-the-box would no doubt reflect this grim reality. Her gaze travelled from the gift to Odysseus's face. His smirk confirmed her worst fears.

He shook the horse. "Come on."

Natasha tried to keep her hands from trembling as she reached out and took the horse.

"Open it," he prompted.

"How?"

"There's a little knob on the side," he said.

"Okay."

"Did you know that your Geronda was involved in extortion? A few years ago, he tried to leach fifty thousand Euros from somebody who came to him and confessed to murder. He threatened that he would go to the authorities with everything he knew if the confessor didn't pay the ransom. Are these the actions of an evolved and illumined person, as you so eloquently put it, Natasha?"

"I don't believe that," she said, opening the little hatch on the horse's torso. "You made that up."

"Did you know that there were allegations of rape brought against him, Natasha?" Odysseus asked. "It would have been about twenty-five years ago when he was a priest serving at Saint Michael's Monastery. My sources tell me he would lure little boys and girls to an eerie and deserted house that lay in an open field between the suburbs of Pikermi and Pallene. Once they were there, he would force them into the cellar, a place which could only be accessed via a chute on the roof. There he would strip them and fuck them…"

"No, no, no!" she yelled.

"Listen to me, Natasha."

"Lies, lies, and more lies!' she screamed

"Why don't you have a little look at what's inside the horse," said Odysseus. "Is that a lie too, is it?"

Her hand groped around the hollow interior until it ran into a folded piece of tattered newspaper. She pulled it out and spread it open on the mattress. It was an article that had been published on page three of the paper "Chronographos" on the 18th November of 1987. An icy chill scuttled up her spine when she saw a much younger and vibrant looking Geronda Demetrios in the accompanying photograph. Her eyes moved to the title printed aside the illustration in block, black, and bold letters:

MONK BEHIND BARS FOR CHILD RAPE

Seeing the words in print was akin to being punched in the gut. It caused all her muscles to tense up. Her breath shortened and, for a second, she thought she might suffer heart palpitations. Dazed, disbelieving, she had to squeeze her eyes shut and open them a few times to make sure she wasn't hallucinating. "No," she said softly.

"That's Geronda Demetrios, isn't it?" Odysseus asked her.

Gritting her teeth together, she whispered, "Son of a gun."

"What?"

"You think you're so smart, don't you?" she asked.

"Just logical."

Tears glistened along the corner of her eyes. "Why are you trying to destroy me? Why can't you just leave me be?"

"Because there are many people out there who really, really love you, Natasha," he said. "They feel what they say. For them, love isn't just an empty word."

"The Geronda's words aren't empty."

"No, they're not, are they?" said Odysseus. "They're full of hypnotic power and will probably drive a mass of bewitched, God-starved souls to commit atrocious acts of death or murder."

"What do you mean?"

"Do you remember the wacky Heaven's Gate, Natasha?" he asked. "Some thirty-nine people of the cult willingly took their lives in Rancho Santa Fe in California because their leader told them that their disembodied souls would be going on a journey abroad the Hale-Bopp comet. What about the incident at Jamestown on November 18th of 1987, the same year your Geronda got done for rape? Didn't nine hundred and twelve members of the People's Temple commit mass suicide at the command of that space cadet, Jim Jones? Two hundred and eighty of them were children, Natasha. Why would parents willingly execute their own children in cold-blooded murder?"

"What's this got to do with the Geronda?" she asked.

"It has everything to do with him," said Odysseus. "These factions were deeply pious and religious, as is yours. And guess what? They all ended in tears. I mean, how much closer can the name of your own brotherhood be to that of Heaven's Gate? They're virtually identical."

"So, what are you getting at?"

"What I'm getting at, dear Natasha, is that those who became involved with these groups surrendered their better powers of discrimination and relinquished their autonomy. In doing so, they allowed a full-time nutter to think for them and think for them he did, didn't he?"

Natasha closed her eyes.

"Which is what's happened to you, isn't it?" he asked. "You've been brainwashed."

She shook her head. "No."

"Oh, yes, you have," said Odysseus.

"You're wrong."

"How did you meet the Geronda?"

"I was introduced through a mutual friend," she said.

"And did he tell you about the Brotherhood of Heaven's Mirror right from the start?"

"No. he didn't," she said. "He just said that he could see that I was troubled and that he could help me find my true purpose in life."

"If somebody came to you asking for help with the written language and later revealed that the only reason, he came to you was to ask you out on a date, you'd be livid, wouldn't you?

You'd be livid at having been lied to and deceived, am I right?"

She nodded. "Yes."

"Then why is this any different, Natasha?' he asked.

She shrugged.

"It's called an Immaculate Deception," said Odysseus. "I could tell you exactly what happened to you."

"Try me."

"You were taken to a place—probably a convent—where everything was lovey-dovey," he said. "What you found there pleasantly surprised you. People chanted, danced, sang hymns, laughed, shared experiences about their misfortunes in the outside world, and recited passages from the Old and New Testaments together. In short, the atmosphere was so merry and electric that it could almost be a little paradise on earth. Right?"

"Go on."

"You were constantly escorted around the convent by monks, nuns, and other people of the Holy Mother Church who were rather superfluous in their concern for your wellbeing. As a newbie, you'd have to have had some healthy, but unwelcomed, doubts about their intent and they would have tried their best to moderate that through positive reinforcement and by keeping you as busy as they could. Having no spare time was good, for it kept doubts bottled up and the charade intact. Once they'd earned your trust, they started planting qualms in your head about the integrity of the world at large. All those closest to you—parents, siblings, cousins, and so forth—posed the greatest threats as the people most likely to burst the delusional bubble which had been contrived by the brotherhood; and so, they would have been the first to face a barrage of relentless contempt. Your family loved you, but they were misguided and didn't really know what was good for you; hence it was best to distance yourself from them. That's what they would have said, right? You were allowed contact with the outside world, but only at certain times and under the guidance of an elder. From that moment onward, your phone calls, e-mails, letters, and dealings with those outside the monastery were supervised by an elder, or by the Geronda himself. After a few weeks of being there, you felt that you'd discovered a serene and blissful mode of being and had no intention of leaving anyway. The convent was your new home and the illumined persons in it your new family. Does that sound about right, Natasha?"

Natasha was completely stunned by what she'd just heard. Her mouth had gone so dry that she couldn't even open it.

Odysseus slammed his fist against the table. "Does it?"

Finally, she looked from the tattered article to Odysseus and began nodding robustly. "I'm afraid that it does. It sounds so uncannily similar to what happened to me that I'm inclined to think that you're talking from experience."

Natasha watched as her kidnappers walked toward Odysseus who had pivoted on his seat to face them. Now was the time to put her plan into action. Moving as furtively as possible, she stooped down to pick up the half-full bottle of orange juice that Odysseus had forgotten was still beside the mattress from when he was questioning her and she hurled it onto the concrete with brute force. The explosion was cacophonous, splattering orange juice and sharp fragments of glass everywhere. She scoured for the sharpest piece, scooped it up with her right arm and charged towards Odysseus, now only about ten feet away. Screaming like a hostage about to clash with an intelligent chainsaw, Natasha lunged toward him. She took a swipe at his arm, attempting to enfeeble him but he anticipated the assault and jumped back in time. With the element of surprise now lost, the odds of everything panning out according to what she'd deliberated were drastically skewed against her. Working with the skill and efficiency of a trained gladiator, Odysseus caught her by the wrist and punched her in the stomach with his other hand. She dropped the weapon the instant the blow racked her body.

"What the hell's gotten into you?" he asked. "Are you crazy?"

"Getting back… some of my own," she wheezed.

She tried slapping him across the face, but he successfully thwarted her attack by lurching backwards. He then thrust his arm out, grabbing her by her black tresses and pushing her toward the ground. Not wishing to relinquish her aggressive stance, Natasha grabbed his forearm and bit it. Odysseus cried out in pain and reeled it back in as quickly as he could, glancing to see if she had drawn blood. The pause gave her just enough time to bend down and pick up her choice of weapon. Subsequent attempts to graze or cut him proved futile. There was no way of inflicting physical damage to a man whose reflexes were about as swift as the mind coming and going of thoughts. Finally, when his powerful arms had succeeded in wrestling her to submission and she could see no other way to facilitate the desired outcome, she clutched the shard of glass in her hand as if it were a matter of life and death and slashed her wrists. Blood spurted from the severed veins like saltwater geysers.

"What on earth are you doing?" he asked.

Natasha laughed hysterically. "Creating a miracle."

Odysseus powered a kick into her arm, knocking the deadly implement from her grasp. Then, turning to his deputies, he issued an urgent order:

"Quick, call the paramedics and get me some bandages and loincloths."

Watching them disappear up the staircase elicited a profound sense of tranquility and empowerment for Natasha. Her redeeming, selfless act ensured that she'd turned the tables on her crafty oppressors once again. The shadowy and insuperable fate to which she'd resigned herself was also an eastern horizon from which the light of new freedom would emerge. She was the one now calling all the shots, an unforeseen turn of the cosmic tide which would allow her to emerge from this scathing encounter triumphant and victorious. The realization sent slivers of ecstasy coursing through her body which drastically lessened the pain emanating from her self-inflicted stigmata.

"It's over, Odysseus."

He shook his head in disbelief. "You're something else."

"That I am."

"You're the devil's doctor."

Natasha grinned. "No, I'm just his executioner."

Odysseus cowered beside her as they rushed through the gates of the emergency department of Saint Demetrios Hospital in Thessaloniki. He was obviously wary of his precarious position, waiting for the moment Natasha would speak up and implicate him as an accessory in her abduction. The manner in which he ran, his back hunched and his head lowered, reminded her of a mischievous boy who had just broken the kitchen window of his own home and was on his way inside to confess the misdeed to his parents.

"Help!" she yelled. "Help!"

The head nurse glanced at her freshly bandaged wrists with

a look of concern plastered all over her face. "What happened here?"

"I really need your help," said Natasha. "I'm being held prisoner against my will!"

"By whom, my child?"

"By Geronda Demetrios, the head monk of Saint Anne's Monastery and leader of the Brotherhood of Heaven's Mirror," she said. "I must report it to the police at once."

"I'll need to have a look at these wounds first, my child," said the nurse worriedly. "I can see blood seeping through the bandages."

"You owe me," said Natasha, turning toward Odysseus who was clearly shell-shocked. "You might be good at what you do, but you obviously need a bit of work when it comes to selecting your accomplices."

"I thought that—"

"They were his people," said Natasha. "I'm talking about the guys that kidnapped me. I recognized them from the convent."

"Oh…"

"I had to pretend your spiel didn't work, otherwise they would have probably done a number on you," she said. "I presume they're at the monastery now, telling the Geronda of your apparent failure. Of course, I would have much preferred you to be the one in need of urgent medical attention at this moment, but your freaky reflexes put that idea to rest quite quickly. The only other option I had was to cut myself."

Odysseus's eyes suddenly lit up like light bulbs. "So, it worked!"

"Yeah, it did," she said.

"Wow."

"But you owe me one."

Shaking his head from side to side, he said, "I saved you and you returned the favor. Why not call it even?"

"Good point," she said. "I'll settle for that."

"Where do you want me to take you after the nurses get you all fixed up and place the call to the police?"

"Home, please," she said. "I want to see my family."

"Would home be an island like Ithaca?" he teased.

"It might as well be," she said, nodding. "Homer did good in portraying a faithful Penelope in need of saving from the Proci. He got the ratios wrong, though."

"Yeah?"

"In real life, it's more like one hundred and eight Penelopes to one Proci."

NYMPHOMANIA

This narrative features a fresh and modern interpretation of Pandora's Box, a myth in which the first woman, Pandora, opens a storage jar entrusted to her by the Olympians that contained all the ills, disasters, and misfortunes set to befall humankind.

"It's all to do with my wife, to be honest," he said.

"Right."

"I think she's cheating on me."

Chris Doumis sat with his hands folded across his lap.

From the little time I had spent with him, I could see that he was rather vociferous, engaging, and forthcoming. He was also young and fairly attractive too. An unbuttoned blue shirt showed off a lithe-bodied leanness and black curls of hair dropped down along a veiny neck to his shoulders, reminding me of Michelangelo's David.

I gathered that the extreme focus and attention to detail regarding his grooming and dress style might have something to do with deep insecurity of some kind or other. Guys and girls of his type weren't anything new or novel to society, and I'd known many like him. They sought to gain approval and validation through the admiration and worship that comes when one possesses, what we call, conventional beauty. In other words, their physical appearance was their primary weapon of assault when it came to the utilization and exploitation of others. Chris was definitely of this plastic mold.

I tried to assume a sympathetic expression, but all I could manage was a wry smile. "That's not very nice of her, is it?"

He shrugged. "Well, no... it's not. But I kind of had this feeling that it was coming, you know?"

"Like an intuition?"

Chris nodded. "Yeah, an intuition."

I struggled to keep a straight face. You couldn't possibly imagine how many times random people waltzed into my office and demanded that I follow their alleged cheating partners around for the sake of catching them out. It was comical, and sad, to say the least. One of these days, I'd have to change the name of my business to, 'Wily Sandra, The Cheating Investigator.'

Resting my chin on my hand, I said, "Is there some valid reason other than intuition that would elicit such suspicion on your part, Chris? Or are your feelings based on intuition alone?"

"They are."

"Based on valid reason?"

"Yeah."

"Care to share an example?"

Chris leaned forward on his seat, as if responding to an unconscious and unrealized desire for complete confidentiality, and whispered, "She goes out an awful lot for a married woman. At first, it would only happen during the day and only for short intervals, but now it's happening all the time, even during the early hours of the morning. Often, she comes back with bruises, grazes, scratches, you name it," he said, raising his gaze to meet mine. "I mean, where the hell does she go during those ungodly hours, pardon my language? What does she do?"

"Bruises?" I asked. "Do you mean um—"

"It's okay, you can say it…"

"Hickies," I said, feeling a wave of heat emanating from my face.

"They definitely look like hickies," he fumed. "And the fact that they're around her neck makes it all the more likely that they are."

"Have you asked her about this?" I asked.

"Sure have," he said. "She says that it's part of some sort of ancient, long-standing dancing tradition that she's involved in. In other words, crap."

"You don't know that for sure," I said.

"Oh, I do," he said, smiling sarcastically. 'Lies are unlike truths, in that they're easily forgotten. When you lie, you get caught out. A few weeks ago, I'd confronted her about a nightlong absence and she'd stated, quite matter-of-factly, that she had to rush to the hospital because a close friend had been involved in a brutal car accident. Last week, I cleverly alluded to the same absence, for which she gave a vastly different explanation. In a few words, she incriminated herself."

I bit my lower lip and dropped my hand onto the table. "I'm really sorry to hear that, Chris. Have you ever accused her of lying?"

"Oh yes, plenty of times," he said. "She just keeps on denying it."

"So, she's a compulsive liar then?"

"Yeah."

I searched his green eyes for any trace of deception. There wasn't any. "Hmm…"

"But to be completely honest with you, I sort of knew it might happen."

"How's that?" I asked. "Have you known your wife to

cheat before?"

"Oh no," he said. "It's got nothing to do with her past or anything like that. I would say it's her own nature that's at fault. She's just one of those types who can't contain herself when it comes to men, especially those who are physically attractive. I mean, she sees a good-looking guy and she'll start to salivate and put on the damsel-in-distress act. She just can't really relate to men unless there's a sexual element to the conversation or the interaction. You know what I mean? She'll forge connections between anything that looks remotely phallic and the male genitalia wherever she can, and she'll compare sights, tastes, smells, and whatever else is on her mind, to sex."

"She's carnally driven then. It must be really difficult for you when you're out in public together," I said, trying to sound empathetic. "Going purely on what you've just said, most people would describe females of that mold as... umm..." I felt somewhat reluctant to use a crass word to describe a woman who was none other than his chosen life partner, his wife.

"Whores?" he suggested.

"Easy is probably a better word," I said. "Much lighter on the soul."

"Yeah."

"Well, Chris, by now it should be fairly clear to you that hiring a private investigator would be futile."

He looked confused. "What do you mean?"

"The answer is more or less self-evident and painstakingly simple," I said. "As much as it might hurt to hear this, it's time to cut the cord of matrimony, say goodbye to one another, and then go your separate ways."

"That's not possible," Chris said, shaking his head furiously from side to side. "We've got children together. Two beautiful boys."

"Without meaning to sound insensitive to your predicament, Chris, you wouldn't be the first or the last married couple with children to file for divorce. It's a dreadful by-product of recognized unions which spans all times and pervades all cultures. When a married couple can't sort out their differences or consent to underlying principles that should mediate their union, then the only solution to their problem, as tragic and unfortunate as it might seem, is a permanent break-up."

Chris wiped the perspiration from his forehead. "But I love her."

"I know that, but it sounds as though the feeling isn't mutual," I pointed out. "It's much better to cut your losses and move on. Find someone who will be faithful and reciprocate that love. You deserve it."

"It's not as easy as that," he said.

"Why not?"

"We're bound together."

"That's very romantic, Chris," I said, "but I don't think romance, or a few candlelit dinners, will be enough to keep the two of you together. From what you've told me, it sounds as though she's already left the relationship and the marriage. I'm not a marriage counsellor or a psychologist by any scope of the imagination, but common sense tells me that your wife is no longer interested in monogamy. It's as simple as basic arithmetic. Better to leave her before she leaves you, I'd say."

He glanced over at me with pleading eyes, seeking the approval that he desired and that I clearly wasn't going to give. "She won't leave me. She's just going through a phase; she'll get over it. I was her first-ever man, the first man to desire her, she knows that. She's not going anywhere."

I regarded him pitifully. "You sound like you're in denial, Chris."

"I'm not in denial."

"Well, I think you are."

"That's just your opinion!" he snapped back.

"Fine," I said, swiveling on my retractable black chair to grab the relevant client file from atop the black cabinet beside my desk. I lifted it up for him to see. "Let's not forget who's who, though. You came to me for help, not the other way around."

"Point taken," he said. "In any case, she's not free to make that choice. Only I can make that choice for her. Her freedom is in my hands."

Chris's statement hit me like a ton of bricks. Until now, it hadn't occurred to me that Chris might be a possessive patriarch whose views and values belonged more to the antiquated vestiges of social conventions where it was considered more than acceptable for a husband to beat his wife for forgetting to cook dinner and use her for his own sexual gratification whenever he so wished or desired. Men like him were liable to think that women were second-class citizens whose only aim in life was to bear children and to be used as footstools. The chauvinistic attitude that had just come to light angered me so much that I could barely look him in the eyes without feeling revulsion.

"So, a woman's fate is wholly dependent on a man, is it?" I asked sarcastically. "Do you honestly believe that a woman cannot be a master of her own destiny?"

"Hey, relax," he said. "That's not what I meant."

"You implied it," I said. "You said your wife doesn't have

any freedom to make choices and that her fate is in your hands."

He smiled. "You're a funny woman."

"How's that?"

"You formulate opinions from things that you've obviously misread and run with them at a million miles per second. Relax!"

"I am relaxed."

He winked at me. "Sure, you are."

I smirked nervously, determined not to cede moral ground in a mini-debate that involved sexism. "Explain what you meant, Chris."

"What I was implying," he said, "was that *she* doesn't have any freedom because of what *she* is. How could she? She's got sex on the mind all the time; she's chained to her own carnal drives. My wife is a slave to her animal instincts, Sandra."

That was the first time he'd used my name. I didn't really know whether I liked it or not. Using one's first name when addressing them introduced a personal element into the picture, and I wasn't sure whether I wanted a man like him to think of me in any other context save for the professional.

"I see your point."

"She is overtly sexual," he went on. "More than any girl I've ever known before. When we first met, she couldn't get enough of it. The passion between us was electric, magical, and mind-blowing. I felt so alive, so intensely self-aware every time we made love it was as if I was having sex for the very first time in my life."

I tried to remain impartial to his boisterous and exhibitionistic banter, but in the end, the fiery compulsion to react got the better of me and I rolled my eyes up disdainfully. Chris pretended he didn't notice.

"She was ravenous all right, and I had no choice but to comply. On some days, we were doing it four and five times a day."

"You're one lucky man then, aren't you?"

"I guess so," he said. "I mean, which guy wouldn't want to be in my situation?

None."

"You're right about that."

"Her sexual appetite was superhuman; a force to be reckoned with. After a while, the repetition of the acts involved started to bore her, so we introduced other things into the bedroom."

I cocked my eyebrows. "Like what?"

"Handcuffs, whips, chains," he said. "That sort of stuff."

"S&M."

"Exactly," he said. "We even tried out role-playing with leather, lycra, satin, and other fabrics and costumes for a while. But no sooner had we started, she would tire of it and look for something new and novel. In the end, I just couldn't keep up with her ravenous sexual appetite. I am only human, after all."

"That you are," I said, tugging at my jade-colored cotton blouse which was beginning to constrict my airway. I gulped and averted my stare upward, trying my best to avoid any eye contact. Before he could pick up where he left off, I changed the trajectory of the conversation to diffuse the sexual tensions and vibrations which were beginning to pulse, unchecked, through the room.

"Have you ever questioned your own behavior when it comes to the recent position of your wife? Relationships are a two-way street."

"Why would I?" he asked. "I treat her well."

"Oh, you do?"

"Very well I might say," he said. "She gets everything she wants."

"Everything?"

"Just about," he said. "She does all the housework and tends to the kids whilst I'm at work. That's a small price to pay for getting everything you want."

"Maybe she doesn't like the fact that you have control over her," I suggested. "Have you ever thought about that?"

"I don't really control her," he said. "She pretty much does what she likes."

"Right," I said. "How did the two of you meet?"

He smiled. "I was just getting there."

"Go on."

"It was a few years ago now," he said, adjusting the collar on his shirt. "It was a midsummer evening in July. I remember there was a full moon that night."

"Sounds very romantic."

"I was out exploring some ancient ruins near our neighborhood. I loitered around the site for some while, listening to the sounds of the night—the irregular hooting of owls and the purring of suburban stray cats. I used to enjoy spending quiet time on my own. On this night, I decided to do some digging near the entrance to the temple, just to see what might be lying beneath the surface there. You'd never guess what I unearthed."

"Try me," I said.

"Guess."

I shrugged. "I have no idea, Chris. You know, the ability to read the mind of another is not on the resume of any private investigator. Not yet anyway."

He ignored my sarcasm. "Well, I ended up unearthing a little wooden chest with a symbol on it—an ouroboros."

"Is that the serpent that bites its own tail?"

"Yeah, that's the one!" Chris exclaimed. "It's a symbol of eternity and eternal recurrence."

"Sounds very esoteric."

"It is," he said. "Anyway, I ended up taking the little chest home and left it on the kitchen table for a few days, wondering what might lie buried inside. For all I knew, the little chest might have been decades, if not centuries, old. The owner may have buried it there with the intention of preserving booty or a personal item of worth."

I frowned. "What's this to do with meeting your wife?"

"Let me finish and you'll see," he said. "I spent many hours debating whether to open it or not."

"As opposed to handing into the authorities, huh?" I asked.

He laughed nervously. "In the end, curiosity got the better of me and I forced the chest open."

"So, you broke it?"

"No, I didn't break it. I managed to figure out how the switch worked without breaking it," he said, looking pleased with himself.

"What was in it?" I asked.

"My wife."

"Huh?"

"She was actually in the chest," he said. "She'd been waiting, since God knows when, for liberation from the eternal darkness. At first, she rose from the space inside like a plume of smoke but then she assumed the form of a woman. I, for one, knew exactly what she was and snatched her veil from her before she could get away." Chris reached into his pocket and pulled out an embroidered white cloth with tassels on it, shaking it in the air like a sentimental keepsake. "From that moment on, she was bound to me. She could never leave me. I made her mine, Sandra."

What Chris said hadn't quite registered yet, although I had a sneaking suspicion that I would soon be tumbling down an invisible rabbit hole and assuming the guise of a passive participant at the Mad Hatter's Tea Party. "I'm afraid you've lost me."

"Why?" he asked.

"Well, for starters, how could she come out of a wooden chest?" I asked. "That's totally unfeasible. Unless you've confused a chest with a life-size coffin or sarcophagus."

"Oh no, it was a chest all right," he said. "And it's very feasible because she's not human."

"Huh?"

"She's a nymph."

"A nymph?"

"Yeah, a nymph. I married a nymph."

From the solemn look on his face, I gathered that Chris had either fabricated the entire story for the purpose of dealing with a scheming wife who he loved and couldn't bear to lose or that he was well and truly crazy. I'd dealt with many men, women, and teenagers who'd regressed into delusional states because of their inability to cope with heart-wrenching truths, so the current predicament wasn't anything new.

Chris may very well have been telling the truth, at least the truth as he saw it. Moreover, one could be sure that he wasn't all there. He was either partly mad or a total space cadet, perhaps even a psychotic rapist and murderer targeting a lone, professional woman like me. The very thought that I might be an intended victim made my stomach lurch and my skin crawl.

I pinched my lower lip between my teeth, thinking about how best to proceed without ruffling his macho feathers or evoking animosity on his part. "So, she's a nymph, huh?"

"Yeah."

"What's her name?"

"Mideia."

"Oh, so she's one of the ancient ones, too. Didn't she have an affair with Poseidon?"

Chris's eyes narrowed. "Are you patronizing me, Sandra?"

"Look, Chris," I said, taking a deep breath. "You seem like a nice enough guy. At least that's what you've projected so far. Sure, you've got your virtues, vices, and hang-ups. You've obviously got your angels and demons; your passions, hopes, ambitions, and aspirations. I guess we all do, hey?"

"What are you getting at?"

"You're much nicer than some big-shot lawyers, doctors, businessmen, and other professionals who waltz in here thinking that my job as a PI is to avenge a wrong or hand out justice. I'm not a hit woman and I don't play God."

He leaned toward me. "What is your job exactly?"

"I help my clients put the pieces of their mystery puzzles together; I uncover dirt on the notorious and the criminal, help in finding long-lost loved ones, and unravel dubious issues to do with finance and inheritance. How do I do this? Well, it's got nothing to do with accessing private records and all to do with following the right leads, engaging the right people, and spending countless hours tracking them. It's a job that involves a degree of imagination, inventiveness, and, most of all, persistence. And I only ever agree to a job when it doesn't go against my morals and standards. Integrity is more important than money, at least to me it is."

"Right."

I rolled my armchair backward, lifted myself up, and proceeded to pace up and down the room.

"So," I said, pursing my lips, "if I'm going to be of any help, I need to know the truth about everything. No lies or eloquent half-truths; I want the truth and nothing but the truth. Honesty is the best policy, Chris. You need to be honest with me, and in turn, I'll be honest about what I can or can't do for you. Agreed?"

"Okay."

"So far so good then," I said. "Now, about your wife. She's been married to you for how long?"

"Roughly two years."

"You have two boys together."

"Yes."

"But she's been cheating on you, or so you claim."

"She has been."

"She also denies all of this and continues to do it."

He nodded. "Correct."

"You also claim that she's a nymph."

"She is."

"Now, what do I know about nymphs?" I said, taking a step toward him. "They live near lakes, ponds, and rivers, in forests and mountains, meadows and prairies. Often, but not always, they'll wear white dresses and veils. Sometimes they wear crowns of garlands. I know that they're light-hearted, whimsical, irrational, and, as you've already pointed out, extremely sexual. They live for hundreds, if not thousands of years, and are as close to immortal as any earthly creature can get. I should also mention that they're masters of the arts—they weave, dance, and sing better than any human being. Some are good-natured, others much more sinister and eviler. The evil ones can drive people mad, strike them mute, abuse them, torment them, toy with them, you name it."

Chris's grave expression morphed into a sunny smile. "For someone that's never met one, you definitely know a lot about them."

"They also have magical powers," I continued, taking another step toward him. "They can turn themselves into anything they want, whenever they want. They can make themselves invisible, too, hitching rides with breezes and tempests, and slipping through nooks and crannies..."

"I've seen Mideia do that," said Chris. "She doesn't like it when I watch though. She says it's similar to her watching on whilst we humans undergo surgery on the operating table in the hospital or something extremely invasive like that."

"From what I remember of my years studying classics, it's possible to bring them under your control by stealing an item or piece of clothing that belongs to them."

"That's right," he said, thrusting his hand into his pocket and pulling out the white cloth again. "See?"

"They're extremely ancient; the belief in them, that is," I said, resting my hands on the back of my desk and lowering myself to his level so that our heads were now parallel. Our eyes locked. "And like any Modern Greek, I know that they don't exist, not in any objective sense anyway. Nymphs are primitive superstitions fabricated by the rustics and villagers to explain two things: natural phenomena and prevailing cultural sentiments of bygone ages toward women. I suppose it was just another ploy used by men to deflect attention away from themselves for being what they are, feeble-minded and sex-driven creatures."

Chris scowled at me. "Mideia is a nymph," he reiterated as if the statement would somehow reverse the composition of my logic.

"She might suffer from nymphomania," I said. "But there's a vast difference between the condition of nymphomania and the condition of being an actual nymph. There's simply no way that she could ever be a nymph. It's just not possible. Ask any sane, rational person and see what they say. Do you want me to call in my secretary?"

"What's the point?" asked Chris, playing with his thumbs. "You're just trying to make a fool out of me."

"Mideia is a flesh and blood woman, Chris, despite what you believe or what you've come to believe about her," I said, refusing to break the eye contact. "She's no more a nymph than you or I."

"No."

"Is that what she tells you, that she's a nymph?"

Chris sighed. "Great."

"What?"

"You think I'm lying," he said, slapping his clenched fists against his knees. "Either that or you think I've lost my marbles."

"I don't think you've lost your marbles. I said no such thing."

"Then help me," he said pleadingly. His eyes looked glassy and his temperament had undergone a transformation which revealed a newfound feebleness and futility. "I love her and want to keep her! If I don't find a way to convince her to stay, she'll just keep trying to lull me into a false sense of security and then take her kerchief back when I'm resting or completely out. I'm much calmer and more collected when I sleep with it in between my legs. I'm a light sleeper and it takes only the slightest movement to wake me. One tug and I'm up."

The sexual innuendo, though unintentional, spurred consciousness of our proximity to one another and I instinctively pulled back.

"Did I scare you?" he asked.

"Umm, no... Uhh... never mind," I said, trying to disguise my blush by increasing the distance between us. I cleared my throat, forced a few coughs, and walked back around to my armchair. "I understand it must be difficult, Chris, but I don't think I'm actually qualified to help you with your problem."

"My problem?"

"Have you ever thought about seeing a psychotherapist to help you with this?"

He frowned. "You mean a shrink?"

"No, not a psychiatrist," I corrected. "A psychotherapist is someone quite like an analyst. They talk you through the circumstances of your situation and do all they can to alleviate your stress. It might help with finding a solution to this dilemma of fidelity with Mideia."

"No, that's not the answer," said Chris, reaching for a glass of water that my secretary had placed on the table for him. After a few gulps, he said, "Some of the stuff that comes out of her mouth is truly perplexing, Sandra. I know she's trying to drive me crazy. After a while, I just tune off."

"What kind of things does she say?"

"Most of the time, it's just gobbledygook," he said. "The other day she was carrying on about our concept of time. She said that time as we knew it didn't exist."

"Is that so?" I asked.

"She said that the smallest moment in time took up no time at all, so it was impossible for something to travel across distances in no time at all, or something to that effect."

"Wow, that's deep," I said, crossing my legs. "Are you sure this is the same Mideia who can't stop thinking about sex?"

"I know, right? After listening to enough of those foolish ramblings, even the soundest person would start to question one's own sanity."

"You've obviously questioned yours, yes?"

"I have."

"If you've questioned that, then why haven't you questioned the fact that she might not be a nymph? Doesn't the rational appeal to you?"

"There's never been any reason for me to question that," he said. "I just know that she's one. I've seen her transform into various animals, objects, and fantastical beings right before my very eyes. I knew from the very first moment I met her that she was a nymph. She came out of the chest, remember?"

"Well, I guess that's where we lock heads then," I said.

"That we do," he said, winking at me. "Anyway, that has no bearing on the plan I've been formulating."

"What plan?"

Chris bent down and picked up an exquisite, brown-tinted briefcase made of buffalo leather from beside his chair, hoisting it up for me to see. He'd positioned it there after walking into my office and before sitting down. Placing it face down on his lap, he clicked open the golden latches on either side and thrust his hand in. My view was obstructed so I couldn't quite see what was in the bag or what he was fumbling for. A few seconds had passed before he withdrew a bottle of methylated spirits and a box of matches and placed them on my desk.

"What are these for?"

"Death by burning," he said.

"Huh?"

"I figured that if I can't have her, then nobody can have her."

"You want me to burn her?"

"Yeah."

"Then you've misunderstood everything that I've just told you," I said. "I don't do anything that goes against my morals. Homicide is, obviously, one of them."

"It wouldn't be a homicide because she's not human," he said.

"She might not be to you," I said. "But to me, and everyone else, she's a flesh and bone woman."

Chris pushed his chosen agents of destruction toward me. "Last night, I trapped her in the chest again. It was quite simple really," he said, smirking. "I asked her to show me how she could have ever fitted inside such a small space, to begin with. When she curled herself into a little floating marble and dropped inside, I snapped the lid of the chest shut. Now all you have to do is burn it and she'll be gone forever. Just say the magic words."

Listening to this elaborately constructed delusion, and the compelling histrionics that came with it, finally convinced me that he was mentally unbalanced. There was no way that the voice of reason could ever burst the bubble of a psychonaut detached from objective reality, and so my only option was to disentangle myself from any imminent commitment and politely show him the door. Only a fool would continue to entertain someone known for walking along the meandering pathways of absurdity.

"Forget it," I said, getting up off my seat. "I've wasted enough time on this foolishness already."

"Please."

I motioned towards the door. "You don't need someone to escort you to your car, do you?"

"This isn't a joke, I swear."

I scoffed at his remark. "And winged serpents once ruled the earth."

"What will it take to convince you?"

"Nothing short of a miracle," I said, pointing at the door again. "I've given you more than enough oxygen today."

"Come on, Sandra," he said. "We go back to my place, I show you the chest, and you dowse it with spirits and set it alight. We can do it outside in the backyard if you want. That way. we can avoid the risk of a house fire. It'll take all of what, two minutes, five minutes at most?"

"Why not just do it yourself?" I asked. "Why do you need me to light the fire?"

"It has to be someone not previously connected to her," he said. "That's why I found you."

"Right," I said. "It makes no sense to me that you love her so much and yet you want her dead. It's irrational, outrageous. Everything about your story is, I'm afraid. I'm just not buying it, Chris."

"Have you ever known true love to be rational?"

"You're right," I said. "That's exactly why I don't partake of it."

"How much, Sandra?"

"No amount can buy my integrity."

"Five thousand? Ten thousand? Twenty thousand? Name your poison."

"I don't do murder."

"It wouldn't be murder," he said. "She's a nymph. The rules of this world don't apply to her, remember? Think of it as a gallant act, a humanitarian act of selflessness for a fellow human being."

"No."

"I'll take you out for dinner afterwards?"

"I'm flattered."

There was suddenly a sparkle in Chris' eyes. "Hey, what if I can prove to you that she's a nymph?"

"How do you propose to do that?"

"You'll see," he said. "Are you up for it?"

There was a swift flutter in my stomach. "What, like now?"

"Sure," he said, dashing to his feet. "Now's a good a time as any."

His house wasn't too far from my office, so we took my car. Neither of us spoke much during the short trip, and then it was only to clarify information regarding the route we were taking. He was too busy thinking about his imaginary wife and predicament, and I was too busy cursing myself silently for having agreed to such a preposterous proposition.

For a while, I found myself questioning the nature of my own actions. Impulses and unconscious emotion sometimes gained the ascendency over the higher intellect, and this was certainly what befell me when I allowed myself to be sucked into this dubious little adventure. It had been quite a while since something novel and exhilarating had transpired in my life, and so the temporary insanity which had possessed me to go along for the ride was probably some unconscious projection of its prevailing absence. Rightly or wrongly, I had taken a huge leap of faith from which there was no turning back.

I swerved into a shadowy side street at his command, decelerating as we pulled into the first driveway to bring the car to a smooth stop. Other than some exquisite English box hedges and topiary that circled the space occupied by the front yard, there wasn't anything spectacular about the brick two-story townhouse that Chris called home. Remarkably, the foliage was trimmed to perfection.

"I'll presume Mideia's the gardener?" I asked.

"You got it," he said, swinging the passenger door wide open. "Come."

I followed Chris along the narrow driveway which split the hexagonal garden from a fence, up along a small flight of steps which veered off to the left, through a tiled patio, stopping before a magnificent glass-framed door, guarded by two marble statues of the sun god, Apollo, and the moon goddess, Artemis.

"Are the boys here?" I asked.

I looked about as he unlocked the door, trying to discern if anyone had witnessed our arrival. I wasn't too sure of my footing in this particular case and didn't know how things might unfold or the outcome. Hence, there was no choice but to proceed with utmost caution.

"They're with my parents," he said.

"Okay."

Chris stepped into the house and flicked the light switch on, illuminating the dark space beyond. I immediately recognized the occupants' love for open style living. The living, dining, and kitchen areas were interlaced into an L-shape which was itself peppered with sliding glass doors and windows. From what I could see, all of the furniture adhered to a corresponding set of black and red colors and was strategically placed to maximize coziness, serenity, warmth, and other sentiments which such a small space invariably evoked. The crème-tinted leather couches, coffee tables, and marble bench tops mixed in well with the crimson-colored kitchen stools, chairs, and watercolor paintings and the whole floor was done in a Brushbox, parquetry style and dressed over with supernal Arabian rugs of every shape, size, and texture imaginable. There was also a play area for very young children, with small plastic balls, a small wooden castle, and a sandpit in one corner of the living room.

Standing before this suburban family sanctuary, I couldn't help but feel a little envious and even resentful of Mideia, if, in fact, she existed.

"Are you all right?" Chris asked, squeezing my arm.

"Yeah, sorry," I said. "I just blanked out for a second."

Chris pointed toward a glass-topped wooden table in the middle of the lounge room. "It's there."

My eyes darted toward a glass-topped table in the middle of the living room. There, in plain view for all to see as they entered the house, stood a rectangular, wooden chest with gilded corners. The ouroboros symbol, the serpent eating its own tail, was intricately carved atop the lid and exhibited life-like scales, teeth, eyes, and other features. The physiognomy of the chest was exactly as Chris had described it in my office, only that it was much more intricate and exquisite than I had originally assumed. Without a doubt, it was impossible to stare at it without feeling awe and admiration for the craftsmanship, talent, and level of skill that went into producing such a fine artefact.

My first instinct was that it was of a great age, much older than what Chris had estimated. It looked like something one might see at the National Museum of Archaeology. In actual fact, the more I gawked at it, the more convinced I became that it was some obscure ancient artefact belonging to a museum or someone's private collection. Perhaps it was a stolen item, the fruit of a crime that he'd come to regret or was now ashamed of, with his only course of action for redemption being to implicate someone else as the thief. Could the story of his nymph-wife, her infidelities, and the chest have been elements of a clever charade contrived to disguise much more sinister intentions on his behalf? Could he be the front of a much bigger conspiracy, one concocted by familiar persons seeking vengeance against my personage and good reputation for reasons that had hitherto not come to light? There was no way I could know for sure.

All of a sudden, I felt really queasy; my vision blurred, my heart raced, my skin grew hot, and the palms of my hands began to sweat profusely. I rubbed them against my black skirt a few times for some traction before zipping open my handbag and pulling out a loaded nine by nineteen millimeters semi-automatic pistol.

Chris' eyes bulged from their sockets. "What the hell are you doing, Sandra?"

I pointed the weapon at him. "Don't move a muscle."

"What's gotten into you?"

"Put your hands on your head!"

"What the…"

"Do it or I'll shoot you," I said. "I'm not playing games."

His eyes drifted from the firearm to my eyes and back again. Scared that I might carry through with my threat, he assumed the proverbial position of surrender. "I don't understand."

"Do you think I'm stupid?" I asked, stepping toward him.

"I know exactly what's going on. I know what you're up to. This whole thing is a massive hoax. There's no cheating wife, no children, and there's definitely no nymph. You want to frame me for that treasure you've stolen. You made up this fancy story to get me here, and as soon as I'd disposed of the chest, you'll be on the phone to the police, telling them how I'd stolen it and then tried to cover up my tracks by burning it in some random yard that happened to be yours. Either that or you've been hired by someone who wants to get back at me for God knows what."

"You're crazy, Sandra," he said, gesturing to me to lower my pistol. "Why don't you just put the gun down, all right?"

"Stay put, Chris."

"Come on," he said. "You're making me nervous."

"Just fess up," I said.

"Are you crazy?"

"No, but you obviously are," I said, laughing. "You're the one who still believes fairies live in gardens and chests, Chris."

"Let's just talk about this," he said.

"We will."

"Please put the gun down," he pleaded.

"After you open the chest."

"No."

I refocused the muzzle of my weapon on his thigh. "I said, open it."

"You're making a mistake," he argued.

"A pretty damn good one."

"You don't know what you're doing, Sandra," he said. "If I open it, she'll…"

"Open it!"

Sighing, he walked over to the coffee table. He bent over, scooped up the chest in both hands, and then turned to face me.

From the grave expression on his face, I thought that he might try his luck with a final objection, but it appeared my firmness had drummed all the fight out of him. Without taking his eyes off my gun, he sidestepped into the space between the table and the couch and slumped back onto a satin cushion. He slid his fingers over to the latch which held the lid tightly shut, shaking his head with disapproval.

"Open it," I urged.

"If that's what you want."

"It is."

Without budging, I watched him flick the latch and lift the lid up. The darkness inside gradually gave way to light, illuminating a cavity shaped to resemble the human heart. There was nothing inside the heart, at least nothing opaque and concrete.

"Where's the nymph, Chris?" I asked sneeringly. "I knew it was bull…"

There wasn't any time to finish my sentence. There wasn't any time to do anything at all because time inverted and began working backwards. Everything was suddenly moving in the opposite direction to what it usually does; in my mind's eye, I glimpsed rivers running uphill, water vapor contracting and condensing as it rained onto the earth, people getting physiologically younger but chronologically older, glass unshuttering, giant trees regressing into seeds and animals into embryos, and deceased scraps scattered in graveyards reconstituting themselves into former living beings. Like an executive producer in possession of a melodramatic script, I could see and feel everything that was about to occur in the immediate future but I was helpless to intercede and alter the ordained course of events or stop them.

This appeared to play out in real-time also. In the flash of an instant, Chris and I were suddenly near the entrance of the house, walking back down the driveway and into the car. Then, we rocketed back over pedestrian crossings, intersections, and other suburban landmarks, up along a flight of stairs leading to my office, and back onto the comfortable chairs which we'd been sitting on during our preliminary meeting. After the conversation between us unraveled in reverse, Chris scooped up his briefcase and backtracked out of my room and into the waiting area, slamming the door shut before him as he went out.

Then, there was darkness.

Somebody nudged my shoulder as I came to. I didn't know for how long I had been out, but it couldn't have been more than a few minutes. Having regained my senses, I realized that my secretary was peering straight down at me, her beady brown eyes full of concern.

"Are you all right?" she asked.

I squinted at the light plunging into the room through the glass window beside me. "I'm really sorry, Liza."

"You weren't answering on the intercom," she said, "so I thought it was best to come and check in on you."

"I can't believe I fell asleep on the job."

"Must've been one hell of a late night," she said.

"Sure was," I said. "Cath and I hung out at a local bar."

She smiled at me. "A few too many drinks, hey?"

"Yeah."

"Meet anyone special?"

"Me, myself, and I."

"Oh, it was one of those," she said, handing me a manila folder. "Here's the next one."

There was a mild discomfort around my ears, so I adjusted the temples of my reading glasses. Feeling a bit peckish, I fished a Mintie out from a Waterford crystal vase which held an assortment of sweets and chocolates on my desk, discarded the plastic wrapper, and popped it into my mouth.

"Who is it?"

"Some guy called Chris," she said.

"He's here now, is he?"

"Yup." She crouched beside me and whispered, "He's a bit of a hunk, too."

"What's his story?"

"He thinks his wife's cheating on him," she said. "Her name is Mideia or something like that. He wants you to follow her."

I didn't respond because the Mintie suddenly became unchewable, the air unbreathable.

CPSIA information can be obtained
at www.ICGtesting.com
Printed in the USA
LVHW041630070423
743803LV00015B/95